An original  Archie HORROR novel

INTERVIEW WITH THE VIXEN

REBECCA BARROW

SCHOLASTIC INC.

FOR MAGGIE, THE B TO MY V.
—R. B.

If you purchased this book without a cover, you should be aware that this book is stolen property. It was reported as "unsold and destroyed" to the publisher, and neither the author nor the publisher has received any payment for this "stripped book."

Copyright © 2020 by Archie Comic Publications, Inc.

All rights reserved. Published by Scholastic Inc., *Publishers since 1920.* SCHOLASTIC and associated logos are trademarks and/or registered trademarks of Scholastic Inc.

The publisher does not have any control over and does not assume any responsibility for author or third-party websites or their content.

No part of this publication may be reproduced, stored in a retrieval system, or transmitted in any form or by any means, electronic, mechanical, photocopying, recording, or otherwise, without written permission of the publisher. For information regarding permission, write to Scholastic Inc., Attention: Permissions Department, 557 Broadway, New York, NY 10012.

This book is a work of fiction. Names, characters, places, and incidents are either the product of the author's imagination or are used fictitiously, and any resemblance to actual persons, living or dead, business establishments, events, or locales is entirely coincidental.

ISBN 978-1-338-56913-1

10 9 8 7 6 5 4 3 2 1   20 21 22 23 24

Printed in the U.S.A.   23

First printing 2020

Book design by Jessica Meltzer

PROLOGUE

THERE'S NO PARTY like a Cheryl Blossom party.

Bass pumping, speakers jumping, bottles spinning in a game that's only going to lead to kissing and crying and somebody breaking up on the front lawn after midnight, but isn't that the fun of it?

It is for me, anyway.

Cheryl's wearing cutoffs—the ones that Mommie Dearest always says are trashy, with that rictus smile she's so practiced at giving her daughter—with a tight white tee and, of course, her signature Bombshell lipstick. Tonight, for the first time in a long time, she feels like a queen reigning over her wild kingdom. There, Chuck Clayton and half the football team playing some stupid game on the deck. Here, Alanna Chiang and the Vixens throwing out tipsy cheers by the pool. And by her side, her sometimes-loyal minions waiting for their next instructions.

She looks at Nancy and Midge and snaps her fingers. "Ladies!" she barks. "Fetch me a drink." Then she turns to the group of girls mingling behind her and throws her hands in the air. "Who wants to play seven minutes in heaven?"

The boys over on the deck look up, jaws dropped, and Cheryl laughs with her red-painted lips wide open. Like she's interested in any of them. "Sorry, boys, this is strictly—"

A scream slices through the night.

"—girls only," Cheryl finishes, but the hairs on the back of her neck are standing up, and she half turns at the thud she hears behind her.

It's some kid, hunched over and staggering toward her.

"Excuse you," she says, her voice loud and sharp to counteract the chill rippling along her spine. "This party is *exclusive*. No sloppy messes allowed. Got it?"

The boy keeps coming, and he's clearly hammered already, from the way he's shambling along, and Cheryl has had enough. This is her house, her rules. No one defies Cheryl Bombshell in her own backyard.

"Hey," she says. "Are you listening? Shoo, little vermin."

There's another thud to her left, and Cheryl whips around.

Another crasher, hunched over in the same way as the first.

"Take him with you, too!" she snaps, but the first one is still ignoring her, and so she takes a few steps forward, hands on her hips, her never-fail power stance. "I said, get—"

The first boy rears up, and now Cheryl is the one who screams, a short wild noise at the sight of the boy's face—one she finally recognizes—contorted into a snarl that shows a row of dangerously sharp teeth that maybe used to be shiny white but are now stained and marbled a deep, dark red.

Almost as red as the color on Cheryl's own lips.

And not teeth.

Fangs.

FIVE DAYS
EARLIER

CHAPTER ONE
VERONICA

"BREAK THAT WALL—make them fall—across the goal line—take that ball—GO, Bulldogs!"

Veronica Lodge swishes, shimmies, and struts through the cheer. When they're done yelling, she drops her poms, winks, and blows a kiss over her shoulder to an imaginary audience. It's only stalling for time while the girls set up for the stunt, and when they're ready, she hops up into their waiting hands, fingers digging into their shoulders for balance, and then she's launched into the air.

Veronica rides the waves as long as she can before twisting and tucking backward, trusting that her teammates will be there to catch her.

They do—they always do—and let her down gently before hitting their final position, shoulders back and smiles bright and shiny.

They hold the pose for a few seconds before releasing, and Veronica claps her hands together. "Okay, girls, let's—"

"Ronnie!"

Veronica glances back and smiles again, wider than her fake-cheer smile. "Stretch it out," she says to the girls, and then spins, throwing her arms open wide. "Archiekins! Shouldn't you be tackling somebody right now?"

Archie Andrews is sweaty and out of breath, a streak of mud across one perfect cheekbone. "Coach finished practice early," he says. "I just came to watch you. Don't you get dizzy when they throw you up there?"

"Nuh-uh," Ronnie says, but she's thinking more about what he just said: *I came to watch you.* Archie came to watch *her.*

Score one for Veronica Lodge!

"It's cheerleading, Archie," she says. "Not for the faint of heart."

"I see that," he says with that smile of his, and Veronica swoons on the inside. This right here, flirting with Archie? It's her favorite part of practice.

"So," she says, stepping up close and sliding her arms around Archie's neck. "Where are you taking me tonight?"

"Tonight?" Archie furrows his brow. "Did we have plans?"

"Well, not as such," she says, pouting just a little. "But I figured you just hadn't asked me yet. So—what are we going to do?"

Archie ducks his head. "Sorry, Ronnie—I would, but I already have plans tonight."

Veronica lets her arms fall back to her sides. "Oh?" she says, careful not to sound like she's bothered by this information, like she wasn't planning on Archie being hers and hers alone tonight. "Who—"

"Archie!"

Betty Cooper's perky blond ponytail almost smacks Veronica in the face as she half dances past her, her Vixens skirt perfectly pressed as always, and slides her arm around Archie's waist. "There you are," she says. "What time are you coming over later?" And then, like she's only just noticed Veronica standing there, she puts her hand over her mouth. "Oh! I mean— Oh, you don't mind, do you, Ronnie? We're just going to watch a movie or something. No big deal."

Veronica flashes a tight grin at her best friend as the stragglers of the football team pass them by, headed to shower off the practice sweat. "Mind? Why would I mind? You two have fun tonight," she says.

"You sure?" Betty makes her eyes wide. "I mean, we could always swing by Pop's after to hang, if you want. I told Jughead we'd go say bye before he and his dad go off on their fishing trip or whatever, and you know he's always at Pop's, so—"

"Don't be ridiculous," Veronica says, and out of the corner of her eye, she spots the one and only Reggie Mantle chugging Gatorade. An idea blooms in her mind.

Perfect.

"In fact," she says, raising her voice, "I completely forgot, but I already have plans, too. With Reggie!"

At the sound of his name Reggie looks over, one lock of dark hair falling perfectly across his forehead, and points at himself. "Me?"

"Yes, you, silly!" Veronica shimmies over to him and throws one arm around his neck. "We're going out tonight. Remember?"

Reggie frowns like he's trying to remember when he asked Ronnie out, except he asks her out at least three times a week—it's just that Veronica never says yes.

Unless she needs a backup, of course.

"Oh, yeah," he says, the confusion clearing from his pretty face. "Like I could forget."

"Perfect," Betty says, her cute little nose scrunched up from the effort of her smile. "I've got Archie, and you've got Reggie. What more could a girl ask for?"

Veronica has to bite her tongue to keep from saying what she wants to. *Yes, I've got Reggie*, she thinks. *What more, indeed.*

Betty slings her bag over her shoulder and waves. "See you later, V."

"Bye, Ronnie," Archie says. "Reggie."

The boys do one of their oh-so-Neanderthal chest bumps, and then Archie and Betty walk away, Betty's arm still possessively around Archie's waist. It's all Veronica can do not to let out a mournful sigh as she watches them go. Why is it always Betty and never her?

What does she have that I don't?

"So." Reggie rakes a hand through his hair and looks down at Veronica in a way she guesses is supposed to be hot but kinda makes him look like a puppy dog. Yes—that's exactly what Reggie is: an overexcitable Labrador with big brown eyes and a deep-seated urge to sniff people's butts. "You have great timing, Ronnie. My parents are out of town all week and—"

Veronica cuts him off. "You wanna go out? Pick me up at eight," she says, all her faux perkiness dropped. "Daddy has a business meeting at the house, and I do not want to get trapped in another one of his deadly boring discussions about town planning regulations or whatever it is."

"But what about—"

Veronica snatches her pom-poms up and shakes them in his face. "Eight o'clock sharp, Reggie. Or don't bother coming at all."

CHAPTER TWO
CHERYL

"UGH!" CHERYL SITS up and launches her phone through the air, not caring if she cracks the screen. Whatever; she can always buy another.

What can't I buy? she thinks. *Besides friends who won't bail on me at the last second?*

She slumps back against the headboard of her bed, pink satin sheets swirled around her legs. Perfect. Friday night and she has nowhere to go, nothing to do, and absolutely nobody to do it with.

This is the problem. Everyone wants to be Cheryl's friend when it's time for a party, when she's offering up her pool on a perfect summer day, when it's late and nobody wants to go home and Cheryl says, *My parents are away for the weekend, everybody come to my place!* Everybody loves the Cheryl who can smack you down with only three words, the Cheryl who'll flirt to pass the time in study hall. But when it comes to anything real—

Everybody disappears.

Even her brother, Jason, is gone, away for the year at boarding school in Switzerland. Stupid Switzerland. At least when he's here she has somebody to bother, but with him gone, she's all alone.

Cheryl forces herself out of bed, because she knows if she doesn't, she'll stay there all night feeling sorry for herself. Maybe other losers stay in on Fridays watching sad movies and crying into their pillows, but she has not reached that stage of desperation yet. Cheryl Bombshell does not cry into her pillow.

She crouches to rescue her phone: no damage done.

No new messages, either. She taps back to her last message to Midge and Nancy, her so-called friends: *I can't believe you're ditching me to go get felt up by some Neanderthal onion-breath Bulldogs. Hello!!! Dinner from my parents' private chef?! Better than hot dogs and a tongue sandwich from those geeks!*

Cheryl sighs, a mournful sound. Of course they haven't replied. This is exactly it: Her girls will come hang out if and only if they have nothing better to do. Cheryl kind of gets it—if she had been asked out by a hot, fun, smart girl tonight, she'd have dropped her friends faster than her mom dropping her credit card for a round of Botox. But the key thing is *hot* and *fun* and *smart*. Nancy and Midge are about to be mauled at the drive-through by Chuck and Turtle, literally the two most boneheaded football players Riverdale High has to offer. That's what offends Cheryl the most. How dare they hold those boys in higher regard than *her*?

"Fine," Cheryl says aloud to herself, dropping her phone onto the cushioned landing of her bed this time. "I don't need you. I have better things to worry about than you. Come on, Bombshell. Get it together."

She closes her eyes for a minute, breathing in and out in a hypnotic sway, until she feels calmed. This Friday night she may have no plans, but in a week's time she's going to be the belle of the ball. Well: star of the gala, maybe. Center of attention at the opening of her family's new hotel, at the very least. And center-of-attention necessitates the *perfect* dress.

Cheryl flings open the doors to her walk-in closet and breathes in the perfumed air, a smile finally settling on her face. She enters, running her fingers along the rows of velvet and leather and silk, most in her signature shade of vivid red, that perfect clash with her bright amber hair.

They think all I'm good for is my mansion and my money? she thinks. *Well, I'll show them. One day I'm going to run this town. And next week, this new hotel? It's only the beginning.*

CHAPTER THREE
VERONICA

"MOM! DADDY!"

Veronica stands in the foyer, fixing her signature pearls around her throat as she calls up to her parents. Reggie should be here any minute, and her parents always get so snotty if she leaves without saying good-bye. Best to keep them sweet.

"Daddy?" Veronica cranes her head back to look up the stairs, listening for any sound of her parents up there.

Nothing.

Huh. Weird. Her father has a meeting tonight, but Ronnie hasn't seen anybody arrive, and before meetings her father always puts an old record on his top-of-the-line turntable and fills the house with Count Basie or Benny Carter as he mixes cocktails for his company.

Maybe whoever he's meeting got here while I was in the shower, she thinks. So maybe they're deep in conversation already and that means Veronica can slip out without bothering to say bye?

She rolls her eyes and groans. No, because then when she gets home later tonight, they'll chastise her for being rude and not introducing herself to their guest.

"So many stupid rules," Veronica says, and she climbs the wide staircase in her spindly black heels. So many rules and yet Veronica tries her best to stick to them all, because her parents are just a *little* old-fashioned sometimes, and playing the perfect-daughter role is something she's willing to do if it gets her points.

Earn points, win prizes. Like, say . . . the new Jaguar she's got her eye on. Metallic black, leather interiors. *I'm going to look so slick cruising around town with the top down*, Veronica thinks as she approaches her father's study.

"Daddy?" She knocks decisively, the way her father taught her— handshakes and knocks and ultimatums all must be delivered with confidence—and waits. "I'm going out now! Reggie's coming to pick me up. So I'll see you tomorrow, probably. Okay?"

She presses her ear to the warm dark wood of the door. "Daddy? Mom?"

Veronica opens the door.

Her father's study is empty. Flames crackle in the fireplace, and there are three glasses on the low glass table between the two tufted leather couches. Three glasses—one for her mother, one for her father, and one for their guest.

Veronica wrinkles her nose in confusion. Where are they, then?

She takes a couple of steps forward, meaning to grab one of the glasses, see whether its contents have warmed or if they're still icy cold. But those two steps bring her to a new angle and a scene unfolds before her and—

Veronica screams.

There, on the floor. Between the table and the couch.

A body.

No. Two bodies; the other is behind the couch, partially hidden. Her mother's hair falls in a wave across the floor, half covering her face, frozen in agony.

"Mom!"

Veronica launches herself across the floor, sinking to her knees at her mother's side. "Oh my god, oh my god," she says, a trembling whisper. "Oh my god, Mom, please—" What is *happening?*

They look . . . but they can't—her parents can't be—

Dead?

No.

"Mommy." Veronica shakes her mother, violently enough to dislodge the pearls, identical to Veronica's, that are wrapped around her neck. "Mom, wake up—"

She stops, her eyes catching on something bright and shining. What's that there?

Below the pearls, at her mother's throat, blooming.

Veronica puts her fingers to her mother's skin, and when they come away wet and red, she isn't sure what to think except for *blood.*

No no no no no, Veronica thinks, and suddenly she is trying desperately to remember the first aid class the Vixens were forced to sit through. In case any of them ever had an accident while there was no teacher around, they'd been told, but the instructor had been *so* unbearably dull and Veronica had whispered to Betty throughout the whole thing, giggling in the back row of the bleachers.

Think, think. "Okay," Veronica says, like speaking it aloud will make it all work. "Find a pulse. First thing, find a pulse, make sure they're breathing." Veronica takes a deep breath herself, but when she puts two fingers to her mother's neck her hand is shaking.

She feels no pulse, no throbbing, beating blood. But—

Veronica shifts on her knees, shuddering as she touches blood again, and she tries not to think about it too much as her fingers feel something else. Lower down, right beneath where her mother's pulse should be—

She leans in, eyes wide, to see what she surely can't be feeling but yes, right there—

Two small puncture wounds in her mother's throat.

"Holy—" Veronica scrambles back. No. That can't be real.

She turns to her father's body now, and beneath him the imported cloud-white rug is stained a deep, foreboding red. "Daddy." Veronica does the same check on him, and it's exactly the same: two punctures, oozing blood, right there in his throat.

Veronica spins away from him, from her mother, from the dead bodies of her parents lying there before her.

Phone. Phone—911—pick up the phone, Veronica—

She has to slide back, find her clutch where she dropped it on the floor upon seeing her parents, but when she has it she scrabbles to find her phone inside. Her hands shake as she dials those three numbers, and as she holds the phone to her ear, listening to it ring and ring and ring, she watches her parents and tries to keep from shattering into a thousand pieces.

"Nine-one-one, what's your emergency?"

The voice on the other end is tinny and faded as the phone slips from Veronica's cold fingers and lands on the floor with a loud bang, an instant spiderweb of cracks shooting across the now-dark screen.

My parents—

My parents are dead.

Veronica clutches her knees to her chest. They *are* dead; she's sure of that. Living people need a pulse. Living people need to be warm, to move, to breathe. She's been sitting here for however long now and neither of them have shown any sign of life remaining. Not a twitch of the fingers, or a fluttering of movement behind closed eyelids. No spark of soul, no firing of neurons or anything deep inside their brains.

So they are dead.

That much is clear to her, however much Veronica wishes it wasn't. But the marks—

Veronica looks blankly at her shattered phone, the voice on the other end of the line silenced. *My parents are dead,* is what she should have told the operator, but maybe it's good that she didn't get that far. Because then what? When they asked what had happened, what was Veronica going to tell them?

She presses up against the closest couch, leaving smears of blood on the dark leather. There is only one creature that makes that kind of mark on people, and it doesn't exist. It is a thing of fairy tale and myth, of creepy midnight bonfire stories, of Halloween costumes.

That much is clear to Veronica, too, but those wounds on her parents . . .

"They don't exist," she says aloud, her voice a breathy gasp in the silence of the study. "It's not real, this isn't real, none of this is—"

And then the silence is broken.

There's a noise behind her, something that sounds almost like a laugh, vibrating through Veronica's bones, and she whips around.

CHAPTER FOUR
REGGIE

REGGIE MANTLE drives too fast.

Always has, always will, probably, no matter how many times the sheriff pulls him over. It's not like he's ever going to get in any real trouble for it. At least, not when he's still a vital member of the Bulldogs. It's a cliché, sure, but the football team is like royalty in Riverdale.

So as long as Reggie keeps making plays and they get to state championships again, he can keep up his favorite illegal pastime.

He's taking a bend in the windy road that leads to the Lodge house when his phone buzzes.

For a split second his heart sinks. If this is Veronica canceling— well, put it this way: It wouldn't be the first (or fifth, or even tenth) time she's done it.

Yet for some reason, Reggie keeps going back for more. His friends roast him for it, but they just don't get it. This thing he and Veronica have—maybe it's not a relationship in the traditional sense of the word, but there's something about her.

Yeah, there's something, *all right,* Moose and Turtle and Chuck all say whenever they bring it up, laughing at him. *Something like short skirts and a superior attitude, huh, Reg?*

Taking the next bend, Reggie smirks to himself. It's not his fault he's so easy to read.

He keeps the car steady on the road with one hand on the wheel and uses the other to check his phone.

The text is only from Moose: *Party at the abandoned bunker,* it reads. *Come by later.*

Reggie tosses his phone back onto the passenger seat and drums on the dashboard. Ronnie might be up for it, after their date. At least it'd be a way for him to get some more time with her.

The moon's high in the sky above, the glow of it lighting the way. He should tell Ronnie to bring a change of shoes, because those heels she likes to wear? They are *not* meant for walking through woods to old fallout shelters.

He reaches for his phone again, stretching his arm and clawing the phone back to his hand. *Maybe a jacket, too,* he muses as he begins to type with one hand. It's early fall still, warm enough, but also cool enough in the evenings and at night to need additional layers. Besides, a cold Veronica is a Bad-Mood Veronica, and he doesn't want that.

Make sure to bring some sneakers. And don't worry: it's for a surprise you'll like, he types, tongue sticking out the corner of his mouth in concentration. Driving and texting simultaneously: Sure, everyone's always trying to stop it, but few realize how hard it is to actually *do*.

Be there in 5, he finishes, and tosses the phone again. He has a good feeling about tonight. Like something big's finally about to happen.

CHAPTER FIVE
VERONICA

THE LAUGH FROM the corner of the office reverberates, and a frozen finger of fear runs up Veronica's spine.

Then a figure appears before her, a calm grin across his face.

"What have you done?" Veronica's words come out breathy, panicked, as she scrambles backward, trying to retreat from danger.

This man is *danger*. Her internal alarm system is going wild, and she's not stupid—here are her parents, dead, and here is a stranger inside her home, and it doesn't take much to put the pieces together.

"What have you done?" Veronica repeats, the question that isn't really a question shrill and piercing as she stares up at the stranger. "You killed them. You *killed them*!"

The man in front of her is tall, white, with eyes like a thunderstorm and one perfect curl sweeping over his forehead. He looks young, maybe midtwenties; too young to be one of her father's business associates. Yet here he is, in sharp black pants and a crisp white shirt, sleeves rolled up to the elbow, and an expression on his face that shows he isn't afraid of Veronica at all, or her screaming, or what he's done.

Veronica notices it a split second later: His shirt is not all white. The cuffs, the collar, a drop on his chest: all bloodred.

"Veronica," the man says, and his voice is low, a twisted smile within it. "So glad you could join us."

"Get away from me." Veronica struggles to her feet, bloodied hands slipping as she grabs for support, or a weapon—something, anything, that she can brandish to show this monstrous creep that she means business. "Get *away*." When she's steady she holds her hands up and takes a slow step backward. "Get out of my house. I'm going to call the cops, and they're going to be here *so* fast, so you should leave, now, unless you want to end this night in handcuffs."

Veronica tries to hide the shake in her hands and her voice. *Great threat, V.* Her phone is still on the floor where it landed before, and unusable, and besides that—

This man just murdered two people. I don't think he's afraid of the cops.

I don't think he's afraid of anything.

Veronica swallows, hard. She wishes she could say the same about herself, but her heart is hammering so violently it feels like it's going to burst right out of her rib cage and land heavily in the already bloody mess in front of her. "Go!" she says, willing herself to sound stronger, more controlled. "*Leave.*"

The stranger laughs, a throaty sound from his wide-open mouth, and Veronica sees two rows of perfect white teeth.

Then she sees the sharp teeth that cap off each row—canines longer than any normal human should possess.

Long, needle-sharp fangs so ready to rip into her.

No no no no no.

That's the running refrain in Veronica's mind when she squeezes her eyes shut. *When I open them, all of this will be gone. When I open them, my parents won't be dead. When I open them, I won't see this man standing in front of me, because monsters like him are not real, Ronnie. They are. Not. Real.*

She opens her eyes.

The stranger is only an inch from her face. "Boo," he says.

Veronica screams, a raspy cry of panic as the man—no, not man, *vampire*—grabs her and laughs. He grips her by the shoulders and shakes her, like that'll stop her noise, and Veronica can already feel the bruises blooming beneath her skin.

"Come, little Lodge," the vampire says, and this close his breath is sharply metallic, coppery. "Oh, this is going to be fun."

He's going to kill me, she realizes. *He's going to use those fangs, he's going to rip my throat open with them, and I'm going to die, all while Reggie freakin' Mantle is coming to pick me up.*

I'm going to die, and when I'm gone Reggie's going to turn me into some lovesick dead girlfriend, isn't he?

It's that stupid thought that does it. Reggie's going to show up here and find her dead, and he'll tell the story a thousand times: how he was on his way to her and if he'd just been a few minutes earlier she could still be alive, and everyone will think he's so pure of heart, and, worst of all, they'll think Veronica *actually* wanted to date him.

"Hell no," she says, half to him but mostly to herself. "I am *not* going out like this." And without warning she rams her knee as hard as she can between the vampire's legs.

It's a classic move, if a little cliché, one that Veronica learned in the self-defense class she actually *did* pay attention in. But it's effective—the vampire buckles the slightest amount, only for a second, but it's all the time Veronica needs.

She uses the distraction to wrench one arm free, about to wriggle from his grasp, but then the vampire forces her back, up against her father's desk.

"You want to fight?" he says, and makes a tutting noise. "I expected better, Veronica. Your father told me such wonderful things about you."

"He did?" Veronica is sidetracked instantly—all she ever wants is for Daddy to compliment her, say he believes in her, tell her how proud he is. She's the heir to the Lodge empire, after all—one day she wants to run it all, and she wants him to know she's going to be good.

The realization punches her hard in the gut, the air rushing out of her in one shocked breath.

Her dad is dead. She'll never get to prove anything to him, not anymore.

"Oh, yes." The vampire grabs hold of Veronica's chin, forcing her to stare at him. His hands are cold, but there's a hum beneath them, like the quiet sound of a power line. "He told me all about how beautiful and well-behaved you are. I guess he was right . . . about one of those things."

Veronica bristles.

Beautiful? Well-behaved?

How about smart, Daddy? How about creative and business-minded?

"Men," Veronica says, disgust mixing with her grief. "You're all so shallow I'm surprised you don't drown in it." That doesn't even make sense, she knows, but it's fine. All she wants is to keep him talking, keep him going long enough to find something she can use as a weapon.

The hand she got free is casting around the desk behind her. Papers; a half-smoked cigar; a handkerchief—

The vampire grips her chin harder and brings his face down, level with hers. When he smiles, Veronica sees those sharp fangs again, and she swallows.

Come on, Ronnie, come on—

"I have big plans for you," he says. "We're going to be friends, you and I."

—pencil, key chain, letter opener—

Letter opener.

Veronica closes her fingers around her newfound weapon at the same moment the vampire forces her head back, exposing her throat. He yanks at her pearls; they scatter, the sound of them hitting the floor like bullets and—

Go, now, do it.

He bites her right as Veronica brings her arms down and drives the sharp letter opener into his back.

Veronica hisses as the pain rips through her neck and up the side of her face; it's like his teeth are molten metal, slicing her and burning her at the same time. The shock of it narrows her vision; she can feel herself beginning to blur, but she can't give in; she can't give up.

With all the energy she has left, Veronica twists the letter opener and rams it as deep into the vampire as she can, and he rears back, releasing Veronica as he searches for the weapon. "You little—"

Veronica doesn't stay to catch the end of that. With one hand clasped to her bloody neck, she takes off.

As she runs, she's aware of the pulsing beneath her fingers and the vampire's thudding steps behind her and that she's leaving her parents behind. But she has no choice—not if she wants to survive.

She uses the only advantage she has: her knowledge of the house. Behind a panel in the upper hall is a set of stairs that goes straight to the garage. That's where Veronica runs, crashing into the panel and leaning all her weight on it so it turns. When she's in, she pushes it closed again and rushes down the stairs. *Get to the car*, she tells herself. *You need to get away, Ronnie. Come on, keep going. Help will come next.*

She knows the vampire isn't far behind; he'll see the blood on the wall, or he'll find the other way to where she is. She can't think too hard about it. She just has to get away.

Veronica grabs the set of spare keys hanging from a hook on the wall and slides into her car, faintly registering the blood she's smearing across the cream upholstery.

Oh, I'm definitely going to need that new Jag now.

The garage door is opening painfully slowly, and Veronica revs the engine, drumming her fingers on the steering wheel. "Hurry up, hurry up," she says under her breath, and glances in the rearview.

Two thunderstorm eyes, tinted deep red now, stare back at her.

"Crap." Veronica punches the gas and rips out of the garage, the bottom of the garage door scraping along the roof of the car, and unsure of whether what she's seeing in the mirror is real or her imagination. Heart pounding so fast she can barely feel each individual beat, she careens down the driveway and fishtails out onto the road.

Veronica drives fast and direct, along the dark road that leads from her house back into the main cluster of Riverdale. It's quiet and lonely on this stretch: no lights, no houses to pass by. Just the woods on either side of her and the rain-slick road beneath the wheels.

After a couple of minutes, her heart begins to slow. There's nothing behind her, nothing in front of her.

"Okay," she says, slumping down a little. "You're okay." Not true: The adrenaline's kept the worst of it from her, so far, but she can feel the wound in her neck, where he sank those fangs into her flesh. It's an aching, burning sting, and with each pulse of her heart, even slowing as it is, a little more blood seeps from the wound.

She closes her eyes, just quickly, just to blink the haze of panic from them. *Just gotta keep driving until I'm far enough away. Then I can get this wound fixed up. Then I can be okay, for real.*

Veronica lifts a hand from the steering wheel and gingerly touches her fingers to her neck, sucking in a sharp breath at the jolt of pain that flashes through her body at the touch.

When she takes her hand away, she can feel the wetness of blood coating her skin, and she glances down to see how bad it is. How deep the red is.

But when she looks back up it's at bright lights, heading straight for her.

Veronica wrenches the wheel, but her hands are sticky with the combination of her parents' blood and her own, and she swerves exactly the wrong way. "Crap, no, no!"

Everything turns in slow motion, the second before the collision stretching out to minutes, hours. She hears the screech of her own tires, feels the air swirl around her and the bite on her neck burning, the rhythmic pulse sending more blood out. *Move*, she's trying to tell her body, except where is there for her to go? And what can she do to avoid what's about to come?

It's too late.

As time clicks back into place, Veronica sees the driver of the other car.

Face frozen in surprise, eyes wide and still pretty, even as he careens toward doom.

It's Reggie. Of course it's Reggie. On his way to pick her up—who else would be on this stretch of road at this time?

"Reggie—" She starts to call for him, but her words are lost in the violent grinding of metal on metal.

The impact tosses Veronica forward. She tries to shield herself, arms over her head, but it's all too fast now, and the sky above her is pricked with so many stars . . . *Or is that a thousand tiny fragments of glass?*

That's the last thing she thinks before everything goes static.

CHAPTER SIX
VERONICA

LIGHT.

Moon. Moonlight.

Cold.

Cold and dark and moonlight—

Look up.

No.

Look away, move away, get away, gotta get away, gotta move—

But it hurts; it all hurts. Every move is like a stab of glass. A stab of icy, icy cold, like midwinter—but winter's far away still, isn't it? Isn't it . . . ?

Crawl.

Crawl over dirt, over stones, crawl, crawl, keep moving—

Follow the way—

Follow the moon.

Crawl, you can make it.

No, no, I can't. Not yet.

Sleep now . . .

CHAPTER SEVEN
VERONICA

DARK.

Moon dark—where is it now, where did it go?

Moon gone.

Wait—

Who's there? Is somebody there? Help me! Help—

Cold gone.

Good.

No more cold. Warm.

Hot, hotter, hottest, nonono—

Burning burning burning—

Nonono, make it stop. Please please please . . .

CHAPTER EIGHT
VERONICA

TREES.

They are the first thing she notices when she wakes.

Veronica blinks, once, twice, a feeling like grit deep in her eyes.

Where am I? How did I get here?

Last thing I remember—

Veronica winces. Her memory, her mind—there's nothing there but a void. She remembers . . . cheer practice. Yeah, there was practice, and Betty and Archie were there, and then—

I came home, right? I must have. But then—how did I end up out here?

She shakes her head; that's as much as she can recall. Whatever happened between practice and now is gone.

She shivers as coldness registers. Cold and damp.

There's an ache deep inside her and a burning in her throat.

She stretches, testing her body.

Head: hurts if she moves too fast, but yes.

Hands: yes.

Feet: whatever shoes she was wearing are gone, but yes.

(Oh, I hope I wasn't wearing my favorite black heels, the ones with the pearl ankle straps—)

Every part of her is here and accounted for.

She feels the ground beneath her: loamy, rain—or maybe dew—dampening her fingers. And then Veronica sits up, a long, guttural moan as she gets there.

Now that she can see herself, she checks herself again and sucks in a breath. In her left arm there's a piece of glass maybe four or five inches long, embedded deep inside her flesh.

Last thing I remember—

It comes back in a tidal wave: her parents, the monstrous stranger, her escape.

And then—

The crash.

Lying on the side of the road.

And—

"Reggie," she says, and her thin, scared voice winds into the emptiness of the woods around her. "Daddy. *Mom.*"

They're gone, aren't they? Her parents, most definitely. And Reggie?

If I survived, then maybe he did, too, she thinks, but it's a shaky lie she's telling herself to cover the fear: the fear that Reggie is dead just like her parents.

Just like—

Veronica puts her hand to her neck, to the bite mark she now shares with her parents.

She feels around, pressing at first softly and then harder all around her throat.

The puncture wounds are gone.

"That's not possible," she whispers to herself. Wait. Is she losing it?

She looks at the piece of glass stuck inside her arm. A small, sensible part of her brain tells her not to touch it, leave it for the EMTs who are surely coming to rescue her, but then the rest of her takes over.

The marks on her neck are gone. Thinking about it, she doesn't even hurt that much. She was thrown from her car, in a head-on collision; she shouldn't even be able to move, right?

Veronica touches the glass, biting her lip reflexively as she waits for the pain to course through her. And it comes, a pain does come, but it's not the lightning bolt it should be. Closer to the sting of a blunt razor clumsily nicking an ankle than the blackout jolt of dislocating her shoulder on a cheer stunt gone wrong.

As before, in her father's study looking over her parents' bodies, Veronica finds herself knowing, deep down, what this means.

As before, she tells herself this isn't real.

It can't be. It's impossible. *Im-pos-si-ble.* As in, things that can't exist, as in completely not even close to being real, as in no one will ever believe Veronica if she tells them what she thinks she is now.

No. Not what she thinks. What she knows her lack of pain and her healed bite mean.

But she wants to test, to be sure.

Without any fanfare, she rips the glass shard from her arm. *"Ahh!"* Veronica makes the noise, but it's a show, really, because just like before, it only hurts as much as a mosquito sting.

And then she watches, equal parts fascinated and horrified, as the gaping wound in her arm begins to stitch itself closed right in front of her eyes.

"Holy . . ." Veronica swallows and watches as the mess of blood and layers of open skin shift and throb, flesh knitting back together, the ooze of her insides vanishing until there's nothing. Only a smear of red that, when she wipes at it roughly, reveals perfect, unmarred skin beneath it.

Her stomach still aches, but it's not from the crash, or the struggle with the stranger back at the house. It's as if it's turning inside out, roiling with hunger.

There's the burning in her throat, too.

Veronica sits there, afraid to move, because if she moves then the night continues on and she has to deal with her new reality. That's what this is, isn't it? Reality. No dream, or nightmare, or concussion-induced hallucination.

All she has to do is add up the pieces.

First: She was bitten by a monster with razor-sharp fangs.

Second: She feels no pain.

Third: There's that ache in her stomach and the fire in her throat that she knows is an insatiable hunger-thirst.

Fourth: She's capable of almost-instant healing.

Veronica squeezes her eyes shut. There is one more thing she needs to check, but she can't, yet.

She doesn't want to.

Instead, she gets to her feet and begins the climb up to the road. "Reggie," she calls, and somewhere in the canopy above her a bird calls back. "Reggie! Can you hear me? I'm coming for you!"

But when Veronica makes it roadside she stops, confused.

Only her car sits in the middle of the road. There's glass everywhere, and the hood is crumpled, clear signs of an accident but—Reggie's car is gone. And Reggie himself is nowhere to be seen.

I hit him, Veronica thinks. She knows she did; she saw him when she did it.

Or she—she *thinks* she saw him, at least.

But if I hit him, where is he?

"Reggie!" She calls his name once more into the dark, but she gets back the same silent answer as before. She turns it over in her mind. Maybe it wasn't Reggie. Maybe it wasn't anybody at all—perhaps it was only a deer that she hit.

Please, Jesus and god and mother Meghan Markle, let it have been a deer.

Veronica stands barefoot on the wet road, lost. Right leads back to home, to her parents' bodies, most likely to the vampire who attacked her. Left leads to town, some kind of civilization.

Any other night, any other accident, Veronica's choice would be simple: go home and call for help.

But what help will come for her now? How can she go home when that's where the danger lies?

Another bird—maybe the same one that called to her—wheels through the sky above her, a dark shape against an even darker night. Veronica watches it for a moment and then looks to the ground.

She takes a deep breath.

Reggie isn't around to help, so there's no more putting it off. She has to know now, once and for all.

She crouches and picks up one of the larger fragments of her windshield. She raises it slowly, the dread of what version of herself

33

she's about to see sitting like a block of cement, deep in the pit of her stomach.

When Veronica finally finds her reflection—*Oh*, she thinks, *well, that myth clearly isn't true; good to know*—she exhales.

Okay. Other than a few leaves in her hair and a smear of blood on her cheek, she looks normal.

A voice whispers in the back of her mind: *The stranger looked normal, too. Until he smiled.*

That's the true test, Veronica knows.

She aims a smile at herself.

The her who smiles back bears straight white teeth, the result of two years of painful orthodontia, and Veronica can't quite believe it. She has no fangs; there is nothing abnormal there at all.

She touches a thumb to her teeth, running the fleshy pad of her finger along the edges as if to confirm what she's seeing.

No fangs.

Could that mean she's . . . *wrong?*

Maybe the stranger isn't what she thought, and maybe the bite on her neck was just the kind of thing a weirdo creep like him would do. And maybe the bite's no longer there and her arm healed instantly because . . . because . . . well, she's been taking a lot of vitamins, lately. Collagen supplements could *totally* turn her into a superhuman wound-repellant machine, right?

Veronica exhales, and then a twist of hunger slices through her. It's physical, like a tear through her torso, and she folds over for a second before straightening back up, catching herself in the glass again. Then it slips from her fingers as she freezes.

Her skin is its usual honey color, but instead of her usual deep brown, her eyes are red. And instead of her perfect teeth, there they are: long, terrifying, sharp.

Fangs.

All the better to eat you with, Veronica thinks, and then she begins to laugh, the only response she has to this new, now confirmed, information about herself.

I, Veronica Lodge, am a vampire.

What now?

CHAPTER NINE
REGGIE

REGGIE COMES TO in the middle of the road. He knows he's in the middle of the road because it's clear in his mind what just happened, even though it probably should be blurry, he thinks—but it's the opposite of that.

Veronica's car coming at him. The screaming of metal on metal. Flying through the air.

Help.

He tries, but the word won't come. His voice won't come.

Help, is what he wants to say. *Somebody please help me.*

He's not sure if he's hurt badly or just bad enough. Won't be playing in the next game, that's for sure.

Where's Veronica?

He'd turn his head to look for her, if he could. If he wasn't afraid of what the movement might do to him.

For a moment he'd thought he had finally done it, gotten Veronica to take him seriously. But now, somehow, he's lying in the middle of an empty road, and Veronica's somewhere nearby, hurt. She must be hurt, and there's nobody around to help them.

Reggie blinks fast, trying to clear the grit—maybe glass—that's lodged itself in his eyes.

And then he feels a weight on his tender belly.

When he focuses, he sees: It's just a bird. A bird, black and shiny-eyed, has landed on him, for some unknown reason.

Go away, he wants to say, and then—*no, don't go. Bring help.* But it's just an ordinary bird, he knows, not some kind of magic message-carrying creature.

It's watching him. Staring at him.

It's just a bird. How can a bird stare? *But it is*, Reggie thinks. Its small eyes are fixed on his and then it hops—no, doesn't hop; it takes two very deliberate steps with its hooked claw feet, along his body.

And then Reggie knows for sure he's in a bad state, because the bird begins to . . . *transform*?

Reggie's eyes roll back as he feels the ground move beneath him—even though that's not possible. Or maybe *he* is the one moving, being dragged into the brush out of harm's way.

His eyes refocus, and the bird—

It had begun to transform, he could've sworn it did. But now it's still sitting there on his chest. Watching him with those pitch-black eyes.

But Reggie is still moving, the trees above blurring as someone keeps dragging him farther into the woods, off the road and out of the way of harm. *Help*, he thinks, but it's relief now, rather than a cry of pain. Somebody's here, somebody's helping him.

He looks up to see the face of his savior, but there's nothing above him except dark sky and the canopy of ancient trees.

And then he feels the fire.

It starts somewhere below, burning through his neck and then racing, impossibly fast, down his arm and across his chest. Then it's everywhere.

Reggie would panic if he could move, but now he's truly trapped, somehow. Locked inside his body as the fire takes over, and if he didn't think he was dying before, he's pretty certain of it now.

Veronica, he thinks, *Veronica, don't let me die.*

CHAPTER TEN
BETTY

"SCOOT OVER." BETTY sets the bowl of popcorn on the table and takes her place on the couch, close enough to Archie to smell the coconut scent of the product he swears he doesn't use in his hair. Like he just looks so carefully, perfectly disheveled every single day by complete accident. "Ready?"

"Are *you*?" Archie unpauses the movie, right as the killer clown's face fills the screen.

Betty lets out a small scream and burrows into Archie's shoulder. "Warn me before you do that!"

He laughs. "You always pick these scary movies, and then you can't handle them," he says. "I'm starting to think this is just a ruse."

"How dare you, Archie Andrews." *Of course it is*, Betty thinks. *What better way to spend a Friday night than letting a boy like Archie protect you from the big, scary movie?* Like she needs protecting. Straight boys can be simple, though: Give them a damsel in distress and they'll try their best to rescue her.

Her mind flashes to Ronnie, out with Reggie tonight instead of where she really wants to be, which is in Betty's exact place. She feels a little bad—but only a little. It's not her fault that Ronnie likes Archie, too, and it's not her fault that Archie said yes to hanging out tonight.

Betty pretends to watch the movie but sighs to herself. *So why do I feel so guilty right now?*

She sits up and grabs the remote, pausing the movie again. "Archie," she says, "do you think Ronnie's mad at me?"

"What for?"

"Hanging out with you tonight."

Archie makes his thinking face, which is to say that he taps his finger against his lips and looks up at the ceiling as if he's a scientific genius pondering a tricky experiment and not a teenage boy ricocheting between two different girls.

"Well," he says after a minute, "me and her went out a couple weeks ago. And she's out with Reggie tonight. So why would she be mad at you? After all, we're all just friends. Aren't we?"

Betty's mouth drops open. Just friends?

Just? Friends?

First of all: to Betty, there is no such thing as Just Friends. *Just* does not belong in front of *Friends* because friends are the most important thing in the world; people are always throwing that phrase around as if to be someone's friend means nothing at all. Betty would do *anything* for her friends because, besides her family, they are her greatest, most valuable thing.

And second of all? Well—unless Archie's out there making out and cozying up on the couch with everybody else he calls his friend, then what he has with Betty and Veronica is *not* as casual as he's acting like it is.

This is typical Archie, she thinks, folding her arms tightly and staring past Archie at the living room window that looks out onto the dark street. *He can't ever decide between us, so he plays it like it doesn't even matter, and then Ronnie and I are the ones who—*

A face appears in the window.

"Oh my god!" Betty jumps, slipping back on the couch, squeezing her eyes shut. "Archie!"

"What?" He laughs, the noise irritating now. "The movie's not even on."

"Not the movie," Betty says, eyes still closed tightly. "There's somebody outside!"

She feels the couch shift as Archie moves and laughs again, but it's gentle this time. "There's no one there, Betty. I think you just got some residual clown scare going on."

Betty cracks open one eye. "Really?" Then she opens both eyes fully and looks out the window. It's dark, only the shadow of trees waving in the wind and the soft glow of the streetlights. No face, no person there.

But— "I swear, there was somebody there," she insists. "I know what I saw, Archie."

He runs a hand through his hair, mussing it just so. "If you say you saw something, I guess you saw something," he says. "You want me to go outside and check?"

Betty has visions of Archie creeping around the house with a baseball bat in his hands, failing to see the trap the murderer has set for him. "No!" She grabs him. "Let's just—close the curtains and ignore it."

"Okay," Archie says. "It's probably just someone playing a prank.

Trying to scare us." He gets up and crosses the room to pull the curtains shut over the window, closing out the night. "Better?"

"Much," Betty says, but the itchy feeling of being watched doesn't leave her.

You're being paranoid, Betty, she thinks. *Nobody's out to get you. There's no one outside. Monsters aren't real.*

There's a rustle outside the window—*a branch? Someone wandering around holding a knife? No, no, stick with the branch idea*—and Betty flinches.

No. Monsters are not real.

If she thinks it enough times, maybe she'll just start believing it.

CHAPTER ELEVEN
VERONICA

VERONICA WIPES HER nose with the back of her hand, leaving Betty's house behind her as she continues her walk into town.

She's been walking for hours. She didn't know where to go— home was obviously out of the question, so she went to the next best place she could think of.

But when she got to Betty's, she saw Archie and Betty cuddled up together on the couch, framed perfectly, and they looked so warm and disgustingly happy together that it only made Veronica feel worse. What was she going to do, knock on the door and say, *Hey, B, sorry to interrupt your date! Long story but I'm a vampire now, can I stay over? I'd go home but my parents are dead and there may or may not be another vampire waiting to kill me, too. Also if you know what I should do about my dead parents feel free to let me know. Sorry about the blood.*

Turning the corner, Veronica actually smiles a little. Well. At the time it seemed ridiculous, but now—that would have been pretty funny, actually. Betty would have *freaked*. Her ponytail would have done a full 360, like that creepy little girl's head in the old movie.

Veronica keeps on walking without any real idea of where she's going. Her house is out, and now so is Betty's. Archie is with Betty. Where else can she go? She's so tired she just wants somewhere to curl up and get some rest. *That's all I need*, she thinks. *Some sleep and then I can figure out what the hell is going on and what I'm going to do.*

Pain twists her stomach and Veronica gasps, stopping to bend over.

Okay, okay, she thinks. *I get it, body. You're hungry.*

So maybe sleep isn't *all* she needs.

She keeps on walking. This whole eating part of her new reality? Already not her favorite. What's she supposed to do? Drink *human blood*? The blood of another living, breathing being? First: gross. Second: How's she supposed to feed from anyone in Riverdale? She can't just attack someone. She's not going to eat any of her friends, and that leaves her with a bunch of kids whose post–gym class sweat-stench she's been subjected to and a bunch of adults who dress like it's still their late-nineties glory days.

Veronica wrinkles her nose. Sure, she may be a vampire, but she still has *taste*.

Taste. Huh.

What *does* it taste like? Is it one of those things where now that she needs it, it'll be like the finest filet mignon? Or will it be more like those überhealthy grass-and-cucumber juices her parents try to force down her? Good for you, sure, but *foul*.

She's tasted blood before. Once, when she and her parents were on vacation in England. They stayed with old family friends somewhere in the countryside near Oxford, and one morning at breakfast, their hosts served a whole spread of eggs and bacon and everything, plus this sausage-looking thing they called black pudding.

Of course Veronica tried it, and of course it was disgusting, and of course she swallowed it even as everybody laughed at her. What she'd wanted to do was spit the gross mush into a napkin, but her parents would have been embarrassed, so her manners won out.

My parents were still alive then, she thinks, and swallows a sob.

At least then, as a human, she'd had the choice to eat something else. Now?

What if I don't feed? she thinks. *Will I die? Starve to death? Or what if I can only hold out so long—what if it gets to a point where my body, or instinct, or bloodlust, or whatever takes over and I have no choice? I might not be able to control myself. What if that's what happens if I don't eat soon?*

Veronica's been walking without any particular direction, and she doesn't register where her feet have taken her until she sees the sign looming: RIVERDALE HIGH SCHOOL WELCOMES YOU.

She looks up at the building, dubious. Well. It's the weekend, technically; no one will be there, so she won't have to see anyone or explain what happened to her. And the couch in the student lounge is pretty comfy, if you ignore that one sharp spring in the middle.

She sighs. "Don't really have any other choice, do you?" she says to herself, and so she heads into the school.

It's easy enough to get in—over the years, with her powers of persuasion, Veronica has learned every unlocked entrance and key code from the sweet old janitor. She gets inside, half waiting for some alarm to go off, but after a minute it's still all quiet.

At least one thing has gone right tonight.

Veronica makes her way to the student lounge and sighs in relief when she spots the old couch, perfectly illuminated by moonlight through the windows, like the night's saying, *Here, rest your weary feet, V.*

There's a box of old costumes in the closet at the back of the room, she knows, and so she roots around inside, looking for something she can change into and another something that will work as a blanket. Veronica strips off her torn and bloodied dress.

"Farewell, fallen soldier," she says, stroking the silky Peter Pan collar sadly. "You worked hard for me. Your sacrifice will never be forgotten." Then she puts on a dress that must have been from an old performance of *Grease*: a long full skirt and a heart embroidered over her left boob. It's not particularly warm, but at least it's clean, she thinks, and then she takes an old coat to drape over herself.

Once on the couch, curled beneath the coat and feet tucked beneath the poodle skirt, Veronica closes her eyes and grits her teeth. If she doesn't think about the hunger, then it doesn't exist.

That'll work, right?

Just a couple hours sleep, she thinks. *Just a little while and then I'll be ready to go.*

Then I can figure this all out.

CHAPTER TWELVE
DILTON

DILTON DOILEY LETS himself into the school building as the early-morning sun struggles up into the sky. He fights back a yawn as he locks the door behind him. Yeah, he'd rather be in bed at this hour on a Saturday morning, but he's in the middle of an extremely sensitive chem experiment, and if he doesn't come in to check it, it could all go wrong. If it goes right, though, it could secure him a college scholarship, and that's why Ms. Arnold gave him a key to get in.

Sure, maybe he hasn't been exactly 100 percent honest with Ms. Arnold about what *exactly* the experiment involves, but the teacher doesn't need to know that yet. As long as Dilton does everything right and keeps the checks regular, then that pesky little risk of explosion won't be anything to worry about.

Dilton's about to head upstairs to the lab when he catches sight of a dark smudge just down the hall to his right. Probably just a stain the janitor missed but—there's something about it that draws him in.

He gets closer, adjusting his thick-framed glasses, and frowns. It's not a stain; it's a footprint. It's the first in a chain of footprints, made in . . . Dilton sniffs and then wrinkles his nose. God knows what that is.

But he follows the trail anyway. Call it the scientist in him—he sees a puzzle and he has to put it together. Give him a mystery and he has to unravel it.

It's silent, and an eerie quiet surrounds Dilton. School's always weird without anybody else in it. It's the kind of place that's built for crowds and loud noises, not for a singular soul creeping around in the dawn hours. He follows the footsteps, his shoes squeaking alongside them, until he's outside the entrance to the student lounge.

"Hello?" Dilton calls into the room, and he swallows. Not that he's nervous, or scared, or anything like that. Of course not.

He steps into the lounge, left in its usual end-of-the-week state: recycling bin overflowing, sticky rings on the tables, a girl on the couch—

Dilton does a double take. Okay, everything *but* the girl is normal.

And then he looks closer and relaxes. "Veronica?"

Veronica Lodge is asleep on the couch in the student lounge, which is a sentence Dilton never thought he'd say. She also appears to be wearing some kind of costume, which makes him smile because the Veronica he knows, the Veronica who's been his lab partner since freshman year, would not normally be caught dead in a cheap, shiny pink dress like that.

Image is important, Dilton, she's always telling him. *Lets you control the narrative. See, in those awful old glasses you had, you looked like a little*

kid who didn't know jack about science. But in these? Chem genius. Fashion is not *a game, trust me.*

Why she's curled up on the couch here, he doesn't know. But Dilton figures he should wake her up. She probably expected to be alone here, and he doesn't want her to freak out if she wakes up later and hears him and his music in the lab. He crouches beside the couch and shakes Veronica gently. "Hey. Veronica? Wake up."

She stirs a little, a lock of dark hair falling over her face, but shows no further sign of waking.

So Dilton shakes her a little harder. "Veronica," he says loudly. "Time to—"

—*get up* is how that sentence should end, but Dilton doesn't get to say it because Veronica rears up, making an unholy noise so loud Dilton has to throw his hands over his ears. "Veronica—*oof.*"

All the air goes out of him as he flies backward, landing on the floor with a thud, and all of a sudden Veronica's on top of him. Except—

She doesn't look like the Veronica he knows anymore. Instead of brown eyes, this Veronica stares with red eyes, and her usual playful smile is replaced with a cruel snarl, showing—

Dilton blinks, like it'll clear his eyes of what he's seeing.

But no. He's seeing fine.

Veronica Lodge has fangs.

Veronica has fangs and they're heading straight for his neck.

"Veronica!" He thrashes beneath her, and, whoa, when did she get so strong? "It's me! It's Dilton!"

She stops, mouth inches from Dilton's neck, and pulls back. Her red eyes are unfocused. "Dilton?"

CHAPTER THIRTEEN
REGGIE

THE SECOND TIME Reggie comes to, he's in his own backyard.

He wakes with a jolt, his eyes snapping wide open.

This time he's able to sit up—wincing as he does it, but he's better than before, that's for damn sure.

Before.

The car accident, and fire tearing through him, and that beady-eyed bird, and—

And *Ronnie.*

"Ronnie!" Reggie whirls into movement and pats himself down, searching for his phone. He has no idea how he got home, and, it turns out, no idea where his phone is.

The last thing he remembers is that intense pain that had spread through him—like he'd been on fire. But when he looks at his skin, he sees no marks, no blemishes. And he feels—*fantastic.* Better than he's ever felt before, maybe—like the adrenaline of scoring a touch-down but none of the pain from the tackles he has to take to get there.

It's as if nothing at all happened to him. Not that fiery pain, not the car accident.

Nothing.

Reggie slowly climbs to his feet. He's way down at the end of their long, lush yard. Up ahead he can see his house, cloaked in clouds. He has no idea what time it is, or even what *day* it is, but nobody in his house seems to be awake or aware of his existence out here.

I have to get back to Ronnie. She must be out there, still, stuck on the road. And the longer I wait around here, the longer she has to lie there, in pain. Maybe—

No. She's not dying. Not if he can help it.

Reggie starts up the garden, his feet dragging through the mud. And then—

A shadow moves across the lawn in front of him.

Reggie freezes. Stiller than he's ever been before. The reflex happens so fast, he's almost shocked by it.

Ahead, the shadow trots out into the foggy morning, the red of its coat gleaming.

A fox.

Reggie locks eyes with the raggedy creature, and everything else around him fades away. All he sees is this animal; all he hears is the steady *thump-thump-thump* of its heart, the dull roar of its blood rushing through it.

What happens next is beyond Reggie's control.

One second he is watching the fox, and the next he has moved; he has leaped on it and pinned the creature to the ground.

It begins to make noise, a piercing shriek, and Reggie grits his teeth as he wraps his hands around its neck and twists and—

Snap.

The fox falls silent.

It's still warm, though, the thrum of life still faint beneath its skin.

There's a gnawing hunger inside Reggie, and something is calling to him. Something about this animal and himself.

And he is starving, suddenly, aching as if he hasn't eaten in days, weeks, months, and before he knows it, he has brought the fox to his mouth.

He bites, fur and tough skin and muscle grinding against his sharp teeth but then, the break, the barrier giving way, and the animal's hot blood gushes into Reggie's mouth, and he lets out a noise of feral satisfaction.

More, more, he thinks as he feeds from this poor creature, alive only a few short moments ago.

He hunches over the animal and does not think about what he is doing, does not consider Veronica, does not notice the hot blood turning to cold stickiness around his mouth and down his neck and all over his hands.

Reggie doesn't notice any of that. He just feeds.

CHAPTER FOURTEEN
VERONICA

VERONICA SHAKES HER head, a face coming into focus beneath her. Glasses, freckles scattered across light brown skin, deep brown eyes open wide—

Dilton?

She becomes aware of their positions: him looking terrified on the ground and Veronica pinning him there.

"Oh my god!" She jumps up and it's like some tide is receding. The red film over her eyes fades to leave the scene before her bathed in its usual Technicolor, and then there's the weirdest sensation as, within her mouth, those brand-spanking-new fangs shift and move, retracting into her gums. Veronica feels it and touches a hand to the outside of her mouth, awed, and then she shakes her head. "Dilton, I'm so sorry."

He doesn't move, watching her from the floor. "Veronica," he says, his normal introspective tone replaced by something a little shakier. "What—your eyes. Your *teeth.*"

"I didn't mean to jump you," she says. Okay, so maybe there's her answer about the whole *what happens if I don't eat* thing. Or maybe it was just because he woke her up—she's never been a morning person. Maybe she can *totally* control her hunger, actually.

Her stomach twists in response, the yawning ache inside her making itself well and truly known.

*Or maybe I need to eat some*thing *before I eat some*body.

Dilton's still eyeing her suspiciously, and Veronica shakes her head. "You—surprised me. I didn't think anyone else was in the building," she says.

If she talks at him enough, maybe he'll forget what it was he just saw. Or—what he thinks he saw, right, because maybe he didn't see Veronica's face all vamped out at all—if she can convince him he didn't see that, then she'll be safe and she won't have to worry about Dilton Doiley.

"I guess you're thinking, like, what the hell is Veronica doing sleeping in the lounge?" Her voice is too high, but she can't seem to bring it down to its normal pitch. "Weird, right? But I mean, it's a funny story, so—I'm heading up the costume department for the musical and I thought I'd get a head start working on things, so I just came in to check out the supply situation and I guess I was super tired or maybe I'm coming down with something, maybe I should go to the—"

"I saw you." Dilton cuts her off, and he doesn't look so terrified now, but he is still staring at her with an intensity that makes Veronica want to run away as fast as she can.

Run, rabbit. Run run run.

"I saw you," he repeats, and he gets up, slowly. "What's going on, Veronica?"

Veronica swallows. "Dilton, I can explain," she says. "I . . ." But she can't explain, can she? The only explanation she has is the truth, and what will sensible, logical Dilton Doiley say when she tells him she was bitten by a vampire and is now a vampire herself?

"Dilton, I didn't mean to—" She cuts herself off and begins to slink toward the door. "Listen. Forget you ever saw me. You don't need to be involved in this."

Dilton moves to the doorway, blocking her in. "I *saw* you," he says earnestly. "Veronica, I'm not stupid. I know—I know what you are."

Veronica stops where she is and raises her eyebrows. "What?" she says. "Dilton Doiley, don't tell me *you* believe in *vampires*."

Dilton reddens a little at the word and straightens his glasses where Veronica had knocked them askew. "Contrary to popular belief," he starts, and Veronica recognizes his lecture tone, "vampires are not solely mythological creatures. There's plenty of historical evidence to . . . what?"

Veronica knows he's stopped because she's laughing, but she can't help herself. It's just all so out-of-this-world *absurd* that the only thing she can do is let the laughter bubble up. If she stops to think about all of this for a moment too long—about the hunger she isn't sure how to feed, and the new world she's in, and her dead parents, oh *god* her dead parents—then she's pretty sure she'll lose it. She'll shatter into a thousand bloody pieces, and as much as this vampire thing has shaken her, she'd still quite like to live, thank you very much.

"What?" Dilton says again, his eyes narrowing. "What's so funny?"

More absurd—a minute ago she was ready to rip Dilton's throat out, and now he's standing there telling her all about the historical legacy of vampires.

"Nothing," Veronica says, covering her mouth. "I just can't believe your immediate reaction to what just happened is 'I completely believe, without even a second's doubt, that what I just witnessed was definitely Veronica Lodge as a vampire' and not more like *my* reaction, which was 'Holy crap I'm either hallucinating or in some kind of fever dream because vampires are not real,' you know?"

"I'm a scientist," Dilton says self-importantly. "I trust the evidence in front of my own eyes, every time."

Her laughter fades. "So you . . ." She isn't sure what to say, really. She likes Dilton, and he's a good lab partner, but they've never really hung out outside of school. She never would have expected that, out of anybody who might find out, he'd be the one to instantly believe her and understand, and most graciously of all, to not make her feel like she's the protagonist in an extended, extremely realistic nightmare. "You believe in vampires, or whatever? You aren't—you aren't scared of me?"

Now Dilton's the one who laughs. "Of course I'm scared of you," he says. "Everybody's scared of you, Veronica. But if you're asking am I scared *specifically* because you're something more than human? No, not particularly."

Veronica is weirdly touched by this—first by him not screaming and running in fear from her, and second, from the acknowledgment that in this school, Veronica's a power player. It makes her feel proud. "Good," she says. "Because the last thing I can deal with right now is making sure you don't freak out."

"But why are you here?" Dilton asks her now. "How come you were sleeping in school?"

Veronica shakes her head. "It's complicated," she says, and then, like she needs to be reminded exactly *how* complicated, a new hunger pang erupts deep in her gut.

She puts her hand on her stomach, as if that'll quiet it, satisfy her thirst somehow.

Except she *knows* what will satisfy it. She's a vampire now, and vampires drink blood.

Well, this is really not going to jibe with the whole vegan-for-the-planet movement the Environment Club is trying to get us all on board with, Veronica thinks. *Although—technically, it doesn't involve eating animals. Just humans.*

She shakes her head, trying to clear the thought. There's no way she's drinking *human* blood. Nuh-uh, not now, not ever.

Dilton's in the doorway, a pink flush to his skin, and if Veronica listens carefully, she can hear the blood rushing beneath it.

Dilton's eyeing her warily. "What is it?"

"I'll make you a deal," Veronica says. She smooths her hands over the slippery costume skirt and locks eyes with Dilton. "I'm really hungry, and despite my personal objections, you look like a very tasty snack right now, Dilton. So if you can help me find something bloody to drink so I don't have to chow down on you, I'll tell you how I got to be this way. Deal?"

She sees Dilton swallow hard, but he nods. "Deal," he says. "I know just the place."

CHAPTER FIFTEEN
DILTON

"MOM?" DILTON CALLS out as he unlocks the front door. His mom shouldn't be there, he knows—her van isn't in the driveway and according to the calendar up on the fridge, today she's delivering three of her custom-made wedding cakes to three different venues. She should be gone until the evening, at least. But Dilton has gotten caught sneaking in from nefarious science projects enough to know he should never assume.

"Mom?" he calls out again. "Are you home?"

No answer.

He swings the door open wide and ushers Veronica inside. "Come on," he says. "We're safe here."

"Thanks, Dilton," Veronica says, and she sounds exhausted.

Dilton isn't surprised. Somehow, she's gone from Veronica Lodge, Head Vixen and Human, to Veronica Lodge, Vampire, overnight. He hopes she'll tell him how, but for now all he can think is that he, too, would be exhausted if he'd suddenly become an immortal, blood-thirsty monster—not to mention spending the night on the *terrible* student lounge couch.

"And thanks for this," Veronica says, holding up the now-empty bag of blood she sucked down on the drive over. "Who knows how much longer I could have lasted without it? I was truly *so close* to ripping your throat out. For which I am super sorry, of course," she adds hastily. "And believe me, I would *not* have jumped you if I were in my right mind. But I better make sure I keep my levels topped up, huh? Can't have that happening again."

Dilton gives a seminervous laugh. Sure, Veronica might be partly joking, but if she *doesn't* manage to keep herself under control, Dilton actually might meet his end. And he *really* would prefer not to die right now. "It's only pig's blood," he says. Pilfered from the bio lab, meaning there's probably going to be a school-wide scandal on Monday morning when Ms. Lemon finds her stash depleted. But what else was he supposed to do? If there's one thing Dilton knows for sure about vampires, it's that they need blood to survive. Animal was the closest he could get without risking his own life—and he quite likes his life, so that was out of the question. He wasn't sure if pig blood would be okay, but it seems to have done the job. At the very least, Veronica doesn't want to kill him right now, and that's good enough.

"The bathroom's at the top of the stairs," he says, pointing. "And my mom's room is on the right. Help yourself to something to wear."

"Will do," Veronica says, and she tosses him the empty blood bag. "You're a good guy, Dilton."

He waves off the compliment as Veronica goes upstairs, and only once she's locked in the bathroom does he let out a giant sigh.

"What the hell is happening?" he whispers under his breath.

Vampires? Veronica in his house, drinking pig's blood like it's nothing?

He makes his way to the dining table and sits, pulling his laptop from his backpack. It's like he's walked into an alternate version of Riverdale, where the paranormal is just . . . *normal*. He would never have believed it if he hadn't seen Veronica transform in front of his eyes . . .

Her face had been hers and yet not, an angry snarl instead of her trademark supercilious smile, her eyes deep red, her teeth stretched into fangs ready for ripping. And then, when she'd realized who he was, it had all shifted back.

Dilton shakes his head as if to clear that image of Veronica from his mind and opens his laptop.

It's like he told Veronica earlier: He's a scientist. He trusts the evidence.

So it's time to find some more evidence.

From upstairs he hears the noise of the shower, and on his laptop he types. Best to start simple, he thinks. *Vampire mythology*, he writes, and hits "Search."

It doesn't take long for Dilton to get sucked in. This is his favorite part of getting to know a new topic—diving deep into the research, both legitimate and slightly less so, and figuring out what's really going on.

Of course, all the stuff he finds at first is about movies and TV and vampire novels, especially the kind where the vampires inexplicably sparkle. (*Sparkle? Why?* he thinks incredulously. *Is there some kind of compound in vampire blood that would cause that reaction with sunlight? What's the logical, physical reasoning behind this phenomenon?*) Even though it's fiction, a lot of the myths are based in real legend, so Dilton reads all about the different methods of transformation and the various "rules"—vampires who can't walk in the sun, who sleep in old-school coffins, et cetera et cetera.

One article mentions a couple of words Dilton trips up on: *moroi* and *strigoi*. "Interesting," he murmurs aloud, opening a new tab.

Always follow the terms, he so often tells Veronica, and when the search loads, he smiles.

This is more like it.

The page he's on is all about early Romanian folklore, and there are those terms again: *STRIGOI* all in caps on one side of the page, and *Moroi* smaller on the other.

Dilton adjusts his glasses and cracks his knuckles. Time to get down to business.

CHAPTER SIXTEEN
VERONICA

VERONICA WAKES UP disoriented, again, but this time it takes her only a second to realize where she is.

Overflowing bookshelves? A desk littered with papers? Telescope set up to look right at the night sky?

Oh, yeah. She's definitely at Dilton's.

More specifically, she's in his twin bed, sleeping off her previous night's adventures. She sits up, blinking at the growing darkness outside Dilton's bedroom window. She really only meant to lie down for a minute after her shower, but judging from the navy sky outside, it's been more like hours.

Oh well. A rested vampire is better than a grouchy, tired vampire, right?

Veronica gets up and leaves Dilton's room, calling out to him. "Are you up here?"

"In the dining room," Dilton's voice calls back from downstairs.

She makes her way down, taking each step with a little bounce. She feels surprisingly and blissfully refreshed. All it took was a shower, a nap, and an outfit change—she's in a Riverdale Class of 1991 sweatshirt that hangs to mid-thigh, just covering the running shorts, and a pair of white socks pulled up to her knees, all pilfered from his mom's dresser. She almost feels back to her old self.

"Good evening," Dilton says as she enters the cozy dining room, and he throws something in her direction.

Veronica catches it and almost immediately begins salivating. "I'm pretty sure throwing bags of blood around is against your mom's house rules," she says, and then she flicks her fangs out so she can use them to pierce the bag of her dinner.

Okay, so maybe not quite *like her old self.*

She sits beside Dilton at the table, trying not to spill on the lace-edged tablecloth as she sucks on the bag of pig's blood like it's a juice box. It does satisfy her thirst, but in the same way a low-fat frozen yogurt satisfies when what you *really* want is a hot-fudge sundae. Has all the look of being the real thing but only a vague shadow of the right taste. That's why one of Veronica's life rules is Eat the Damn Dessert.

She's not sure if she's ready to Drink the Damn Blood just yet, though. So, for now, piggy will do.

"You know, even a few hours ago the thought of drinking blood made me wanna hurl. But it's actually not so bad." She squeezes the last few drops out and tosses the empty blood bag in the trash. Then she concentrates on pulling her fangs back in. It still feels weird, but she has to master it. She can't be running around town fangs out all the time.

She turns to Dilton. "What do you think?" she asks, fanning her hands around her face. "Back to my usual self?"

"Can barely tell you're a vampire," he deadpans, and then his face changes.

Veronica knows what's coming. "Oh, fine," she says.

"What?"

"You're gonna ask me how I got this way," she says, and the look Dilton gives her is somewhere between ashamed and eager. Of course he's eager to hear the story—it's *Dilton*. The boy thrives on the weird and the wonderful. "Okay. I'll tell you. But no interruptions, okay?"

She tries to clear her throat, but there's a big old lump in it.

It's not hard to know why. It's one thing for her to think about her parents being dead; it's another thing entirely to say it out loud to somebody else. It makes it real, and Veronica's not sure if she's ready for it to be real.

But she takes a deep breath and starts from the beginning. "Reggie was supposed to pick me up at eight," she says, toying with a loose thread on her borrowed sweatshirt. "So I went to see my mom and my dad. I went to say good-bye . . ."

CHAPTER SEVENTEEN

VERONICA

VERONICA DOESN'T ENJOY filling Dilton in, but she has to do it—has to tell him about the stranger vampire who'd killed her parents and would have killed her, too, if she hadn't gotten away. All color faded from Dilton's face when she told him how she'd found her parents' bodies strewn across the study floor, how it had hit her that they were really dead.

"I'm so sorry, Veronica," he says gravely now, once Veronica finishes the first half of her story. "Your parents—I'm so sorry."

"Thanks," Veronica says, with all the weight of a deflated balloon. It feels wrong to say thank you, but what else is there? Her parents are dead.

They're *gone.*

It hits her so hard and so suddenly that Veronica feels like her heart's going to explode. Maybe they weren't perfect, and sure, she got frustrated with her dad and the way he treated her, but they were still her *parents.* They were the ones who tucked her in when she was little, and gave her everything she ever could have wanted, and raised her to be a Lodge through and through.

And now, she thinks, a shocked emptiness in the rest of her mind, *I'll never get to talk to them again. I'll never see my dad smile, or hear my mom's laugh. That's all over.*

"So"—Dilton shifts—"what are you going to do? Should we—should I go . . . get them?"

The image of Dilton dragging her parents' corpses out of the mansion, as creepy as it is, is maybe the only thing that could put a dent in her sudden melancholy. "What, and put them in your mom's deep freezer?" Veronica manages to crack a small smile. "I don't know what I'm going to do yet. But thanks for offering."

"It's the least I can do," Dilton says, and then they both paused, fixing each other with a strange look, and burst out laughing. Like he was just offering to pick up milk at the store or something, not the corpses of her mom and dad.

My capacity for the absurd is truly *being pushed to season-three* Glee *levels*, Veronica thinks.

What happened after all that is easier to talk about—her escape from the stranger, the crash, waking up in the woods to find that she was no longer human.

Still, Dilton lets out a low whistle.

"So it wasn't Reggie that you hit?" he asks.

And Veronica shakes her head. "Can't have been," she says. "There was nothing there when I went back to the road. Maybe . . ."

She trails off, but Dilton reaches out and taps her elbow. "What is it?"

"Maybe it was a hallucination or something," she says. "I don't know. It was like he was right there, except he wasn't. Maybe the vampire . . . he wanted me to see that, or something. Can they do that? Make people hallucinate?"

"Huh," Dilton says, and he taps his finger against his lips thoughtfully. "Well . . ."

He's got a gleam in his eyes. It's the same look he gets in class when he's about to make a breakthrough on an experiment, or tell Veronica all about some weird cult video he found on some creepy secretive part of the internet.

"Spit it out, Dilton," she says. "What did you find?"

"Well, while you were asleep, I did some research," he starts. "So, when we think of vampires, we think of the movie kind, right? Or maybe the TV kind of more recent years. Get turned, feast on blood, can't walk in the sun, you know the drill."

"Sparkly skin," Veronica says, holding her arm out. *Hmm. Time for some bronzer shopping, perhaps.*

"Right," Dilton says with a laugh. "But if we dig back, we find the earlier discussion of vampires has similarities with what we think of now, but it's more grounded in realism. Here's the main thing I found: Eastern European tales of vampires talk about two different kinds. The first one is the moroi. They're people who've died—or been killed, more likely—and then been revived with a vampire bite. The moroi are undead creatures, and some of the tales talk about them being more malleable and easily controlled."

"So they're dead and then come back to life?" Veronica frowns. That doesn't explain her change: The vampire's bite didn't kill her, nor did the crash, and yet she's still here, a newborn vampire.

"Not exactly," Dilton says. "They're alive, but not alive. Dead, but not dead. The *undead*."

Veronica arches an eyebrow. "So like zombies? You're telling me moroi are like zombie vamps?"

"Something like that," Dilton says, his fingers flying over his keyboard. "Okay, and then you have the second kind: strigoi."

He says it with reverence, and Veronica shifts. When she speaks, it's quieter. "Something tells me these ones are less zombie, more monster."

Dilton nods at her. "Strigoi are *living* vampires. The folktales say the first strigoi were souls who had been cursed, to live in immortality and to drink the blood of humans to survive. Some of that old stuff we've always heard is true, according to this. 'Weakness against garlic, silver, holy water, and crosses.' But that's not all—they're way more powerful than the moroi. First, they can exhibit a kind of telepathy, the tales say. They can control the moroi—make them bend to their will."

It's starting to make a kind of sense to Veronica. "So instead of a shambling zombie-vamp gang," she says, "a strigoi can turn moroi into . . . an army. With mind control."

"Right." Dilton turns his laptop around so Veronica can see the images he's found: crude, faded drawings of half-human, half-beast creatures, sporting fangs and wings and pointed ears. "In early myths, the strigoi were sometimes referred to as sorcerers or shape-shifters. Their other power, see, is their ability to appear in other forms—sometimes as animals, sometimes even as other people."

Bats, Veronica thinks. *That old classic.* "But they can only use mind control on moroi?"

"So far as I can tell, they aren't able to fully control other strigoi," Dilton says. "But they *can* be susceptible to a strigoi's powers of persuasion. More mind *tricks* than mind control."

"Mind tricks," she repeats. "Telepathy. Powers of persuasion . . ."

She bites her lip—with her regular teeth, not her fangs. "So what I thought I saw *could* have been a hallucination. Or not a hallucination exactly—a vision. Whatever the stranger wanted me to see."

There's something clawing at the edge of her memory, but she can't focus on it. All she can think now is that the vampire that killed her parents—he'd *wanted* her to crash. She'd thought she was getting away, while really, she was playing right into his hands.

I woke up in the woods, she thinks. *But how did I get there? How did I change?*

Just like that, the memory snaps back.

After the crash. Lying in the road, and feeling cold—colder than the fall night should have made her. The kind of cold you feel when your body is in shock, when you're losing the blood your heart needs to keep you alive.

Then—someone moving her, the sky shifting above her, and the cold transforming to a heat so burning, so searing hot, that she'd cried out in pain.

"That's it," she says, quietly, to herself, like she's forgotten Dilton is even there.

"What's it?"

Veronica looks at Dilton sitting beside her. It's so incongruous, to be discussing the finer points of vampire transformation in the dining room his mom's clearly taken a lot of time and effort to decorate. To be talking about this in front of a row of school portraits chronicling Dilton's growth from a curly haired, gap-toothed little kid to the serious (still curly haired) boy he is now.

"I think I remember turning," she says slowly. "It felt like . . . burning. Like I could feel a fire spreading through my body, and then I must have passed out again—or passed out for the first time, who knows—because when I woke up, I didn't remember what had happened. I saw how I had healed, faster than any normal person should be able to, and then I saw my fangs and I knew what had happened."

She screws up her face. "But I didn't die. I'm certain about that part. So that means I'm not a moroi, right? But then—how does someone become a strigoi? You said the first ones were cursed."

Dilton nods. "Only the first, though," he says. "After that, they could create strigoi in a similar way to moroi. But instead of the bite reviving them, it's the blood that's key. To create a strigoi, they must be bitten and then ingest vampire blood. They don't have to die first. It almost seems like it's a virus—"

"Okay," Veronica says, cutting him off before he can get too deep into his nerd theory. "So if I'm a strigoi, that means he . . . fed me his blood." That makes her want to throw up more than her original horror at the idea of drinking blood did. From *him*? The man who attacked her, who killed her parents?

And now I have his blood coursing through my system? she thinks. *Now I am what I am because of him?*

"Okay," she says again, but it's steely this time. "So how do I undo it? Do I kill him? And how—stake through the heart?"

Dilton holds his hands up. "Whoa, whoa, slow down," he says, and spins the laptop back around. "I don't know about undoing it, but as far as I can tell, yes, you're right—a stake through the heart would kill a vampire. That or decapitation."

"Take his head off?" Veronica leans back. "So that'll kill him, but it might not fix me. That's what you're saying, right?"

"There doesn't seem to be much literature on the vampire-back-to-human process," Dilton says with an apologetic shrug.

Veronica drums her nails on the table as she tries to process all that Dilton's telling her, a terse staccato beat. "Let me see again," she says after a moment, and Dilton slides the laptop across to her.

She scans the page he's on quickly, only seeing all that he's already told her. But none of it is what she really wants to know.

How do I get my life back?

On the sidebar of the page, there's a collection of links. Veronica hovers over them for a second before deciding to click on the very last one.

When the new page opens, it's full of images. Veronica squints, leaning in to see better, because they all look old and like they've been scanned in from ancient books or something. It's mostly more of the kind of images Dilton had found—drawings of vampires in all different forms, some more human-looking and some more monster. Interpretations of a myth, Veronica thinks.

But it's the image at the bottom of the page that catches her attention. It looks like a family tree, almost, with one shadowy fanged figure at the top, *strigoi* written beneath it, and tiers of similarly fanged progeny spreading out beneath. Then the same image is mirrored, but this one has a red *X* laid over the fanged drawing, and each descendant drawn differently—no fangs.

Veronica, like everyone in Riverdale, had to do a family tree project way back in fourth grade. It was easy for her, seeing as how her family was among the founders of the town—there was plenty of history for her to research. She'd spent hours painstakingly cutting and pasting family photos and inking their names and relationships to one another in careful cursive.

But this tree is way less thorough than her project, and the words there aren't in a language Veronica can read. All she can do is interpret the images, and what they seem to be saying to her is how to take down a bloodline.

"Look," she says to Dilton, turning the laptop so he can see and tapping a finger on the image. "I think this is showing us how vampire lineage works. See the strigoi at the top? Underneath are the vampires they've created, I think, and then the vampires *those* ones have created, and so on."

Dilton nods. "So they're all traced back to one strigoi sire. One bloodline."

"Right," she says. "And then look—" She points at the second version, with the sire crossed out. "I'm pretty sure this says that if the sire of a bloodline dies, then all their progeny reverts to their human form."

"That makes sense," Dilton says. "Cut-the-infection-out-at-the-root kind of thing."

A plan is solidifying in Veronica's head, and for the first time since the previous night, she feels a sense of control coming back. "The vampire who attacked me and killed my parents," she says, "he's gotta be the sire. And once we kill him, I'll go back to being human. And everything will be back to normal."

Except for my parents being dead.

Veronica shakes her head. Can't think about that now. First, get her humanity back. Then deal with the earth-shattering loss of her normality.

"I'm sorry, did you say 'once *we* kill him'?"

Veronica covers her grief with a grin at Dilton, flashing her fangs. "What's wrong, Dilton? You scared?"

He sits up straighter, holds his chest out. "What? No way."

"Good." Veronica reaches out and pats his cheek. "Because we're going to need some weapons, my friend."

CHAPTER EIGHTEEN
VERONICA

WHEN DILTON'S MOM gets home later that night, he tells her that he and Veronica are working on an extremely important science paper and he knows the rules about girls staying over but would it be okay, just this once, for this extremely important school reason?

Veronica listens in on the stairs, trying not to laugh at Dilton's earnestness. What does his mom think, that she's going to corrupt her baby boy? Dilton's cute and all, but he's not Veronica's type, and besides, they have way more pressing issues to deal with.

Namely, killing one strigoi sire and returning Veronica to her regular ol' human self.

"Okay," she hears Dilton's mom say. "It's just so nice to see you have a friend over, Dilly!"

Now Veronica feels a pinch of sympathy, but she squashes it. *Focus on the most important thing.*

"Weapons," she says again, when she and Dilton are up in his room. "We need all that stuff you said—garlic, holy water, silver, crosses. Obviously, you'll have to handle all that." She smiles, with her fangs this time. She's getting pretty good at flicking them out and pulling them back in.

It would make *quite* the party trick, if it wouldn't also send everybody fleeing in terror. Or—actually, maybe that's a bonus.

"And then I can have the stakes," she continues. "That should give us a good shot at taking this creep out."

Dilton's already busy on his laptop again. "There's a store that carries everything we need about an hour and a half from here," he says.

"Wait. Seriously?"

Dilton nods. "There's an active paranormal community out there, Veronica. You can never be too prepared."

She rolls her eyes. "This isn't Adventure Scouts, Dilton," she says. "This is Slayer Scouts. And our motto is—"

She pauses. *What is their motto?*

And then it comes to her, and she runs her tongue over her fangs, feeling every ridge and edge, and her smile this time is sharp. "Death to sires."

CHAPTER NINETEEN

VERONICA

IT'S TOO LATE to go on a weapon-buying spree tonight—the paranormal supply store would be closed by the time they got there—so she and Dilton agree to go first thing in the morning.

Dilton's mom insists on Veronica taking Dilton's bed while he takes the couch downstairs. Veronica spends the night sleeping fitfully, woken by dreams of her parents' empty eyes, until she gives up on sleep entirely. She spends the next few hours waiting for the sun to rise, staring at Dilton's ceiling, marked with glow-in-the-dark stars. They're just like the stars Betty used to have, before they decided she was too old for such things, and looking at them now fills Veronica with a soothing kind of nostalgia. Memories of sleepovers at Betty's, being nine years old and desperate to make it past midnight.

When she hears Dilton's alarm going off downstairs, Veronica goes down and makes sure to feign tiredness, yawning the same way he does. "Being up at this hour on a weekend should be outlawed," she says to him, and he just nods blearily as he stumbles upstairs to the bathroom.

They set off not half an hour later and make good time on their way there. They stop first at a clothing store, so Veronica can outfit herself appropriately. "I mean, I can't fight a strigoi in *this*," she tells Dilton, gesturing at her sweatshirt-and-knee-socks combo—an extreme social-media-cool-but-won't-be-cool-in-six-months look. "What have I taught you about fashion, Dilton?"

What she eventually decides on is not quite like her usual style, but it feels perfect for her vampire self on this sire-killing mission: tight jeans with rips at the knees, a ribbed tank, and a cropped leather jacket with zips all over, all black, naturally. And she adds the killer finishing touches: boots with a chunky heel, perfect for stomping Big Bads, and a pair of pearl hoop earrings.

Drinking blood, wearing ripped jeans, and *leather*? Oh, she's doing *all* kinds of new things lately.

When they finally arrive at the paranormal store, the gray-haired woman behind the desk eyes them suspiciously when they enter, like she thinks they're going to steal something, and Veronica sniffs. As if she, a Lodge, can't afford to pay for a few wooden stakes and a pile of garlic.

And also, if she wanted, she could steal this stuff and scare the living daylights out of this woman, she realizes.

Huh. Maybe there's a small upside to being a vampire.

"Don't forget the crosses," Dilton says to her, arms full of liter bottles wrapped in red plastic and proclaiming themselves full of *Father Frank's Certified Holy Water! Straight from the Source!*

She stares at Dilton. "I can't get the crosses," she says. "Remember?" She lowers her voice. "That whole I'm-a-*vampire* thing?"

Dilton looks like he'd smack himself in the head, if his arms weren't full. "Oh, yeah. Well, you find us some flashlights instead. I'll be back in a second."

Veronica drifts around the store as Dilton disappears, scanning the shelves. Silver bullets, for werewolf killing; all manner of herbs and crystals, for spell casting; guides on dealing with faeries and various other beings. *There really is nothing you can't buy*, Veronica finds herself thinking.

When they have everything they need, they pay the grumpy old woman and make a quick escape. The drive back feels longer, but Veronica knows that's her nerves. Okay, so maybe she's a *little* scared of the Big Bad Strigoi. He did almost kill her less than two days ago, after all.

It's okay, she tells herself. They're only going back to her house to look for clues—something to tell them who this sire vampire is, and where they can find him. Because once they find him, Veronica can kill him.

Payback for stealing her humanity.

Payback for taking her parents from her, forever.

Veronica shakes her head violently. She can't think about them now. Once she's dealt with the strigoi, she can figure out how to tell everyone that Hiram and Hermione Lodge have been murdered.

Dilton pulls up outside the Lodge mansion, and Veronica's heart is in her throat. "Okay," Dilton says. "I got us these, as well."

Veronica bursts out laughing when Dilton hands over a walkie-talkie and a matching Bluetooth earpiece. "Are you for real?"

"We're gonna need to communicate," he says. "These are more reliable than our phones. Also, you don't currently *have* a phone."

She eyes him. "You're enjoying this. This is like your superhero final-battle dream come to life, isn't it?"

"I will not dignify that with a response," Dilton says, and he knocks his walkie against Veronica's. "You ready?"

"As long as you are," she says. The plan is simple enough: This is the last place Veronica saw the strigoi, so it's the first place it makes sense for them to search for clues. She'll go in, and Dilton will act as lookout.

If the strigoi is here, or shows up and tries to attack again?

Dilton has the holy water, the silver crosses, and plenty of garlic to pelt the strigoi with. That should weaken the strigoi, and then Veronica will have her chance to stake him, right through the heart.

And then, for good measure, she'll take off his head, too.

(She hasn't told Dilton about that part. That's just a little extra personal revenge, on behalf of her parents.)

Veronica flips the passenger-side visor down and checks the makeup she applied in that first clothing store. Her eyeliner is perfectly winged and her lips painted deep, almost purple, red.

She has her weapons and her armor. "I'm ready. Let's do this."

CHAPTER TWENTY
VERONICA

IT'S CREEPY QUIET when Veronica enters her house.

Well—what else was she expecting?

Go quietly, Dilton had reminded her. *Just in case the strigoi is still hiding out here.*

Veronica steps lightly through the foyer and heads up the stairs. She has a stake, sharp and menacing, tucked in the back of her pants—it'll be the perfect magic trick, when she reveals it and uses it to kill the strigoi, if he shows up.

Lights up onstage and the showgirl takes a bow!

Veronica slows as she approaches her father's study. This is the part she's dreading the most. She doesn't know what her parents' bodies will look like now, what they'll *smell* like, or how she'll react when she sees them. But she can't afford to fall apart; she can't let her guard down and give the strigoi the opportunity to get the drop on her.

She hesitates outside the half-open door, left where she'd flung it on her way out, a bloody handprint just visible on the dark wood. Her breath comes fast, and then she makes an executive decision and turns away.

I'll come back, she tells herself. *I'm not avoiding it. I'm just being thorough, careful with the plan.*

The walkie in her hand crackles. "Veronica?" Dilton's voice is reedy through her earpiece, but at least only Veronica can hear him. "What's going on?"

Veronica quicksteps down the hall, toward the library, and brings the walkie to her mouth. "Checking things out," she says quietly. "No sign of him up here, and nothing useful that I've seen yet."

She makes her way through the house, going methodically floor by floor, but there's no sign of the strigoi anywhere, and nothing to indicate why he chose her home to invade or where he might be now. She radios back to Dilton: "It's empty. I'm going to go down to the basement. It's the last place to check." *Well. Last besides the study where her parents' bodies are.* "Get ready, just in case."

"Basement? Might not be a good idea," Dilton walkies back. "He may be hiding out down there. Older strigoi often retreat to dark, damp spaces."

Veronica would roll her eyes if he were in front of her to see. "Are you just reading the Wikipedia entry to me?"

There's a moment's silence before Dilton speaks. "I mean—"

"Dilton, you know better than that," Veronica says. "Always cite a reputable source. Get it together, kid."

She heads down, despite his warning, taking the back way through the kitchen and then creeping down the basement stairs. Veronica never goes in the basement; there's nothing in there besides the housekeeper's cleaning supplies, boxes full of her father's business documents, and the expensive art her mother collects but never seems to hang. But now she makes a circuit of the dank space, shining her flashlight into the cobwebby corners. It's as she expected: boxes and paintings and—

Veronica squints. Wait.

There's a box in one corner that doesn't fit with the rest. She gets closer, aiming her light right at it, and lets out a slow breath.

Of course it's not a box like the rest at all.

It's a *coffin*.

"Really?" Veronica looks to the ceiling and exhales noisily. "A coffin? *Really?*"

The walkie crackles. "Did you find anything?"

Veronica picks it up. "Only that vampires really love dramatics," she says.

"What?"

"There's a coffin down here." She approaches slowly. The strigoi could be inside. Right? That's what old-school vampires do, or at least that's what all the scary stories talk about—vampires sleeping through the day in their plush, velvet-lined coffins. "I'm thinking this is our Big Bad's bed."

Dilton's voice comes through excited. "If he's asleep, that's good," he says. "You can kill him without him even knowing it's coming."

Veronica runs her fingers across the top of the coffin, and they catch on something, grooves in the wood. She leans down and narrows her eyes. It's some kind of etching, a symbol, like an old crest of arms or something. Veronica speaks into the walkie again. "There's something on the coffin—"

A crash comes from above.

Veronica jumps and then freezes, staring up at the ceiling, the house above her.

"Veronica?"

"Shh," she hisses into the walkie. "I think there's someone in the house."

The strigoi. Is he back?

"Remember the plan," Dilton says, but Veronica takes her earpiece out and shoves it in her jacket pocket, silencing him. She doesn't need to be told what to do.

Veronica creeps back upstairs, trying to pinpoint where the sound came from. It was loud enough for her to hear all the way down there—maybe a window breaking? Why would the strigoi need to break a window to get in? Maybe it's not him. Perhaps somebody has sensed that the Lodge house is strangely still and thought it'd be a good time to loot something.

You picked the wrong time, monsieur cat burglar, Veronica thinks, and she pulls the stake from where it's tucked at the small of her back.

But she slows as she goes up the main stairs. The sound is coming from the study.

Of course, she thinks, heart sinking. Of course it is.

At the top of the stairs she stops, allows herself a minute to steel her nerves. She is Veronica Lodge, head cheerleader, future business tycoon, queen of the coordinated accessory.

I am going to go in there and I'm going to kick ass and I will not be intimidated by some robber or some old-timey vampire or whatever else might be waiting in there.

There's a second crash, and Veronica doesn't wait another moment.

She launches herself at the door to the study, kicking it wide open with one of her stompy boots. "Hey! Time to—"

Veronica freezes, her mouth still open, and gapes at the scene in front of her. "Mom? Daddy?"

CHAPTER TWENTY-ONE
VERONICA

NO. NO.

This is not possible.

It's maybe the millionth time Veronica has had that thought in the past two days, and shouldn't she know by now?

There's no such thing as impossible, not in this monster-filled world.

"Mom," she says again, taking a faltering step forward and sliding the stake back into her jeans. "Daddy?"

Of all the scenes Veronica had anticipated, this was not one. Her parents' slowly decaying bodies, still laid out on the floor? Sure.

But her parents standing together in front of a blazing fireplace?

Her parents, not dead?

Her parents watching her with extremely red eyes, and smiling at her with fanged teeth?

No. None of those scenarios had been on her list.

"Veronica!" Her father holds his arms out wide. "What took you so long?"

"Daddy?" Veronica takes a step forward, breathless. She isn't sure whether to be joyful or terrified. On the one hand, they're not dead, but on the other—

Those eyes and fangs say it all. But Veronica remembers how she found them. How they were lifeless, completely lost to her, and that means—

Dilton's words from yesterday come back to her. *The first one is the moroi. They're people who've died—or been killed, more likely—and then revived with a vampire bite.*

Veronica wants to smack herself for taking so long to put this together. Of course her parents aren't dead.

They're *undead.*

"I thought you were gone," Veronica says now, still a little breathless. "I thought I was never going to see you again."

Her mother laughs, but it's not the sound Veronica had mourned only one day ago. It's flatter, meaner, altogether colder. "Dead? Oh, sweetie. Did we scare you? I'm sorry!"

"Come, my love." Her father holds a hand out to her. "Don't be afraid."

Veronica begins to move toward him, an instinctive response, but something stops her.

What else was it that Dilton had said? *Some of the tales talk about them being more malleable and easily controlled.*

Zombie vamps, Veronica had called them. And about the strigoi Dilton had said, *They can control the moroi—make them bend to their will.*

Her parents are watching her, rictus fanged smiles on their faces, but Veronica doesn't move another inch.

These aren't her parents.

Not really, she thinks. Their bodies, sure, but their minds? She saw it for herself: the two of them killed, but both with bite marks. Who knows how close they'd been to coming back—to transforming—when she'd found them?

But to be brought back means they're one of those zombie vamps, and that also means—

Like her thoughts have summoned him, he melts out of the shadows. "Hello, Veronica. So nice to see you again."

Veronica shifts into power stance without even thinking. The strigoi looks just as she remembers: handsome, charming, with a poisonous smile and that singular perfect curl sweeping across his forehead.

How long does it take to get that in place? Veronica thinks. *I wonder if he uses a curling iron or those pink plastic rollers my grandmother used to use.*

She has to stifle a laugh at the thought of this so carefully composed man—no, not man, *vampire*—sitting in front of a mirror like her old-lady grandma, and suddenly she's not so afraid of him.

"Last time we met, I told you to get out of my house," Veronica says. "Oh, yeah, and I put a knife in your back. Are you here for round two?"

"Whoa there." Her father steps in between them, chuckling. "Veronica, my love. Why don't we all sit down?"

"Sit down?" Veronica stares at him. "There's no time for chitchat and cocktails, Daddy. I know how to turn us all back to our regular human selves, okay?"

Hermione Lodge smooths her perfectly blown-out hair and perches on the edge of the couch. *For a woman who died two days ago, I gotta say, she looks pretty good*, Veronica thinks. *Whatever concealer she's using is doing the lord's work. You can barely tell she'd started to decompose!*

Her mother frowns ever so slightly. "Turn *back*?" she says. "But—why would we want to turn back?"

Veronica points at the strigoi, calmly standing there rocking on his heels with a smirk that she wants to slap off his face, like he belongs there. Her parents haven't even reacted to this intruder in their midst. "Because *he* turned us all into monsters against our will and—"

Now her father laughs again and takes her hand. "Against our will? Oh, no. You've got it all wrong, Veronica. Don't you remember that important associate I told you I was meeting on Friday?"

Oh.

Oh no.

Veronica takes a step back, uneasy. Suddenly she wishes she hadn't shut the walkie off; she's pretty sure she's about to need Dilton's backup. "What about him?"

Her father grins, and with his new fangs protruding it's profoundly unsettling. He holds a hand out in the strigoi's direction. "Meet Theodore Finch," he says. "He and I have some *very* exciting plans in store for Riverdale."

CHAPTER TWENTY-TWO

ARCHIE

ARCHIE WHISTLES AS he slams his car door shut and straightens out the bunch of flowers he's brought along.

Usually he doesn't feel bad about the little triangle he and Betty and Ronnie have going on. Why would he? The girls never say anything to him about it, and it's not like they're serious—he just really does enjoy hanging out with both of them. They're his friends, and maybe sometimes they go on dates or make out a little, but it's not a big deal.

Or at least Archie never thinks of it as a big deal, but he's starting to think maybe he's wrong. Ever since Friday night when Betty asked if he thought Ronnie was jealous of them being together, he's been wondering if maybe things aren't quite as cool as he's thought.

The fact that Veronica hasn't responded to any of his *or* Betty's texts all weekend seems to point that way, at least.

Maybe she's with Reggie, he thinks. Not like he's jealous or anything. Whatever, the two of them can do what they want. It's just weird that he hasn't heard from him, either—usually he'd be texting with updates as his night with Veronica went on. *Or maybe it didn't go so well, and he's too embarrassed to say anything.*

Archie smirks a little as he bends to check his reflection in the wing mirror, fixing his hair. His dad always says to get flowers when you think you might have done something wrong. That way, if you did, then you're apologizing, and if you didn't, then you just earned yourself some points for coming home with flowers.

He straightens up and looks at the imposing mansion before him. If Ronnie is mad at him and Betty, then maybe this will be a good start.

Archie walks up to the house and goes to ring the bell, but the front door's already open. Weird. And there's a car he doesn't recognize in the driveway.

"Veronica?" Archie calls, and he steps into the house.

CHAPTER TWENTY-THREE
VERONICA

VERONICA STARES AT her father. "You can't work with a *vampire*." And then she draws her stake again, flips it around, and raises an eyebrow. "Not when I'm here to kill him."

The atmosphere changes instantly. It's that stake in Veronica's hand; she can feel the energy coming off it, and suddenly everyone's in attack positions: her father, her mother, and this Theodore Finch.

"Kill him?" Hiram Lodge narrows his eyes. "I don't think so."

"Yes." Veronica keeps her voice strong. "That's how we turn back. And maybe you two agreed to this, for whatever bonkers reason or plan you've come up with, but I sure as hell didn't." Veronica shifts her weight from side to side. "So yeah, I'm gonna kill him."

Her father grins again, rolling up his sleeves. "Well, you'll have to get through me first."

Now, when Veronica walked into the house earlier, did she expect to be faced with fighting her own father? Possibly to the *death*?

Abso-*freaking*-lutely not. But seeing how things have been going lately, this turn of events weirdly makes sense.

Become a vampire, clear out a paranormal monster hunting store, physically fight my dad, she thinks. *Just a regular weekend!*

She eyes her father as they prowl circles around each other. "I'll try not to hurt you," Veronica says, and her father snarls.

"I'll try not to kill you."

Then they're on each other. Veronica tries not to think about the absurdity of the moment and concentrates on dodging her father's grabs. He wants the stake, she can tell; disarm her and she's not a threat anymore, right?

That's the problem with her father. He always underestimates her, like how he never lets her sit in on those business meetings, how he tells his associates like Theodore all about her looks and her neat behavior rather than her instinct for problem solving.

Veronica's always planned on showing him how wrong he is about her. She just hadn't planned on doing it *quite* this way.

Hiram lunges for Veronica and she dives sideways, rolling as she hits the floor and springing straight up, your basic cheer-dance transition. "Is that all you got, Daddy?" She pulls the walkie from her back pocket and flicks it back on. "Dilton! Time to move in!"

She flings the walkie to the floor as her dad aims at her again, his fingers grasping her wrist this time.

Veronica twists, his fingers burning her skin, and sweeps a leg at her father's feet. He drops but only to one knee, and uses his grip on Veronica to yank her closer.

"Bad idea," he growls. "I was going to go easy on you—"

Veronica doesn't let him finish. Instead she drives her shoulder into his face, knocking him back and surprising him enough that he releases her wrist, and Veronica flexes. Her heart's pounding, but it feels good. Adrenaline, like the kind she gets being thrown in the air under the Friday-night lights, or when she found the last pair of limited-edition leopard print Louboutin slingbacks in her size. But there's something else behind it, too, and as she spins the stake in her hand and drops back into attack position again, she understands.

She feels *strong*, and fast. Every blow her father lands on her hurts only as much as a mosquito sinking its little teeth in. Her dad feels like a gnat she can squash with just a flick of her hand.

I'm enjoying this, she realizes, a glee to the thought. *I'm having* fun.

"Come on," Veronica says, mimicking her father's grin from before. "You wanna fight? Let's *fight*."

And then a call comes from outside. "Veronica?"

Dilton. "In the study!" she calls, and catches her father's fist on the side of her head.

Crap.

It's dizzying but she's fine. *I'm fine, I'm fine*, she thinks as she spins for a second, *I'm fine—*

She sees a flash of red hair in her confused eyes. *Wait. That's not Dilton. That's—*

"Archie!" Veronica throws herself at the door right as Archie comes through, but maybe that hit got her a little harder than she thought, because she falls at his feet. "Get out, now!"

A look of horror unfolds over Archie's face. Veronica watches it, and then watches as her father leaps neatly over her and catches Archie in a headlock before anybody else can move.

"Veronica!" Archie says her name, but it's strangled, desperate, and he reaches out.

She gets to her feet and flips the stake so it's pointing right at her father, but he tuts. "I wouldn't do that if I were you," he says, and visibly tightens his hold around Archie's neck. "You want your friend to live, don't you?"

"Daddy." Veronica stills—the whole room stills, and tension balloons. But Veronica doesn't put down the stake. "You don't have to hurt him."

"No?" The word comes from behind Veronica, and she spins.

Theodore leans against the wood-paneled wall, watching with amusement. "No, I suppose he doesn't have to hurt your friend. But, see, if *I* decide he should, then he will."

Veronica's stomach sinks. "This *is* you," she says, breathless, looking around at her dad holding Archie captive and her mom, motionless on the couch, and this vampire lounging like it's all so entertaining. "All of it. You're controlling them."

Theodore Finch begins to clap. "Brava! You've figured it out," he says, pushing off the wall. "But have you figured out *why*?"

"I don't care," Veronica says. "Whatever your little plan is, it doesn't matter to me at all."

"Well, it should." Theodore comes closer. "Because I've got a very important part for you to play, little girl."

Veronica pauses and lets her stake hand lower a fraction. Little girl? Jesus, what a dick.

But she can't let herself get distracted. She needs to keep herself together—no, actually, what she needs is Dilton to be here so they can commence the pelting-with-garlic part of their backup plan and take this monster out for real.

There's no sign of him, though. And Archie's face is getting redder by the second in her father's chokehold. *Okay*, Veronica thinks, calling up all her performance skills. *Let's try something else.*

According to what Theodore said during their first meeting, he thinks she's a demure, well-mannered girl. So fine. Let him see what he wants to see.

"Important?" she repeats, making her voice high and full of disbelief, as if she can't fathom that someone like *him* would care anything about a stupid small girl like *her.* "For me?"

Theodore comes closer still.

Come into my web, Veronica thinks.

"Yes," he says. "See, I think it's about time Riverdale got some new blood. For too long it's been the same old people ruling over this town, and they don't see its true potential. But I do. And I need somebody smart like you on my side. After all, who knows this town and its residents better than the reigning social butterfly of it all?"

"You think I'm smart?" Veronica says, staring up at Theodore and blinking.

Theodore brings a hand to her face, stroking a finger down her cheek.

It takes a mammoth amount of effort for Veronica not to gag. *Good* lord, *men are silly. How is he eating this up so easily?* As if Veronica is suddenly going to switch and drop the idea of killing him, abandon the hope of getting her parents back to their human selves, just because he paid her one teeny-tiny compliment that she knows he doesn't even mean.

But it really seems to be working.

"What do you want me to do?" Veronica drops her hand, like she's dropped the idea of killing him entirely.

Theodore leans down. "Stop pretending I'm stupid, for a start."

"Wha—"

He has her in a vise grip before she can react, almost a mirror of how her father's holding Archie. "Please," he says. "Did you really think I was buying this act?"

Veronica's glad she can't answer, his arm across her throat. She *did* think she had him, and now—

Theodore presses his arm tighter across Veronica's throat. She tries to pry his fingers off her, but it doesn't seem to make any difference. Theodore ignores her struggling and laughs. "Why don't you fill her in on how things are going to go, Hermione?"

Her mother seems to flicker to life then. She rises from the couch and approaches Veronica, struggling in Theodore's arms. "It's very simple," she says. "We're going to turn everybody who matters in this town. All of our friends. The mayor and the sheriff. Everybody on *our* level. Then not only will we be among the richest and most important in Riverdale—we'll be in true control, too."

Veronica arches her back, trying to break out of Theodore's hold, but if anything, it only makes it worse. "You won't be in control," she says to her mother, the words just about rasping out. "*He* will. He's *controlling* you *now*."

Hermione smiles, her red lipstick so perfect and shiny. "Oh, no, my love," she says. "This is the plan we agreed to *before* we were reborn. We were aware that Theodore could exercise his powers over us, and we welcome it. This is everything we've ever wanted. Don't you see? We'll live forever now. The immortal Lodge family, rulers of Riverdale. What more could we possibly want?"

She keeps on smiling, a rictus grin, and Veronica doesn't know what to think. It's possible her mom's telling the truth, that it's really her speaking—an agreement with Theodore, in exchange for the power her parents are always chasing? That, Veronica can believe. But she can't put aside the theory that Theodore might be controlling them in all ways, at all times.

It could be her dad with his arm pressing against Archie's windpipe, or it could be Theodore's influence. Either could be true. "I won't—let you do this," Veronica says, fighting to get the words out.

When Theodore speaks, his silky voice is right in her ear, breath hot on her skin. "I don't think you're really in a position to threaten us," he says.

And then there's a spray of water that skims Veronica's cheek, leaving a stinging pain there. *What the—*

Dilton's in the doorway, holding what looks like a neon water gun. *Water gun*, she thinks, beginning to smile. *Dilton, you genius!*

Theodore yelps and releases Veronica, a hand on his face where Dilton's blast of holy water hit. His skin's smoking a little, and it's all the time Veronica needs to get across the room. "Dilton!" she calls. "My dad!"

Dilton pivots quick—

Hermione lunges and knocks the water gun out of Dilton's hands. "Stop right there."

Veronica skids to a halt in front of her father.

In front of Archie, his face almost as red as his hair while her dad continues to hold tight around his neck.

Oh, Archie, you really have the worst timing, she thinks.

Veronica eyes the distance between her and the stake she dropped, her and the walkie she threw across the room. "Don't even think about it," her father says, eyes laser-focused on her. "Here's how it's going to work. You leave us alone, and we won't hurt little *Archiekins*. But if you try to interfere in our plans again, Veronica—" He bares his fangs. "Archie will die."

Veronica wants to say a lot of things, most of them involving cursing, but it's clear to her that she's beaten. Dilton has no weapon; she's lost hers. They're outnumbered, three vampires to her team's one. And Archie—

She heard what her dad said, loud and clear.

Veronica jumps when she feels a pair of hands settle on her shoulders, but it's her mother. "I suggest you run along now," she says. "We'll take good care of Archie, don't you worry. As long as you stay out of our way, he stays alive. Doesn't that seem like a reasonable deal?"

She looks at Archie. "Sorry, Archiekins," Veronica says softly, and she tries to believe that there's forgiveness in his eyes, but maybe that's just her guilt talking.

She leaves him there, in the grip of her mother, her father, and Theodore, Dilton following, and as the two of them rush from the house, the anger she feels at Theodore Finch hardens into a righteous, burning-hot rage.

He won this time, but she'll come back for Archie.

And next time, she's not leaving without him.

Whatever it takes.

CHAPTER TWENTY-FOUR
VERONICA

VERONICA IS SILENT on the drive back to Dilton's.

Well, silent on the outside. On the inside, her mind is yelling a thousand different things about the events that just took place, about the scene they're fleeing from.

So her parents aren't completely lost to her. That's a good thing. But they're also completely in the grasp of a power-hungry ancient vampire.

That's pretty *not* good.

And now they have Archie, and Veronica doesn't doubt that Theodore meant exactly what he said. He won't hesitate to kill Archie—or more accurately, to force her father or her mother into killing Archie. She's torn, because that's something she *really* doesn't want to happen, but at the same time, she can't take the risk of following Theodore's instructions and leaving him there.

So I either try to rescue him and risk him dying, or I leave him there . . . and risk him dying.

Great choices.

It's getting dark by the time they pull up in front of Dilton's house, and only then does Veronica look over at him. "Water gun?" she says.

"Seemed like a good idea at the time," Dilton says, a little sheepish.

Veronica cracks a small smile. "It was," she said. "You just, uh . . . maybe we need to do a little training on those. Your fight skills leave something to be desired, Dilton."

"I'm big enough to admit that's true." He clears his throat. "So. Your parents."

"Yup," Veronica says. "Not dead! Extremely not dead!" She pauses. "Okay, well, *technically* I guess they're a little dead, being moroi and all. But that's for sure not what I expected to see when I walked in there."

"At least they're *kind of* alive, though," Dilton says. "I mean, that's a good thing, right? It means they're not completely lost to you. You can get them back, Veronica."

She looks sideways at him. "Can I?" she says. "They're completely under Theodore's control. And he's making them act like . . . *super* jerks. I mean, sure, they annoy me sometimes, and me and my dad don't always get along, but they're still my parents. Except he's turning them into monsters, literally and emotionally. And taking Archie hostage? Threatening to *kill* him—permanently?" She shakes her head. "I just abandoned Archie there, and god, what if I never get to see him again, and I never—" Veronica stops. It feels petty somehow, irrelevant and self-centered, to be thinking about how Archie's death will affect her. Their romance. How she'll never get to kiss him ever again, or throw popcorn at him instead of watching a movie, or take him to prom and be crowned king and queen in front of everybody they know.

But that's what she's thinking about. That's what's making her heart hurt right this moment, and that's what will happen if Theodore gets his way.

Dilton cuts the engine, and the sudden silence seems loud to Veronica. "Hey," he says quietly. "I know he means a lot to you. I know what's happening sucks. But I also know that you—we—didn't leave him there by choice. You didn't abandon him. And it's not your fault you couldn't take the strigoi out. You were outnumbered."

Veronica nods, but it still stings. Even after she'd been surprised by her parents, there'd been that moment when she thought she might pull it back. But of course, he'd seen right through her.

"Theodore," she says. "The strigoi. His name is Theodore Finch."

"And what does he want, exactly?" Dilton raises an eyebrow. "I mean, I'm assuming he's following the villain handbook and told you all about his nefarious plot?"

"Yeah, he villain-splained himself, all right," Veronica says, rolling her eyes. "He told me he's going to turn everybody in town so he can rule Riverdale. Well, actually—my mom is the one who said that. And she said that they agreed to this plan before he turned them, while they were still human. But I don't think I believe that at all. I mean, yeah, they like being powerful, but they essentially run Riverdale already. So—"

"What?"

"I feel like that can't be *it*," Veronica says. "Say my parents did agree to this deal. That would mean that they effectively gave up their free will to serve under this guy. For what? So they can live forever?"

"A lot of people would say yes to that," Dilton says. "In terms of immortality, I'd say being a vampire ranks up there with finding the holy grail."

"And then . . . there's me." Veronica drums on her knees. "I can't figure it out, Dilton. Why he'd make me a strigoi instead of a moroi. He could have had me under his control, too, but he chose not to. Did he just mess up? Or is there some bigger plan I'm not seeing?"

Dilton's quiet for a moment, and when he speaks, it's thoughtful. "Could be," he says. "Then again, it could be that there's some kind of quota he needs to make. You know, gotta create one strigoi for every two moroi, something like that, or he'll be in trouble with his vampire bosses."

It's not even that funny, but Veronica laughs anyway, because she appreciates that Dilton's trying to lighten things up a little. "Who knows," she says when she's stopped laughing. "But what I *do* know is that there's no way we're leaving Archie there with them." She turns and grabs Dilton by the shoulders. "Time for a new plan."

CHAPTER TWENTY-FIVE
CHERYL

CHERYL TURNS LEFT, then right, checking her lipstick in the mirror stuck to the inside of her locker. Perfect and pristine, as always.

"Cheryl?"

She doesn't turn away from her reflection, but she doesn't need to. She can see Betty Cooper's worried little face over her shoulder in the mirror. "Betty," she says. "To what do I owe this pleasure?"

It's Monday morning and Cheryl is back on track. Sure, she was feeling mopey on Friday night, but that was an *eternity* ago. Since then, she's had a full-body massage, packaged up a bunch of old clothes she sold online, and used the money from the sale to make a not-insignificant donation to GLAAD. Now she's back in the swing of things—today is tumbling practice, and she's going to nail her double-full *finally*; she can feel it. And then the rest of the week, when she's not back in the gym or scrolling Insta in class, is all about prep for the gala this Friday. She's picked out a hot dress—red, of course, silk and vintage-inspired with delicate lace around the sharp V of the neckline—and the spiked heels to go with it. On Thursday she has her slot at the salon to get her nails fixed up and her face serumed to perfection, and then she'll skip school Friday to go over to the hotel and make sure every little detail is perfect. Sure, her parents are technically in charge of the gala opening, but when it comes to décor and finishing touches, they have nothing on Cheryl.

Back in the corridor, Betty's still waiting, and Cheryl's still bored.

Cheryl stares at Betty in the mirror. "What? Is there something in my hair?"

Betty shakes her head. "I was wondering—have you heard from Veronica?"

"Me?" Cheryl frowns. "No. Why would I?" She and Veronica aren't those kind of friends. More like frenemies, really: Cheryl was cheer captain last year, and Veronica won it this year. Veronica was center flier last year, and now Cheryl reigns up in the middle. The Lodges opened a new restaurant in the spring; the Blossoms will have their hotel to overshadow it starting this Friday. *It's just friendly competition*, she thinks. Always good to have somebody snapping at your heels to make you want to be the best even more.

Their frenemy status definitely has nothing to do with the fact that Cheryl is jealous of Betty and Veronica. Just because they're thick as thieves and go almost everywhere together and do almost every little thing together. Probably tell each other all their secrets and all their dreams, too. Whatever. Doesn't bother Cheryl at all.

"It's just that I last saw her when we left practice on Friday," Betty's saying, "and then I haven't seen her all weekend. I haven't heard from her at all, actually."

"Aw." Cheryl slams her locker shut and turns finally, pinning

Betty with her brown eyes. "Did you and your bestie get into a tiff? Don't worry, I'm sure you'll work it out."

"I'm serious, Cheryl," Betty says, and she twists her ponytail around her fingers. "It's not like V to go so long without saying anything at all. I'm starting to worry about her."

Cheryl rolls her eyes. "She's a big girl. She can take care of herself. And I don't know what went down between you two, but with your endless 'We Love Archie!' drama, I can't say I'm surprised." She brushes past Betty, maybe more of a push with her shoulder than she really meant. (Or maybe not.) "If she wanted to talk to you, then she would. Trust me, Betty. Don't worry your pretty little head about Veronica Lodge."

The bell rings as Cheryl begins to walk away.

"Fine," Betty calls. "But I'm telling you, she won't be at practice later."

"Good," Cheryl calls back. "Then I can take back my rightful place as captain." *And as center of attention*, Cheryl thinks, and she smiles.

CHAPTER TWENTY-SIX
REGGIE

HE'S BEEN tracking her.

Veronica.

He couldn't find her for the past couple of days. He even went to the hospital to see if she'd been brought in after the accident, but nothing. And when he went to her house, nobody was there.

But then he heard her voice. This morning, as he tried to sleep on an uncomfortable bench shielded by a low tree, he could have sworn he heard her voice. And when he sat up and looked through the branches, he caught a glimpse of black hair swinging as she entered the laundromat.

Now he's watching from the grungier end of Main Street, the part where it's not really Main Street at all, where several of the stores stand empty. Only the old faithfuls are hanging on: a pizza place, a shoe repair store, and the laundromat. He hasn't been home since the other night. He hasn't known where to go or what to do because he killed that animal and *ate it*. He did it; he actually did it. And what does that mean?

The way he feels stronger than ever, but simultaneously ruled by this feeling that comes in knockout waves every few hours, a feeling he's come to know is *hunger*.

And when he got a glimpse of himself in a dark window . . .

The fangs. The red eyes.

He knows what he thinks it means, but what he thinks can't be real. Can't be possible.

So he's come looking for Ronnie. Maybe she can tell him what's going on, since she's the one who left him in the road and she's the one who hasn't bothered to come find him and she's the one who started all this.

He wouldn't have gotten into the accident if he hadn't been on his way to see her. If she hadn't crashed into him.

He wouldn't be . . . whatever it is that he's become, now.

She hasn't even tried to contact him at all, he's realized. He's been running around town trying to find her, worrying about her, but clearly she's not doing the same for him. Clearly she's got better things to do than worry about the mess she's caused.

Reggie steps up to the window of the laundromat and presses his face to the glass, cupping his hands against it. "Ronnie, Ronnie, Ronnie," he says softly. *Look at her, sitting there, like nothing at all is wrong.*

Something *is* wrong with Reggie, and he's going to get answers.

CHAPTER TWENTY-SEVEN
VERONICA

VERONICA'S IN THE last place anyone would think to look for her: the musty old laundromat. She could have just hidden out at Dilton's, but she couldn't sleep last night for how bad she felt about leaving Archie behind. And when Veronica feels bad, there's only one thing that makes her feel good again: clothes.

In the back of her mind, she kept thinking about the dress she'd been wearing on Friday night, the one that was meant for her date with Reggie. After her run-in with Theodore, she left it for dead in the costume closet at school. But this morning, as the sun came up, Veronica kept thinking that if there's a chance for her parents to come back to life, then maybe there's a chance for the dress, too. And honestly? She'd just wanted to take a break from thinking about vampires and decapitation and do something familiar. Do something *normal*.

So she crept out early from Dilton's and ran over to the school, sneaking in and out as fast as possible before anyone else got there, and now here she is. Everyone knows that if you bring your clothes in here, old Mr. Gunderson will dry-clean them on the spot with no questions asked. He doesn't have time for questions, not when he could be watching the English soccer he loves so much.

Now that her dress is being taken care of, Veronica's sitting at one of the tables at the back of the store, working on a plan to save Archie back. The only problem is that Veronica's struggling to think clearly past the rage she's feeling.

Except she can't decide whether she's angrier at her father or Theodore. Her dad's the one who threatened Archie's life—but he only did it under Theodore's control. So Theodore's the one she should hate the most. But—

It's like Theodore's seen inside her brain, somehow. He knows just how to make her father act to get under Veronica's skin the most. The way he'd smiled at her while he talked about killing Archie; the way he'd seemed to take such pleasure in knowing the threat would work on her—

It's like Theodore knows every little sore spot I have, she thinks. *He knows what will hurt the most and who it'll hurt coming from. And he thinks I'm weak, like using Archie against me means I'm going to stop coming for him entirely. But I'm not weak just because I have emotions and feelings for my friends.*

She guesses that's something he and her father have in common—they think the only way to succeed is to be like them, cutting people out and thinking only about themselves. Ruthless, Daddy always calls it, but it's not. It's sad, really. Sure, he's successful, but everything he does seems to hurt somebody along the way. Usually—his own wife and daughter. How is *that* winning?

I won't do that, Veronica thinks. When she's in charge of the Lodge empire, she'll rule it *her* way, not his. They'll fear her, but they'll admire her, too. They'll wonder how she became so calculated yet caring. She'll remember the names of all her employees' kids and ask about them between cutting multimillion-dollar deals.

She sighs. *Yeah, right.* Her dad's never going to hand the company over to her, not willingly, at least. And besides, all that is kind of irrelevant right now. That whole issue of her dad being an immortal creature is probably going to get in the way of him passing the torch. You don't have to give up being the boss if you figure out how to live forever.

And you certainly don't give up being the boss if you're being controlled by an all-powerful vampire beast.

Theodore's the real problem now. "So first things first," Veronica says under her breath. "Take him out."

But before she can do that, she and Dilton have to get Archie out of harm's way. Veronica drums her fingers on the yellowing table, nails clicking on the chipped surface. Her parents are still back at the house, and that's where they're keeping Archie. If she can get in without them noticing her—if she can slip in undercover and find her way to Archie—then she can release him. But how is she going to get past them?

Sneaking out of the house without them noticing is a specialty of Veronica's. But sneaking *in*?

She casts her gaze up at the water-stained ceiling. *I'm going to need a distraction*, she thinks. *Something that will*—

A hand claps over her mouth. "Don't try to struggle."

Veronica of course does exactly that, her heart racing, but the hand quickly leaves her and its owner slips into the seat opposite, raking a hand through his floppy dark hair. "What did I say?"

"Reggie?"

It all comes back to Veronica in an instant: her car fishtailing across a rain-slicked road, Reggie's surprised face illuminated by her headlights, the crunch and shatter and grinding of the cars as they collided.

But then the rest comes back, too: waking up in the woods, finding her way back to the road, the absence of Reggie and his car. She had hit a deer or something, or it was Theodore manipulating her thoughts. The proof is right here: Reggie sitting in front of her now. Not a scratch on his pretty-boy face, so there's no way that memory is real.

The relief that floods her slows her heart back down to its normal, steady beat. Okay, okay; everything is okay.

Act normal. Because for Reggie, everything is normal, and she is the normal Veronica, and that's how it needs to stay.

"Reggie," she says, her voice calmer now. "Cutting school? I thought Coach made a rule about attendance and eligibility to play in football games. What, you don't want me cheering for you next game?"

"Football? That's what you want to talk about?" He leans back and studies her. "How about we talk about something real, Ronnie. Friday night?"

Veronica sighs. Friday night, when she was supposed to be out with Reggie but was in fact busy being turned into a vampire. "I'm sorry," she says, and she tries to sound as sincere as she possibly can. She really needs to get Reggie out of the way, so she can get on with figuring out this plan. "I should have called, I know. I'll make it up to you. Next week—we'll go out again next week, for real this time—"

"You think this is about us going out?" Reggie leans over the table, and his eyes darken.

Veronica swallows. "What else—"

"Ronnie." He says her name like she's some kind of monster, and heat prickles up her spine. "Why are you acting like nothing happened? We almost *died*."

The car accident. So—it was *real*?

"I don't know . . . ," she begins, slowly, but then she shakes her head. "Wait. So it *was* you that I hit?"

Reggie rakes a hand through his dark hair. "Yeah," he says, like *duh*. "And then—"

"And then what?"

He shakes his head again. "Look at you. You're completely fine. I thought you might've died, but here you are. Good as new."

Good as dead, Veronica thinks, but she can't say that, can she? "Guess I got lucky," she says lightly. "You did, too."

And now the way he looks at her matches the way he said her name. "Lucky?" he says, and laughs. It's a bitter sound, something cruel to it. "I guess so. Although I don't know if anybody else would call us lucky."

"We survived a—"

"Cut the crap, Ronnie," Reggie interrupts. "We both know how we got out of that car wreck alive. Don't we?"

He snarls, suddenly, and Veronica gasps.

Because instead of his pristine braces-straightened teeth, Reggie's sporting two new, blinding-white accessories.

Fangs.

"So," he says, "maybe now you'll tell me what the hell is going on."

CHAPTER TWENTY-EIGHT
VERONICA

VERONICA KNOCKS A hand against her forehead. She glances to the front of the laundromat to make sure Mr. Gunderson's still not paying them any attention.

No no no. What happened?

"Come with me."

She grabs Reggie by the wrist and drags him out the back of the laundromat, into the alley filled with overflowing trash cans and an old broken-down oven from the pizza place a few doors down. "Hold up," she says to Reggie, trying not to let her panic show too much. "You're a *vampire*?"

Reggie Mantle is a vampire.

Well, if this isn't *absolutely* the last freakin' thing Veronica needs right now.

Reggie's staring at her. "So I'm not losing it," he says. "We really are vampires, then. *I* am a *vampire*."

Veronica waves a hand in the air, dismissive. It's bitchy, but she really doesn't have time for Reggie's existential crisis— not when Archie could be killed at any moment and her

113

parents are walking, talking playthings for a monster.

"Yeah, I know, it's a lot," she says. "But when did you—"

"I was on my way to pick you up," he says. "You came out of nowhere, and I couldn't stop. I woke up on the road, and I thought that was it; I was gonna die." Reggie's gaze drifts somewhere distant. "Then I feel someone pulling me off the road and into the woods, and then there's this weird—burning? And next thing I know, I'm waking up again, but I was in my own backyard. And then—"

Veronica waits for him to finish, but he doesn't say anything more. Only swallows hard and shrugs. "Then what?" she says, pressing him. "Reggie. I need to know."

"I had this urge to . . . to *feed*." Reggie's eyes shine now, like the memory of it has awoken some new joy in him. "So I did."

"What?" Veronica hisses. "You *killed* someone?"

Reggie shakes his head. "A fox," he says. "It came in my yard."

And Veronica slumps back. At least there's that.

So me and Reggie both went for animal blood first. But how long can that last? she wonders. *How long can a vampire resist until they give in, find the human blood they so desperately want? Are we both destined to give in, eventually?*

She eyes Reggie. So he's a vampire, too. Theodore must have done to him exactly what he did to Veronica—pulled him from the crash, turned him.

But what does Theodore want with Reggie? Yet another mind to control? *What's Reggie gonna do, score a touchdown for you?* Veronica thinks. *Scarf down seven hot dogs in under two minutes? The boy has limited skills.*

She widens her eyes. "Wait," she says. "This is going to sound—just go with it, okay?" She pauses before she asks the question. "Did you die?"

And Reggie raises his eyebrows. "Did I *die*?"

"I know it sounds weird, but it's important. When you get turned, it matters if—just tell me," Veronica says. "Did you die? In the accident, before you were turned."

Reggie eyes her cautiously and then shakes his head. "I mean, I don't think so," he says. "I thought I was going to. But then everything changed."

Veronica exhales, relieved. That makes him a strigoi, like her, and that means that Theodore doesn't have another member of his mind-control army ready to go. Reggie's free to do what he wants, not what Theodore would have forced him to do. "Have you seen him again?" she asks quickly.

Reggie frowns. "Who?"

"The guy who found you. Who turned you."

"No," Reggie says. "I mean, I didn't see anybody that night. I have no idea who rescued me."

Rescued. Like Theodore is some good Samaritan just stumbling on half-dead kids and turning them out of the goodness of his unbeating heart.

Wait.

A thought hits her, and Veronica bites her lip. If Reggie didn't see who found him—

Is there a possibility it wasn't Theodore at all? Could there be more than one vamp out there turning people?

She exhales. *Occam's razor, V,* she thinks. They learned about it last year in English class: the idea that in an unexplained situation, the most obvious answer is usually the right one. *When you hear hoofbeats, think horses*, she remembers. *Not zebras*. Or in this case, vampires.

Veronica leans across the table and fixes her gaze on Reggie. "Listen. You need to lay low, okay? I'm gonna take care of everything."

"What do you mean, take care of it?"

"I know how to undo all of *this*," she says, snapping her own fangs out and pointing at them. "Trust me."

"Undo it?" Reggie says. "How? What are you even talking about?"

Veronica resists rolling her eyes again. Yet more vampire lore she really doesn't have time to be delving into, but okay, fine. Only because she remembers how adrift she felt before she knew. "There are two kinds of vampires," she starts. "There's a kind called the moroi, and in order for them to change, they have to die first, and then they're brought back to life by a vampire bite. They can be mind-controlled and stuff. But you and me, we didn't die, right?"

"So . . ." Reggie furrows his brow. "We're not that kind."

"No. We're the *other* kind: strigoi. We were turned because we ingested vampire blood. Now, see, I have no memory of that actual moment, but what I do remember is being on the road after the accident, then waking up in the woods later and this intense feeling of being—"

"On fire," Reggie finishes softly.

Veronica locks eyes with him. *Yeah, that's the transformation feeling, all right.* "So now you know. Since neither of us can be controlled, we're okay. And I know how to undo all of this, turn us back to normal. But I need some time. So, just—keep your head down, don't go looking for trouble, and don't let *anybody* know that you're a vampire."

Reggie's silent for a minute, and Veronica would believe he's thinking it over if she didn't know that Reggie's internal monologue is more *football girls food football girls food* than *Do I agree with the advice my good friend Veronica is giving me? Oh me, oh my, I wonder what I should do.*

"You want me to act like nothing's changed?" he says eventually.

"Unless you want to be at the center of a neighborhood-watch mob wielding pitchforks, then yeah, I want you to act like nothing's changed."

Reggie grits his teeth—his fangs. "Fine," he agrees. "But in the meantime—I'm *starving*, Ronnie. What am I supposed to eat?"

Veronica throws her hands up. "Go to Pop's," she says. "Get a burger, *super* rare. That should tide you over."

"A *burger*?"

Veronica's own stomach growls in response, and she presses a hand to it. *I need to eat, too*, she thinks, and reminds herself to text Dilton and get him to swipe some more pig's blood from the lab.

She eyes Reggie again. She could spare some of it, she guesses. Especially if it means he's not running wild around town, getting in the way of her dealings with Theodore.

"Listen, maybe I have something that can help you. I'll have to check with my supplier," she says. "But until then, Reggie? Lay *low.*"

She flips her hair one last time and stomps back inside, leaving him alone in the alley.

CHAPTER TWENTY-NINE
REGGIE

LAY LOW, Reggie thinks.

What's he supposed to do—go home and sit around in his room waiting for Veronica to call him and tell him he's allowed out again? *Nah.*

She left him out on that road to die, after all. She doesn't get a say in what he does now.

Reggie smacks a hand against the wall and stalks out of the alley. Fine. She can do whatever she wants, and he'll do whatever he wants.

Right now, what he wants?

Blood.

Around the front of the building, Reggie sits for a minute in the chill air. *Eat a burger.* What a joke. Sure, the fox and the couple of other things he's caught since then have kept him going, but it's not exactly satisfying.

He might have been bewildered by the change in himself but he's not beyond understanding. He has to eat, or he'll weaken and starve. He has to eat something *real.*

Vampires don't live off dead meat.

So he sets off, walking fast, with purpose.

Soon he finds himself at school, on the football field. It's where he always goes when he needs to think. Being out on the field, being alive and connected with his teammates, listening to the cheering from the stands and feeling the pure life of it all—sweat, breathing, heat. Man, there's nothing like football.

It's the middle of third period, and the field's empty. Reggie stands right there in the center, wondering what he's going to do next. Go home? Then he'll have to face his mom, her constant pecking at him. Go to class? Nah—he's on high enough alert around all the girls in school on a regular day. Who knows what would happen with him in full vampire mode.

Vampire.

And not only is he a monster now, but so is Veronica. Although—how much of a monster is he, *really*? It's not his fault he was turned. It's not his fault he needs human blood to survive. He didn't ask for any of this; he just has to live with the consequences. That doesn't make him a monster, does it?

"Hey."

The call slices through Reggie's thoughts, and he looks in the direction it came from.

Jessica Hayes is sauntering toward him. She's wearing gym shorts and a tank top tied into a knot above her belly button. There's a jewel in it; it flashes at Reggie, gleaming under the low sun.

"What are you doing out here?" she calls again, closer this time. "Shouldn't you be in class, Reggie? I know Coach docks your game time if you don't play by the rules."

"I could ask you the same thing," Reggie says, letting his eyes run over Jessica's body. Letting his nose pick out her smell. "Or are you into cutting class all of a sudden?"

Jessica stops in front of him and bends over, catching her fingers underneath her running shoes in a deep stretch. "Nope," she says, and then flips back up, her short hair fanning through the air. "I have study hall third period, and since I'm—how do they put it—a *star athlete*, I get to come and train." She shrugs, putting a hand on her hip. "Or do whatever, really. No one ever checks that I'm out here. They just assume I'm doing what they told me to do."

A grin spreads across Reggie's face. Jessica's a sprinter, on the track team, and he's a Bulldog: rarely do they cross paths in the athletic department. But he's seen her—around school, hanging out at parties.

A runner like that, she's bound to have some good blood in her. It's like when you buy the milk with the supplementary vitamins—she's got that good added nutritional value, Reggie thinks.

His stomach growls.

"So," he says, "what do you feel like doing today? You wanna run? Or—"

Reggie steps up to her, looking down. She's almost as tall as him. Her eyes are a clear, focused hazel.

"Or what?" Jessica gives him a coy smile. "What did you have in mind?"

"It's easier if I show you," Reggie says. These are lines he's practiced in using, lines that have worked more times than he can count, on all kinds of different girls: book-smart ones, athletes, popular, outcast, everyone. Because all the girls want Reggie Mantle when it comes down to it.

He runs a hand down Jessica's arm, from her shoulder to her wrist, where he takes hold.

Her pulse thrums beneath his fingers.

"Come on," he says, and begins to lead her toward the bleachers.

It's a strange kind of quiet underneath the seats, like they're sealed in their own little world.

They start out slow, soft.

Jessica's a good kisser. Reggie finds himself thinking that as her hands creep up his back, as he grabs on to her waist and begins to moves his mouth away from hers.

She's a good kisser, but kissing is not what he came for.

He pushes her shirt off her shoulder and puts his lips to her skin, eliciting a small gasp from Jessica. "That tickles," she says, a lilt to her voice that Reggie knows is supposed to hypnotize him. Would work on him, if he were the Reggie of only a few days ago.

But now he's not thinking about how far they'll go, or what's beneath her shirt.

No. He can only think about what's beneath her *skin*.

Just a taste, a voice in the back of his head says. *Only a little. I just want to know what it's like . . .*

"Jessica." He speaks her name into her skin, and then looks up at her.

She smiles.

He flicks his fangs out.

And Jessica screams.

The noise is loud, but short, because Reggie sinks his fangs into her throat and she is silenced.

He feels her vein pop, the fizzy gasp of it, and her blood explodes into his mouth.

The world around Reggie dissolves.

It is the most glorious thing he's ever tasted, the most amazing sensation he's ever felt, and as her blood fills his mouth, slides down his throat, he feels relief.

Around them is nothing but dizzying blackness: there is no football field, no bleachers; no time, no space.

Only the sweet, hot blood he feeds on and the lightning-fast realization that he cannot go back.

No; it's more than that.

He doesn't *want* to go back.

The animal blood he'd had before was like . . . a sloppy joe, and Jessica is a perfectly rare T-bone steak. At first he means to keep to his plan, to only taste a little of what she has to offer, but he finds that he can't stop. He just drinks and drinks, swallowing as fast as he can, each drop sweeter than the last.

Until a time comes when nothing more seems to be reaching him, and Reggie opens his eyes, finally.

He unlatches his teeth from Jessica's flesh and lifts his head. He watches the way her head falls back, loose and uncontrolled. How her eyes are locked in a wide-open gaze, focused on nothing.

She's dead, he thinks. *I killed her.*

And some part of him knows he should feel bad about it, but he doesn't. After all, they don't live in a kind world: It's all about animals, power. He needs to eat, and she's his food source.

Simple as that.

Reggie lets her body drop to the ground, landing with a muted thud. He wipes the back of his hand across his mouth and lets his fangs retract, the red film over his eyes dissipating, and then he uses the toe of his boot to kick at Jessica's dead body. "What am I going to do with you?" he says, and folds his arms.

So much for lying low.

And then Reggie hears the familiar sound of somebody running up the bleachers, and he looks up.

The footsteps pause.

A face appears in the gap between the rows. Moose Mason peers down at him. "Reggie?"

Reggie grins.

CHAPTER THIRTY
DILTON

THE LIBRARIAN PASSES by Dilton, and he clicks out of his browser window quickly. Not that she's paying any attention to him: With his studious reputation, Dilton often finds himself getting away with things. No teacher thinks that a kid who comes in on the weekends to do extra-credit experiments could ever be any kind of trouble.

That comes in useful, especially for times like now, when instead of finishing his English paper, Dilton is using the library computer to research the strigoi.

When the librarian's gone, Dilton opens the browser again and resumes reading. Theodore Finch, he's discovered, is no stranger to Riverdale. In fact, the Finches were one of the founding families of the town, way back in the early 1900s. So were Veronica's family, he knows, and the Blossoms, too—everyone knows that both of their families helped put Riverdale on the map, after the Lodges first came to America. But unlike the Blossoms and the Lodges, the Finch name—and their lineage—has disappeared into nothing.

Dilton taps *finch riverdale death* into the search bar and then looks up when he hears the door smack open. He stands when he sees who it is.

"Veronica!" he hisses. "Over here."

He drops down and waits for her to join him. He has some blood bags in his backpack, and it feels like he's lugging contraband around. As long as she's here, she can take them—and feed, too, so she won't accidentally vamp out if somebody gets too close.

Veronica plops down in the chair beside him. "I know it's not exactly the safest thing for me to be here," she says, holding a hand up. "But it's kind of an emergency."

Dilton turns away from the computer, the Finch history forgotten for now. "What emergency category does this fall under?" he asks. "Like you-lost-another-pearl-necklace kind of thing, or like there's-an-old-vampire-running-around-trying-to-take-over-the-town emergency?"

"The second kind," Veronica says. "And I did not lose my necklace. Theodore Finch *broke* it. Yet another reason he must be stopped."

Dilton pushes his glasses up his nose. "So . . . emergency?"

"Right." Veronica takes a deep breath. "Remember how I said I was supposed to be going out with Reggie on Friday, before the whole found-my-parents'-dead-bodies thing, and I thought I crashed my car into him but then I realized I was seeing things?" She lowered her voice. "Turns out I was *not* seeing things, and the reason there was no sign of Reggie is because our friendly neighborhood strigoi sort of rescued him and sort of made him into a vampire, too."

Dilton's jaw drops. Great; this is *exactly* what they need. "*Sort* of?"

"Completely," Veronica says. "Yeah, that boy's one hundred percent vamp now."

More wreckage, Dilton realizes. Theodore's beginning to really piss him off. First Veronica, and her parents, and now Reggie? He's just going to keep going, until all of Riverdale belongs to him.

Unless they stop him first.

"We need to end Theodore," Dilton says. "But we can't do that until we get Archie out of danger."

"Don't you think I know that?" Veronica snaps. "Don't you think I've been trying to come up with something all day?"

"Ah, but you don't have to plan anymore," Dilton says. "I think I *have* come up with something."

Veronica widens her eyes. "What? Tell me," she says, and then in the same breath, "Also I'm starving. Did you get the—"

Dilton kicks his foot against his backpack on the floor. "But not here," he says. "Can't have you doing the vampire snarl where anybody might see."

"Vampire snarl?"

"You know, when you go all—" He makes the face Veronica had worn when he'd woken her in the student lounge, all bared teeth and creepy staring eyes. "Like that. And then your eyes go red, and the fangs come out, and you generally look like you're about to eat someone."

"I do not," Veronica protests. "Whatever. Tell me about this idea of yours."

Dilton runs a hand through his hair. "It involves distracting your father for long enough that you can get in and out of there without him realizing. I figured if we could send someone in there to occupy him, get him talking, then you might have a shot."

"You think he can be distracted just by talking about something?"

"Not about *something*. His favorite topic," Dilton says. "Himself."

A smile spreads across Veronica's face. "Oh, perfect," she says. "And we're going to do this how?"

"We call him and say we want to interview him for the school paper," Dilton says.

Veronica nods. "That'll work. He always says those kinds of interviews, puff pieces with nobodies, are stupid, but he actually *loves* them. Why wouldn't he? Somebody who wants to hear all about how smart and rich and talented he is? No questions about offshore accounts or union busting? It's his *dream*." She pauses. "But who's going to go in? He'll recognize you from the attack, and obviously I can't go."

Dilton shifts excitedly. Here's the part he's most looking forward to, inspired by his research.

Veronica's a strigoi, and strigoi have special powers.

"Here's what I'm thinking," he says. "You go in. But not as you. As somebody he won't know." Veronica's frowning, and Dilton leans in to clarify. "You *shape-shift*."

Now Veronica begins to laugh. "Are you for real? Wait, oh my god, you are. Dilton!"

"What?" he says, trying not to be too hurt by how clearly hilarious his plan is to Veronica. "You're a strigoi, and that's one of the powers I read about. It makes sense."

"It makes zero sense!" Veronica stops laughing and looks at Dilton seriously now. "One: I have no idea how to do it. Two: We have no idea if there are restrictions on it, limits on who or what I can shift into or for how long I can stay shifted. And three: I'm certainly not trying it for the first time on my own father, currently under the control of Theodore Finch."

Dilton slumps back. "Fine," he says, disappointed. Is it so bad that he wanted to see how the whole transformation thing worked? Maybe not the *simplest* plan in the world, but it would have been *great*.

"Back to the drawing board," Veronica says.

Dilton thinks for a moment, and like a flash of lightning, the perfect candidate comes to him. In fact, it's so perfect, he can't believe he didn't think of it sooner.

Only problem is, Veronica won't like it. And, truth be told, he's a little afraid of Veronica now. Well—he was a little afraid before, but now she has the added bonus of being able to literally eat him if she wants.

He exhales and says it anyway. "What about using a real reporter?" he says. "What about Betty?"

Veronica pushes away from Dilton. "No way," she says. "No. I'm not putting Betty in that kind of danger. Anything could happen to her! What if Theodore gets her? She could end up being under his control."

"But she's the best," Dilton says. "If there's anyone who can keep your dad talking, it's Betty. She's so good she'll have him thinking he's doing a *Vanity Fair* profile, not a fake column for the school paper."

"Archie's already in my father's gross little clutches," Veronica says. "I can't have Betty getting caught up in all this, too. I mean, if something happened to her . . ." She looks at the worn library carpet and then back at Dilton. "She's my best friend. I can't live without her."

"We'll give her weapons—holy water, a cross," Dilton says. "And we'll be there to protect her, if we need to. But we won't need to, because the plan will work."

There's a shushing noise, and both of them look over to the desk, where the librarian is giving them a stern look. Veronica looks up at the ceiling, like she's weighing whether she wants to do this. Whether she wants to endanger her best friend—because, Dilton knows, that's what he's proposing they do. There's no such thing as absolute safety, not when monsters are involved.

And then Veronica sighs, air hurtling Dilton's papers across the table. "All right," she says. "I guess I'm about to tell my best friend that I'm a vampire."

CHAPTER THIRTY-ONE
CHERYL

CHERYL'S EYES ARE wide as she turns in a slow circle, taking in the soaring ceilings and gold filigree outlining the arched windows of the ballroom. "It's *perfect*, Mom." She whirls around, her hair spinning behind her like a red ribbon through the air. "Don't you think?"

Penelope Blossom purses her lips as she looks at her daughter, and for a moment Cheryl thinks she's going to disagree. But then Penelope smiles, her lips painted with her signature shade of red, a habit Cheryl has inherited. "You're right," Penelope says. "It's perfect."

"And it'll be even more perfect for the opening." Cheryl strides over to the nearest window and stands with her back to it, holding her arms out wide. "The tables are going to be set up here with space for dancing up at the top, and the stage should be done tomorrow."

Her mother nods as she takes the space in. "And the menu?"

"All set," Cheryl says. "With vegetarian, vegan, and gluten-free options, of course."

"Excellent."

Excellent. Cheryl has to fight to keep the beaming smile off her face. It's a big deal that her parents let her take control of the gala, and it's a bigger deal that it goes well. With her brother at boarding school, sometimes it seems like he's all her parents can talk about. *Jason's doing so well in Switzerland. Jason's really picking up French quickly. Jason's school is going to be excellent for his college applications.* Sometimes it's nice to know her parents remember she exists, even if she's not becoming bilingual or whatever. And won't *this* look great on her college apps? Not only can she plan a hotel opening, but she can also make sure it doubles as a philanthropic venture—everyone will have the chance to make a generous donation to a community-based charity. See? Glitter and glamour and good deeds.

Her mother sighs and turns back to Cheryl. "It's just a shame your brother can't be here with us on Friday."

Cheryl grits her teeth. *Of course.* "Well, you can always Skype him in," she says with a false brightness. "I'm sure that's exactly how he'd love to spend his Friday night!" Or day, or whatever the hell time it'll be there.

Penelope claps her hands together. "That's an excellent idea!"

Excellent.

Cheryl turns so her mom doesn't catch the angry look on her face, or the muscle that's jumping in her cheek. What more does she have to do to make sure she's center of attention? What else can she do to make sure her parents notice her and *only* her on Friday?

She turns back to her mom, her face under control. "It's going to be quite the night," Cheryl says. "Just you wait."

CHAPTER THIRTY-TWO
VERONICA

AFTER SHE LEAVES Dilton, Veronica heads to his house so she can feed without any danger of interruption or, as Dilton has so delightfully taken to saying, "going vamp."

What, like I'm supposed to not *look like a scary killer when I'm drinking blood?* Veronica thinks. *Pshh. Imagine expecting me to look pretty and put together while I'm just trying to eat. Misogyny at its finest.*

She spends an hour or two attempting some more research on Dilton's laptop, trying to dig into Theodore Finch. The Finches were a founding family, Dilton told her, but Veronica has never heard of them, which is especially weird considering that Veronica also belongs to a founding family. It's like they've been completely erased from Riverdale history.

There's not much online, either—almost like they've been completely erased from the entire internet. Well, *almost.* Veronica finds a handful of mentions of Theodore in different historical society columns from way back in the early 1900s: *Magda Lefleur, accompanied by Theodore Finch; Lorena Kitt and Theodore Finch demonstrate their waltz abilities; Theodore Finch and unknown companion enjoy all the casino has to*

offer. Seems like he was quite the playboy, back in his day.

Dances, dinners, and gambling, Veronica thinks. Great. That tells her almost nothing—and certainly not anything useful about how *that* Theodore became *this* Theodore.

A society gentleman whose family has disappeared from memory, who became a vampire and a monster.

Veronica exhales a gusty sigh. Great research.

She slams the laptop shut. It's time for her to head back to school, anyway.

This time she doesn't venture inside but instead waits behind Betty's car, picking the polish from her nails. When she realizes what she's doing, she makes a noise of irritation. That mani cost forty bucks and was supposed to last until the gala on Friday.

But then she looks at her chipped nails and realizes that the irritation she thought she felt was more of a reflex than a real feeling. She doesn't really mind the way they look. Usually the sight of chipped polish puts her on edge because it goes against everything she's supposed to be. Veronica Lodge, always styled to perfection, with her short skirts and heels, flouncy blouses, and velvet headbands. The ever-present pearls that should live in the now-empty space around her neck.

There's something refreshing about the lack of all that, though. The old Veronica never would have gotten into a physical fight with her father; the old Veronica would have turned her nose up at the thought of killing someone. But it's almost as if being a vampire has shattered her shell. There's no space for perfection when the stakes are life and death.

And plus—Veronica the Vampire Slayer is so far providing plenty of new and interesting costume opportunities. Before she found Dilton in the library, she had swung by the department store downtown, just to get a few essentials. Sure, it wasn't exactly the *low key* she'd lectured Reggie about, but what was she supposed to do, live in her one pair of ripped jeans and a leather jacket? No, thank you.

Now she's in a skirt similar to Old Veronica (*Human Veronica?* she thinks), except instead of plum corduroy or pleated chiffon, this one is pink and pleather, with a gold zip running down the front. She has on the same boots, but a new white sweater with an upside-down cross stitched into it (seemed appropriate, no?) and a leopard-print faux-fur coat, the kind her mother would burn if she saw.

She's smoothing her fingers over the fake fur as she waits for Betty to leave Vixens practice and come back to her car.

Veronica does *not* want to involve her. And not because she's mad at her anymore, either—god, Betty and Archie, their love triangle, and the constant wonder of which of them Archie likes more is the last thing she cares about now. All of that feels an absolute lifetime away. No—she's more worried that bringing Betty into this bloody mess is going to end up hurting her, somehow, and what she said to Dilton is true—Veronica doesn't know if she can live without Betty. They're two sides of the same limited-edition coin. B and V, light and dark, Vixens together. It feels safer to keep her out of this. If Veronica could, she'd lock Betty in her bedroom until all of this was over.

And honestly—it's not just about Betty's safety.

What will she think when she knows I'm no longer human? What will she see when she looks at me, once she knows the truth?

There's more than one way to lose a person.

She sighs to herself. But Dilton does have a point. Betty *is* a great reporter, and she's the only other person Veronica trusts to get the job done.

If Betty loves her as much as Veronica believes, then her being a vampire won't change anything.

She sees a familiar blond ponytail bobbing through the parking lot, and Veronica steels herself. *Remember*, she thinks. *All of this is so I can return to being human. I'm a vampire now, but I won't always be. If Betty helps us, everything can go back to normal.*

Normal Old Human Veronica.

Why does it sting a little to think of that?

There's no time to dwell on it; Betty's on her then, relief written all over her face. "V!" Betty throws her arms around Veronica's neck with such strength that the two of them almost topple to the asphalt. "Oh my god, I was so worried about you! I thought maybe you were mad at me, or maybe something had happened to you, or—"

Veronica untangles Betty's arms from around her neck and looks her best friend in the eye. "B," she says, her breathing uneven. "Something did happen to me."

Betty's eyes widen. "Oh my god," she says. "What? V, what happened? You're scaring me."

Veronica bites the inside of her cheek. *If you're scared now, wait until you hear this.*

"Give me your keys," she says, holding her hand out to Betty. "I think you're gonna want to sit down."

CHAPTER THIRTY-THREE
BETTY

BETTY GRIPS THE sides of the car seat and stares straight ahead. Across the parking lot is a little bird, maybe a robin, hopping from puddle to puddle. It's all she can focus on while her brain processes what Veronica just told her.

A vampire. Veronica is a vampire. Veronica's a vampire? Vampires are real. Vampires are real, and Veronica is one and so are her parents and now they, plus the vampire who turned them all, are holding Archie hostage so that Veronica won't interfere with their plans to turn more people and take over Riverdale with their vampire gang.

Betty blows out a breath. Simple, right? Not a big deal. Her best friend is dead—undead? Living dead? Something like that—but it's *totally* not a big deal *at all*.

"Betty?" Veronica sounds anxious. "Are you freaking out? I knew this would freak you out."

Betty shakes her head almost violently. "I'm not freaking out," she says, in an extremely freaked-out voice. "I'm fine!"

"B, it's okay. I know you think I'm a monster now—"

Betty whips around to look at Veronica. "A monster?" she says. "Oh my god. Why would I think that?"

"I mean . . ." Veronica bares her teeth and in a split second, with a sharp *thwick* sound, her fangs shoot out. Betty swallows. Oh, yeah. Oh, those are some rip-your-throat-out vampire fangs right there. "I'm a literal monster. So."

"But you're still you," Betty says. "Right? Aren't you?" *Isn't she?* She looks it—or, she looks like a version of it, at least. Her outfit's a little more Cheryl Blossom than what regular Veronica Lodge would wear, but those are just clothes. On the inside, she's still Veronica.

"I think so?" Veronica plays with the hem of her sweater. "I mean, I feel different, but I still feel the same, too."

"And you're—" Betty squints, trying to straighten it all out in her head. A moroi is a vampire who can be controlled; a strigoi is one who can do the controlling. "You're a *strigoi*, right? You're not, like, under mind control from the one who turned you?"

Veronica shakes her head. "Operating under my own free will," she says, and as if to prove it, mimes part of the dance section of their latest cheer routine, flipping her hair and rolling her shoulders. "See? No musty old vampire could ever dream of puppeteering that choreo."

Betty laughs, relaxing finally. "I was worried about you," she says. "I even asked Cheryl about you. I thought maybe you were mad at me."

"For what?" Veronica asks.

"You know. Me and Archie. Our date." Betty coils the end of her ponytail around one finger. "I felt really bad, you know. When we were together. I felt . . . guilty."

Veronica looks at her, a small smile on her glossed lips. "You shouldn't feel guilty," she says. "I mean . . . yeah, I was a little mad before, but not *really* mad. And I don't even know why I was mad at you, because Archie's the one who keeps stringing us both along."

"Right?" Betty turns her body and pulls one knee up onto the seat. "You know what he said to me on Friday? That we're all *just friends*."

"Ew!" Veronica makes a gagging sound. "Oh, you know, it makes me so sick when people blow off friendship like it's nothing, and also, hello, Archie, you don't get to date two different girls for a long-ass time and then pretend like there's nothing romantic going on at all."

"That's exactly what I said!" Betty frowns. "Well, I mean, I *thought* it. I didn't say it. But I *should* have."

Veronica curls her tongue behind her teeth, a wicked smile. "Maybe we should just leave Archie exactly where he is," she says. "I don't know if he deserves to be rescued."

Betty laughs but shakes her head. "Tell me the plan again," she says. "So I go in and pretend I want to interview your dad for the paper? Won't he suspect I'm lying?"

"Not when you show him the mock-up of the Entrepreneur of the Year feature you're running," Veronica says. "Which Dilton is already hard at work fabricating."

At Dilton's name Betty narrows her eyes. "How exactly did Dilton Doiley become your number one partner in crime on this?" she asks Veronica. "I know he's your lab partner but—"

"I told you," Veronica says. "He found me the morning after and then he was actually helpful. As partners in crime go, he's pretty decent." Then she shimmies her shoulders. "But he's not a patch on my number one, Miss Elizabeth Cooper."

Betty sticks out her tongue. "Okay," she says. "I'm in. But you have to teach me everything to protect myself in case it all goes wrong. Like those self-defense classes we took last year, but for paranormal creatures."

"Of course," Veronica says. "Dilton and I have a whole armory going on."

Now Betty eyes her. "Seems like that's not all you two have going on," she says. "I mean, Dilton's kind of cute, with those glasses and his freckles. Don't you think?"

"Dilton's cute," Veronica agrees, "but I am not interested in anything other than being friends with him. I think maybe I'm swearing off boys forever. They're so much more trouble than they're worth."

"True," Betty says. "Besides, you have the whole vampire thing happening, it's really a lot."

"Very stressful," Veronica says, mock serious. "So very challenging for me right now; please, if you could just give me some space during this difficult time, it would be much appreciated."

Then she breaks and starts to laugh, and Betty does, too. Yeah, her best friend may be an undead creature, but at least the girl knows how to make a joke.

CHAPTER THIRTY-FOUR
ARCHIE

SWEAT TRICKLES DOWN Archie's temple, and he grits his teeth.

Come on, come on. Just a little more, almost there . . .

But the rope slips out of his grasp, and he slumps in the chair he's tied to, exhaling noisily. He almost had it that time.

Except that's what he's told himself every time he's tried to undo the knots around his wrists—and he's lost track of how many times that is, over the two days he's been stuck in this room.

He's tired and hungry and maybe a little delirious. Has to be, right? Because if he's not that means what he saw when he showed up to apologize to Veronica yesterday was really real: vampires and Veronica fighting her father and Dilton Doiley, of all people, mounting a rescue attempt.

Vampires, in Riverdale. *A lot of weird things happen here, but this really beats them all,* Archie thinks. *Next thing there'll be freakin' were-wolves in town.*

He looks around the room he's trapped in, like maybe in the past hour something will have changed. But it's still the same stuffy guest room, a bed and a large ornate dresser and a velvet couch his only company.

Archie tips his head back. If he strains, he can just about see out of the window, overlooking the circular driveway and the trees beyond it. At least he has this; at least he has the ability to tell what kind of time it is. To count how long he's stuck here until somebody comes to get him.

Somebody will come and get him. Right?

Archie begins working at the knots again. Maybe he's his only way out of here.

But then he catches a flash of something moving outside.

He drops the rope again and stretches as far back as he can, almost tipping the chair. It's a car, he thinks, and the recognition clicks.

No. It's *Betty's* car.

Horror takes over him. If Betty comes inside the house, there's a strong possibility she's going to end up exactly as trapped as he is.

As he watches, Betty gets out of the car and starts up the steps toward the house. She's probably here doing exactly the same thing he was, except she's not going to find Veronica, either.

I have to warn her.

"Betty!" Archie calls, and then stops. What if Mr. and Mrs. Lodge hear? Or that other guy, the creepy one who seems to be running things—is he still around? If they know Betty's out there, she might not get the chance to get away.

Archie thinks fast and begins to shuffle the chair closer to the window. It takes more effort than he expected, or maybe he's too weak after two days with no food or water. But he eventually gets up to the window, and from this angle he can see Betty almost directly below him, waiting outside the front door.

He slams his shoulder against the window. *Look up, Betty. Look up.*

CHAPTER THIRTY-FIVE

BETTY

IT'S TUESDAY, AFTER school, but Betty didn't go. They had too much prep to do, and besides, Betty wasn't sure she could get through a whole day of classes and Vixens practice acting like everything is exactly the same, without using her cheer voice to yell, "THERE ARE ACTUAL REAL-LIFE NOT-IMAGINARY BLOODSUCKING VAMPIRES RUNNING AROUND THIS TOWN!"

Now Betty pastes on her parentally approved smile as she rings the bell. She's trying her best to be calm, to be completely on board with this new world she's suddenly been thrust into. She's nowhere near as freaked out as she was when Veronica first told her, but it's still . . . *weird*. That monsters are real.

She thinks of Veronica and what she'd said yesterday. *I know you think I'm a monster now.*

She'd sounded so sad when she said it.

Betty shakes her head. Veronica is not a monster. Sure, in the literal sense maybe she is, but she's still the same V Betty's always known and loved. Just now with a few . . . bonus features.

Betty scans the grounds as she waits. It's quiet out here, at the Lodge mansion. She's always known that, but never before has it seemed so sinister. Usually coming to Veronica's means they can be as loud as they want and no neighbors will complain. Now she realizes that there's no one to help if things go wrong. No one to hear if she screams.

A thud comes from somewhere above, and Betty's about to look up when the imposing front door swings open. "Mr. Lodge!" she says brightly. "Thank you so much for agreeing to speak with me."

Hiram Lodge is wearing what Veronica always calls his Off-Duty Look: a dark shirt with the sleeves rolled up to show off his watch, black jeans, and dark loafers that probably cost more than Betty's beat-up car.

"No problem at all," Hiram says, beckoning her inside. "You know it's always a pleasure to be interviewed by my favorite journalist in town."

Betty laughs as she follows him inside, playing her part carefully.

Act like you're just doing a profile on him, Veronica has told her several times. *Just get him started talking about his life and keep it going. Oh—ask him who his biggest inspiration in business is. He loves talking about Elon Musk, god knows why.*

"Can I offer you a drink?" Hiram takes the stairs two at a time as he leads Betty to the study. "Water, soda, fresh juice?"

Betty slows as she comes to the study entrance. This is where Veronica was attacked by the strigoi guy. *Is he here?* He's running the whole operation, according to both Veronica and Dilton. Maybe he's in the house somewhere, just waiting to get Betty, too.

And where is Archie? Down in the basement? Locked away in the attic? She can't hear him at all, and wouldn't he be calling for help? If it were her trapped, she'd be screaming, yelling until her throat was raw and going until she ran out of energy to continue. But no; it's silent.

Maybe he's already dead.

She's aware of Mr. Lodge watching her, and Betty crosses the threshold, bright smile back in place, willing the thought out of her head. "Juice is fine," she says. "Is Mrs. Lodge around? I'd love to get a couple comments from her, too."

"She's at a board meeting right now," Hiram says. "But I'm sure she'd be happy to chat another time."

No Hermione. Betty's not sure whether that's a help or a hindrance. It makes one less person for Veronica and Dilton to avoid, but it also means that Betty's truly alone with Hiram.

It wouldn't matter if she was *here,* Betty realizes a split second later. She's a vampire, too. She can't be trusted any more than he can.

"Make yourself comfortable," Hiram says. "I'll be back in a moment."

As soon as he's out of the room Betty drops her smile. She doesn't sit but instead rifles through her bag for the vial Dilton gave her before she left, holding it up to the light so the clear liquid inside gleams.

Just for precaution, Veronica had said as Dilton gave her the holy water and pure silver cross and a small bag of crushed garlic, mixed with other herbs. *You only have to use them if things go bad. Otherwise, just stick to the plan. Keep him talking, me and Dilton get in and out with Archie, and then you leave once you get the all clear from me. Understood?*

Betty had nodded and said yes.

But now she looks at the holy water sluicing in the vial as she turns it end over end. She's going to stick to the plan, all right.

Only, her plan's a little different from V's.

Steps sound outside the study, and Betty hides the vial in her palm. Hiram reenters holding two glasses: one with orange juice, and the other with a dark amber liquid inside. "Here you go," he says, holding the glass out for Betty to take.

But she puts the hand without the vial in it up to her mouth. "Oh," she says, "is that orange juice? I'm so sorry, I should have said. I'm allergic."

Hiram raises his thick eyebrows. "Allergic to . . . orange juice?"

"I know." Betty shakes her head. "Weird, right? There's some kind of enzyme in it. I can't eat oranges at all. Gives me hives."

"Oh." Hiram takes a step back at that, as if Betty might burst into an itchy rash right then and there. "Would you like something else instead?"

"Water would be great."

She sees his nostrils flare, no doubt annoyed at her fussiness. But he can't act on that annoyance, can he? Not if he wants a glowing profile in the paper. "I'll be right back," he says, and sets his own drink down.

Yes.

Betty watches him leave again and wastes no time. She darts over to the glass table and unscrews the lid of the vial. The weaponized water slips into Mr. Lodge's Scotch with barely a sound, and she picks the glass up to quickly swirl the liquid around.

The idea came to her as soon as Dilton showed her the vials he was keeping in an old test tube holder. If holy water burned on skin contact, Betty thought, then it made sense it would burn on the inside, too. And maybe more—it could act like any kind of drug, possibly knock him out or make him unable to control his body. (Okay, so she's making a giant assumption here, but she's not a science genius like Dilton.)

Even if all it does is hurt, then it'll be enough. A person—well, a vampire—burning from the inside out is not going to be hard to get past. Then she won't have to worry about keeping him occupied long enough for Veronica to release Archie—he'll be incapacitated, and she can help V and show her that she's taught her father a lesson.

Maybe then he'll learn to stop assuming that girls like her and Veronica are not a threat to him.

She swirls the liquid some more and then sets the glass back down, carefully centering it in the ring the condensation had left on the table.

By the time Hiram returns with her water, Betty's sitting on one of the uncomfortable couches, her notebook and phone ready to record on the table. "Thank you *so* much," she says, accepting the fresh drink from Mr. Lodge. "Okay. Are you all ready to get started?"

Hiram sits on the opposite couch and pushes his sleeves up, then reaches for his glass.

Betty holds her breath as she watches him raise it to his mouth, take a large sip, and swallow. "Ready now," he says with a sleazy grin.

And Betty grins back. *Yes. Enjoy your poison.* "Perfect," she says. "So, first of all: Who would you say is your biggest inspiration as an entrepreneur?"

CHAPTER THIRTY-SIX
VERONICA

VERONICA AND DILTON wait until at least ten minutes have passed since Betty entered the house, and then Veronica leads Dilton to the garage.

They take the back stairs up to the second floor, and Dilton says they should separate but Veronica stares at him. "Are you kidding me?" she whispers. "I'm not having you die on my watch. I've met your mom now. She's very nice. I'm not telling her I let her son get eaten by a stray vampire."

She's not sure where her father will have put Archie for safekeeping, so the only option is to check everywhere. They go room by room, avoiding the study, where Betty surely has her father deep into telling childhood stories by now, and with each empty space Veronica gets more frustrated.

It helps a little when she gets to her own room. For a moment she wonders if her dad might have put Archie in there, some kind of silly little message, but when she opens the door it's the same as always. She wants to run in and dive beneath her crisp white covers, gather up all her clothes and accessories and vital beauty products, but it would take time they just don't have.

She darts in and grabs a lipstick anyway, and when Dilton frowns she flips him off. "This is important," she says. "Stop devaluing femininity because you think it equates to weakness, Dilton."

"I wasn't!" he protests, but Veronica is already on to the next door, slipping into the library.

The room with its tall shelves of books is empty, and she's about to leave when she takes a second look at the papers strewn across the table in the center of all the books she knows neither of her parents have read. "Dilton." She waves him in. "Shut the door."

Dilton does as she says and stands beside Veronica, leaning over the papers the same way she is. "What are these?" he says. "Blueprints?"

Veronica runs a finger over the thin paper covered in blue lines, mapping out a tall building. "Yes," she says, "but not for one of ours." That, she's sure of—Veronica knows the ins and outs of every building her family has developed. Sure, she's had to sneak into her father's study and steal peeks at the documents to do it, but she does it anyway. Her father is always telling her that she doesn't understand the intricacies of his projects, that she doesn't have the right kind of business brain to click in the company. Sometimes she thinks—hopefully, wrenchingly optimistically—that he says those things deliberately, knowing that they fuel her, knowing that it only makes her want it more. But deep down she knows he says them because he really thinks that about her. To her father, she's *just* smart enough to be the face of Lodge Enterprises, smart enough to network well at the various receptions and galas they have, but that's where it ends—

She stops. "Wait." Beside the blueprints is a sheet of names that she hadn't noticed before, and Veronica picks it up. She scans through the list and—*of course.*

"I think this is the Blossoms' new hotel," she says, the realization sparking and settling into truth. Flipping through the blueprints, it starts to come together in her mind: the tall arched windows on every floor, the entranceway with its fountain and columns, the double-height ballroom. Veronica's watched it going up, day after day for the last six months, and it's done now, finally, ready to be unveiled.

This Friday. The gala.

"It's Friday," she says to Dilton, slapping the list down. "The opening of the Blossoms' hotel. *That's* where they're going to get everyone. Think about it—everyone important in town's going to be there. *And* my dad was pissed that the Blossoms didn't cut him in on the development. That's where they're going to hit."

"And do what?" Dilton says.

Veronica glances up at him, her eyebrows pulling together. "Turn them all," she says.

There's a loud crash from somewhere upstairs that makes them both jump, and Dilton looks up and then back at Veronica, his serious eyes narrowed. "Archie," he says. "Let's go."

Veronica leaves the plans where they are and follows Dilton, both running as fast as they can, all attempt at keeping quiet abandoned. There's no way her dad didn't hear that noise, too, Veronica thinks. *Keep him there, B. We're almost done.*

They go up another flight of stairs, and Veronica looks from door to door. Behind the middle door is her parents' bedroom. The one on the right is a guest room, and on the left, their screening room. Then the hall goes on, leading to a guest bath and another unused room.

Another thud comes.

It's definitely from down the hall, so Veronica takes off, and when she reaches the last door, she tries the handle only to find it locked. "Archie?" She presses close to the door. "Are you in there?"

"Ronnie!" the muffled call comes back, and Veronica pulls a bobby pin out of her hair. It's been a while since she's picked a lock, but the muscle memory is there.

Veronica slides the pin into the lock, and the tip of her tongue sticks out of her mouth as she twists and angles just so, waiting for the tumblers to fall. Dilton leans close, watching over her shoulder. "Do you know what you're doing?"

"Yes," she says, "but maybe I could concentrate more if you weren't right in my face—"

She hears the sweet sound of the lock opening. "See?"

Veronica pushes the door wide, and there's Archie, tied to a chair fallen on its side. "Oh, hey," Archie says, looking up at them. "What are the odds of seeing you two here?"

Veronica ignores his pathetic attempt at a joke and sets to work untying him. "I know you're probably wondering what the hell is happening," she says as she unties his wrists and Dilton works on the ropes around his ankles, "but right now we just need to get you out of here."

"No," Archie says, and he tries to stand but topples sideways. "Damn. I can't feel my foot."

"I'll carry you," Veronica says impatiently. "But we have to go, now."

Archie looks up from the floor. "We can't," he says. "Betty's here. We need to get her before we can go."

"Don't worry about Betty," Veronica says. "She's part of the plan; she's fine. You, on the other hand, are dead meat if we don't leave *right* now."

"Yeah, don't worry about me."

At the sound of Betty's voice, Veronica whips around. "B!" She rushes to her. "What are you doing? Where's my dad?"

Betty gives her a sly smile. "Passed out," she says, and produces an empty vial that Veronica is pretty sure used to be filled with holy water. "I spiked his Scotch."

"And it knocked him out?" Dilton shifts, looking intently at the glass tube. "Interesting. Not a result I would have predicted, but then it's possible that a metabolic reaction follows a different pattern than a—"

Veronica smacks him. "Science later," she says. "Escape, now."

Together she and Dilton take hold of Archie, and the four of them navigate their way back down through the house. Passing by the study, they hear a groaning noise, and Veronica stops short, leaving Dilton bearing the entirety of Archie's weight.

"Whoa," Dilton says. "A little heads-up, next time."

"Go on," she says. "Get to the car. I'll be there in a second."

Her friends take the last set of stairs down, and Veronica slips into the study.

Her father's lying on the floor, and she has a moment of déjà vu. Except the first time she saw him in this position she was heartbroken, numb at the realization that she'd lost both of her parents. And now?

Veronica walks over to him. He's semiconscious, drooling as his eyes struggle to focus on her. "Hi, Daddy. Or—should that be 'Hi, *Theodore*'?" She's not sure how it works, exactly, or if Theodore can hear and see and experience everything that her father does, but if not, her dad will at least be able to relay this message to him.

On the floor her father moans, no real words coming out.

"Shh," she says. "Don't try to talk. I have a message for your master." She crouches down so she can look at him as close to eye level as possible. "You know, I didn't plan on Betty poisoning you, but I have to say, it's a gold-star move. That girl is *so* smart." She claps her hands together. "Anyway, I have Archie now, which means you have no leverage, and as such I *will* be going ahead with the general interference with and destruction of your 'turning everyone into vampires and taking over the town' plans. Sound good?" Veronica stands and uses the toe of her boot to push at her father, for once so weak.

He'd be beyond embarrassed if anyone could see him now. And Veronica is embarrassed for him, too, a little, but also—

There's another part of her that kind of enjoys seeing her father like this. Hasn't she always secretly fantasized about what Hiram Lodge would be like stripped of his strength? When he's needling her, or belittling her, or undermining her—hasn't she thought: *Take away all your privilege and power and what would be left of you, Daddy? Nothing but a pathetic shadow of yourself, like you always accuse me of being.*

Of course, she never thought those fantasies would be real, but here he is. And here she is, a newborn powerful vampire girl. She's a strigoi: more powerful than him, and nobody can control her.

How the balance has shifted.

She looks down on him and shakes her head, her dark hair swimming in a veil. "You're pathetic," she says. "Tell Mom I said hi."

CHAPTER THIRTY-SEVEN
VERONICA

BY THE TIME she gets outside, Dilton has Archie in the backseat of Betty's car and Betty's behind the wheel.

Veronica gets in and slams the door, then drums her hands on the dashboard, triumphant. "Gun it, B."

"Your wish is my command." Betty hits the gas and the car squeals off, and Veronica adds her voice to the whine of the wheels. She feels electric. Old Veronica would never have had the guts to tell her father what she thinks of him straight to his face. Old Veronica would never have said *You're pathetic*, but New Veronica did. Vampire Veronica looked down at her father and said exactly what she was thinking, and oh, it felt wild. Like the biggest release—like she'd been forcing herself to stay silent for so many years that she hadn't even realized how much pent-up rage was inside her. Yes, her dad *is* pathetic and *does* belittle her, and she *does* deserve better than that and he will, he will, he *will* get what's coming to him. Just like her mom will. Just like Theodore Finch will.

She flexes her fingers, curling them into fists as Betty whips through the woods. This strength, this newfound fire—

If this is what being Vampire Veronica is, then maybe I like it, she finds herself thinking. *Maybe I don't—*

Betty lets out a small yelp. "What is that?"

Veronica snaps back to the moment and looks ahead, where Betty's wide eyes are focused.

There's a figure in the road.

It's dusk, the sky growing darker and the trees stretching high around them, and anyone else might think it's just a shadow, just an illusion, but Veronica remembers.

Theodore's eyes in her rearview. Standing behind her, waiting.

It's him.

Veronica feels the car slowing, and she grabs Betty's elbow. "Don't slow down," she says. "Keep going."

"But I'm going to—"

"Yes." Veronica puts a hand on the wheel now, her fingers curling over Betty's. "You're going to hit him."

"Have you lost it?" Betty shakes her head. "You want me to—"

"It's not a person," Veronica says. "That's *Theodore*."

They're getting closer, and Theodore only waits in the middle of the road, unnaturally still. Veronica can tell it's him by the lean of him, the energy emanating from his statue pose.

"That's him?" Archie leans forward from the backseat. "That's the guy we're so afraid of?"

Veronica holds on to the steering wheel harder. "You might be afraid of him," she says. "But I'm not. Drive, Betty."

Betty squeezes her eyes shut but the car speeds up. Veronica guides them as they race through the bend, and then she's close enough to lock eyes with Theodore.

They're twenty feet away.

Fifteen.

Ten.

"Veronica—"

She ignores whichever of her friends said her name, keeping everything aimed at Theodore.

His lips curl into a smile.

He doesn't think I'll do it, she realizes. *He doesn't believe I have the guts.*

"V, please." Betty's fingers tremble under hers, and Veronica only clenches tighter.

Five feet.

Got you now, Veronica thinks, and she smiles, fangs and all.

Four—

Three—

Two—

"Veronica."

They brace for impact, even Veronica braces for impact—

—except—

There's a long moment of motion, a swooping sensation as Veronica waits for the glorious smash but—nothing comes.

Veronica blinks and Theodore is gone. That's it.

One second he's right in front of them, and the next, the road is empty and they're speeding head-on toward the woods. "Betty, brake!"

Betty slams on the brakes and Veronica feels the car begin to spin out, barely slowing. There's a wall of trees waiting for them, and she bites her tongue, hard, as she realizes what she's just done.

She meant to kill Theodore, but instead she's killed them all.

Sorry, Mrs. Cooper, she thinks. *Sorry, Mr. Andrews. Sorry, Dilton's very nice mom.*

And then the car comes to a shuddering halt right before the tree line.

There's only shocked silence for a second, two, three, and then Betty punches Veronica in the arm. "You almost *killed* us! V! Oh my god!"

"Ow!" Betty's punch doesn't really hurt, but Veronica rubs at the spot where her fist landed anyway, her heart pounding still. "Sorry. It seemed like a good idea, in the moment."

"Where did he go?" Archie says, a tremor in his voice. "He was right in front of us, and then he—vanished."

"Into thin air," Dilton says, and he rolls down the back window, sticking his head out of it as if searching for Theodore. "Interesting."

Betty puts the car in reverse and eases back onto the road. "Let's go home," she says. "Before we almost die another time."

They're almost back in town when Veronica notices it.

Wheeling in the sky above, but following the same route as them: a jet-black bird, wings wide and sleek.

It lands on the sign welcoming them to Riverdale, THE TOWN WITH PEP! Floats down on an invisible breeze and perches there, its claws gripping the metal of the sign, and it's just a bird, but—

There's something about the way it moves. As if with purpose, a greater meaning than simply flying and surviving.

Veronica tries to look away from it, but the way it's sitting so unnaturally still now keeps her gaze fixed on it.

And then it *looks* at her.

Its head snaps around and its beady eyes meet hers, she could swear it.

Veronica presses back against the seat, like that'll make a difference, and then she watches the bird's eyes track them until they round the bend and are out of its sight.

She shivers.

CHAPTER THIRTY-EIGHT
REGGIE

FROM THE BACK of the truck, Reggie has a good vantage point of Moose.

Moose—one of them now.

Well—what else was Reggie supposed to do? He couldn't let Moose walk away after he'd discovered Reggie standing over Jessica's body yesterday. Especially not when Moose had started freaking out, saying things like he was going to call the cops and that Reggie was a monster.

Reggie hadn't meant to kill him, just like he hadn't meant to kill Jessica.

It seems like being a vampire comes with a body count.

Moose had started to run, and Reggie had no choice but to go after him. He'd tackled him halfway across the football field and grappled Moose into a chokehold, one that he only meant to subdue his friend, but maybe he was stronger than he realized now, or maybe he'd just been scared enough that the force he put on Moose's windpipe was enough to choke him completely.

It had happened so quickly, and for a moment Reggie had felt a panic threatening to enter him. But then as he looked down at Moose's unmoving body, his eyes frozen wide open in fear, Reggie had remembered what Veronica had told him:

There's a kind called the moroi, and in order for them to change, they have to die first, and then they're brought back to life by a vampire bite.

So he did what he had to do. He turned Moose.

It was easy, really. All Reggie had to do was bite Moose, and for a while he'd thought nothing was happening because Moose was still dead, but soon after that he woke up. Changed. And now it's like Moose will do whatever he wants. They make a good team—just like they do on the football field.

Football is part of the reason they're at the drive-in now. It's kind of a two-birds-one-stone situation. Moose needs to feed, and Reggie heard that their football rivals were going to be here tonight. That quarterback Blake Elroy is always talking smack about them, playing dirty, and he gets away with it because his dad happens to be the district superintendent.

After tonight, he won't be a problem anymore.

Reggie thinks of last night: him and Moose digging a shallow grave among the trees that border the high school and shoving Jessica's body into it. He regrets it a little, but only because now that she's dead, he won't ever get to taste her blood again.

Maybe I'll keep the next one alive, he thinks, but deep down, he knows he won't. It's way too hard to stop once you've started feeding, once their hot blood is filling you up.

The drive-in is loud tonight, the Midvale team paying zero attention to the movie—but also zero attention to Moose.

Reggie watches him now, sneaking through the cars parked

erratically across the field. All he has to do is time it right and he'll be feasting.

Moose reaches the tall black truck nearest the Midvale team and waits alongside it.

It doesn't take long for their target to wander off, separating from his team as he heads toward the snack stand.

Get him, Moose, Reggie thinks. This will be his true test—can Moose make the kill? If he's good enough, Reggie's thinking he'll get some more of the guys on board. No need to keep all the fun for himself, and besides, no one really likes eating alone.

At the truck Moose still waits, and Reggie can see the coiled energy within him, waiting for the right moment.

Then—

Blake Elroy passes by.

Moose jumps on him, bringing him down way more easily than he ever has in a game before. For a moment there's a struggle— Reggie thinks the quarterback might get away—but then Moose rears up and brings his teeth back down into the boy's neck, a violent tear of the flesh.

The boy kicks and flails as Moose eats, but he soon stops moving. Moose keeps going, and Reggie can tell it's happening.

Moose feels the power flooding through him—the same power Reggie felt when he had drained Jessica.

Reggie ducks down in the bed of the truck and eyes the shovel he's stashed in there. Soon they'll need to find a place to start digging, dispose of the body.

Reggie sits back. He'll give Moose some time, though. Won't interrupt his first blissful meal.

CHAPTER THIRTY-NINE
VERONICA

BETTY PULLS UP in front of her house and parks, her head dropping back against the seat. "Finally," she says.

Veronica looks up at the Cooper home, the whole thing so warm and inviting with the glow of lights behind pulled curtains, the autumnal wreath hanging on the front door. They dropped Dilton at his place and took Archie back to his house to recover and explain his absence to his dad—cover story provided by Betty, because who knows what nonsense Archie would have come up with on his own.

Betty had said—no, insisted—that Veronica stay with her tonight, and Veronica had almost cried in gratitude. Not that she isn't thankful for all of Dilton's help and the chance to have somewhere to sleep, but right now, she needs the familiar comfort of Betty's soft pink bedroom, the scene of so many sleepover crimes.

"I'm sorry," she says to Betty again. "I kind of got a little out of control back there."

"Stop apologizing." Betty gives her a tired smile. "I get why you did it. I mean, once you take Theodore out, all of this goes away, right? You get to go back to being human, and your parents will go back to their normal selves, too, and *we* can go back to focusing on school and the Vixens instead of, like, vampire-killing weaponry."

Veronica pushes her hair behind her ear. "B," she says, "do you really think we can go back to normal after this?"

"What?" Betty gives her a sharp look. "Of course. Once we stop Theodore and your parents, it'll be like none of this ever happened. No vampires, no strigoi or moroi, no shape-shifting or mind control or whatever other wacky business is involved." She tips her head to the side. "What is it, V? You know, no one's going to see you any differently, if that's what you're worrying about. Sure, right now you're Vampire V, but that's only for now. We'll kill Theodore and get our regular old human V back and nothing will have changed. I promise you."

Veronica looks away, pretends like she's watching the neighbor taking out their trash cans. *Nothing will have changed.* That's what she's worried about, actually. Not that everyone will see her differently but that they *won't* see her differently at all. That they'll expect the old, perfect Veronica to reappear and everything to return to the way it was pre-strigoi. Except Veronica's not sure that she can do that, and more important, she's not sure she wants to.

"Come on." Betty taps Veronica on the knee. "You can borrow some pj's."

The idea of curling up to sleep on Betty's bedroom floor, like they've done for years, pulls her back. "The fluffy ones?"

"Sure," Betty says with a laugh. "And tomorrow, you can borrow whatever you want, too. Where did you even get that outfit?"

Veronica pauses, looking down at her short black pinafore dress, under which she's wearing a black off-the-shoulder top and black fishnets. "What's wrong with my outfit?" She'd been particularly proud of this look when she put it together this morning; kind of an edgy Brigitte Bardot, if she'd taken a detour through post-punk London.

"Nothing!" Betty says, maybe too brightly. "I mean, it's cute, sure, but . . ." She makes a face, scrunching up her perfect nose. "It's just not *you*."

Veronica says nothing. *Not me*, she thinks, anger rising in her. *Okay. Well, what is me, then? Prissy pearls and pleated skirts? Am I not allowed to step outside of that for one freaking minute?*

See, this is what she's worried about. Already Betty wants her to shift back, become somebody she isn't. Because that isn't her, not really; not anymore. Old Veronica is gone, but she's all Betty wants, and she's going to be all everybody else wants, too. When this is all said and done, she'll have to go back to pretending to be everything everyone always thinks she is: smart but not too smart, confident but not arrogant, tough but with the edges filed off. Don't intimidate anybody too much. Don't ruffle anybody's feathers.

That's the me everybody likes, she thinks. *But what about when I'm different? What if I don't go back to that version of myself? Do people like me or have they only ever liked the version of me that I pretended to be?*

Even her best friend wants her to be different. Veronica slides a finger inside one of the holes of her tights. It's only clothes, sure, but Veronica has always known that there's no such thing as *only clothes*. They're how you choose to present yourself to the outside world, how you show yourself. The inner exposed on the outer, however you choose to, so it stings for Betty to dismiss them so easily.

"V?" Betty's looking at her intently. "What's wrong?"

Veronica looks back up at the house. Now it doesn't seem so comforting and cozy; it feels claustrophobic. She knows what awaits her in there, and it's the place where she played her old self so convincingly that every Cooper fell in love with her. If she goes in there, she'll sleep on the same old blow-up mattress she always does, under the gingham comforter like always, and Betty will wish her sweet dreams the way she likes to, and in the morning Betty's mom will make them blueberry pancakes.

The rhythm of it used to be sweet, but now it's off.

"You know what?" Veronica opens the car door and swings her legs out. "I don't think I'm going to stay. I think I need to take a walk, you know? Clear my head a little."

"V," Betty says again. "Are you mad or something? Did I say something to upset you? If I did, then I'm sorry."

Veronica ignores both Betty's question and her apology. How can she be sorry if she doesn't even know what it is that's upset Veronica? How can she apologize when it isn't really even her fault but more about Veronica realizing that maybe she's not the girl everybody thinks she is?

"I just need to take a walk." Her stomach growls, and Veronica sighs. *Yeah, yeah, Hunger. I hear you.* "I need to eat."

"Are you sure?" Betty says. "Are you sure it's safe?"

Veronica whips around and bares her fangs at Betty, so fast and ferocious that Betty lets out a little scream. *Don't forget who I am now,* she wants to say. *Don't forget what this monster can do.*

But she doesn't say it, instead laughs like she was just messing, and Betty laughs too as she puts a hand to her chest. "Okay," she says, breathless. "But call me if you want me to pick you up."

Veronica slams the door. "Sure," she says, keeping what she's really thinking inside.

I don't need you to save me.

I can save myself.

CHAPTER FORTY
CHERYL

CHERYL'S PANTING, LEANING over with her hands on her knees. There's something about the last twist in her double-full that she just can't get. She's not whipping it around fast enough, she knows, but when she does that she always under-rotates.

She straightens up and starts over, powering down the tumbling track.

Her steps thunder in the quiet of the empty gym. There's no Vixens practice today, and everybody usually loves Wednesdays precisely for this reason. It's a rest day, time when they can ice their sore ankles and hips and hang out at Pop's with the rest of the after-school crowd instead of sweating through practice. But Cheryl likes to use the time to get better. No, not better. *Best*. She wants her captain spot back, bad.

Although if Veronica keeps on the way she has been, it won't be hard to snatch it. Veronica hasn't been at practice for the past two days, or in school at all this week. Even Betty missed practice yesterday, and the last couple of days of school. So did Archie,

Cheryl noticed, and no doubt they were all off together. Well, fine by her. They can have their little triangle of drama—it only clears the way for her.

Cheryl whips through the air, round off to back handspring to layout to the double-full that she pulls, *hard*. But then there comes the under-rotation, and she lands on her knees, the impact jarring through her.

"Crap!" She smacks the mat, breathing heavily, and then glances up at the large clock above the scoreboard.

Time to go. Her parents are out of town tonight, and Cheryl has felt the pressure creeping up her spine all week. So she's doing the best thing she knows and throwing an impromptu rager. Sure, mid-week pool parties aren't the smartest, but right now Cheryl doesn't care about being smart. She just needs to blow off some serious steam, before it cooks her from the inside out.

She hits the showers, rinsing the suds out of her long red hair and singing tunelessly. What? There's nobody else around. Nobody can judge her rendition of "Black Velvet," so yeah, she's going to sing.

She's toweling off her hair on her way to her locker when she catches sight of them.

A pair of feet in chunky boots, sticking out from behind the lockers.

Cheryl pulls her towel tighter around her body and creeps forward. "Hello? Is somebody here?" She looks around for a weapon, suddenly aware of how alone she is. If some creep has snuck in here and is lying in wait for her, there's nobody to help. Only Cheryl can defend herself.

She spots a stray hanger on the floor by Chelsea Montez's locker and snatches it up, brandishing it ahead of her. "Show yourself," she demands. "I'm not afraid of you."

There's a rustling sound, and then the skulking figure appears around the edge of the locker bank.

"Jesus, Cheryl. You could take someone's eye out with that thing."

Cheryl's heart slows and she drops the hanger. "Veronica! What the hell are you doing?" She narrows her eyes. "More important, where the hell have you *been*? You know you've missed two practices, right?"

"Yeah." Veronica leans against the lockers, an insouciance to her that Cheryl hasn't seen before. "I'm aware."

Cheryl tosses her hair back. "Well, since you're here," she says, "I'm having a party tonight. Everybody's coming." Not everybody, obviously, but Veronica will know who she means: everybody who matters, everybody in the upper social echelons of Riverdale High. Of course that includes Veronica Lodge, and of course she'll come—

"Pass," Veronica says. "Thanks, though."

Pass? Cheryl puts a hand on her hip and stares Veronica down. "What, you have someplace better to be?"

"Something like that," Veronica says, and she pushes off the lockers. Cheryl notices what she's wearing for the first time: an entirely grungy twist on a Veronica look, including those chunky boots and a short zebra-print skirt that clashes with her faux-fur leopard coat.

"Are you channeling Courtney Love or something?" Cheryl says. "Is this your attempt to go alternative? Because I don't think anyone's going to buy it."

"Buying people's opinions is what *you* do, Cheryl. Not me."

"Excuse you?" she says, keeping her voice steely. *Show no weakness to Veronica.* That's one of her most important rules. The Lodges, like the Blossoms, are cutthroat people. If Veronica sees any crack in Cheryl's armor, then she'll use it to her advantage. That's what Lodges do.

Cheryl rearranges herself, a flash of thigh as she moves, and puts her own cutthroat vision back on. "Don't be at my party tonight, then," she says. "But you better be in practice tomorrow, or the team will have no choice but to discuss your standing as captain, Veronica. It's your job to set an example to everyone, to stand as our leader. Can't do that if you can't even get your ass in the gym."

Veronica glares at her, and for a moment Cheryl wavers. It's a trick of the light, or maybe a trick of her own mind, but for a second she could have sworn Veronica's eyes flashed red.

"You try that," she says. "Run your little coup, Cheryl. See how that works out for you."

And then Veronica storms out, knocking Cheryl's shoulder, and Cheryl gives an outraged gasp as she watches her go.

Wench, she thinks, and flips her hair back again. She hadn't really been thinking about any kind of coup before, but now?

Oh, now, I'm out for blood.

CHAPTER FORTY-ONE
VERONICA

VERONICA HURRIES OUT of and away from the school, trying to put as much distance between the building and herself as she can. Trying to put as much distance between herself and Cheryl, really.

It was risky to go back there, she knows, but she had to. It was the only place with a readily available supply of pig's blood, and after all the action of yesterday followed by walking around town by herself all night, Veronica had been *starving*.

It should have been perfect, chowing down in the locker room that would be empty because there was no Vixens practice today. Except of course Cheryl had been there anyway, and Veronica couldn't believe she'd almost let herself get caught. She'd managed to stuff the empty blood bag into her locker and clean any remnants from her face before showing herself to Cheryl, but it had been way too close.

And then there was the problem of her lingering hunger. Sure, she'd fed, but the pig's blood had barely taken the edge off. And then Cheryl had been there going on and on about her party and the

Vixens, and all Veronica had been able to think about was sinking her teeth into Cheryl's pale, pulsing throat.

She speed-walks through the parking lot. She'd had to get out of there.

She's halfway to the town library when her phone buzzes in her pocket. Thank god for Daddy's insurance plan that allowed her to order a brand-new phone to be delivered to Dilton's—more than two days without checking Insta and she starts to get the shakes. Her problem now is that all day the phone's been going off, but Veronica's ignoring everyone. Well: Truth be told she'd been asleep in the laundromat for a large part of the day and then she'd woken up hungry, and cue school/Cheryl/escape.

So she's only glanced at her phone—increasingly impatient messages from Betty and Archie and mostly Dilton, asking where she is and if she's okay and what their next move's going to be.

Veronica feels exhausted by it all. She didn't ask to be leader of their pack. Honestly, part of her wishes she could just go it alone: Having her friends trailing her is beginning to feel like it's slowing her down. After all, she's a vampire now and they're still weak little humans.

The thought enters her mind unbidden. *They don't have to be.*

Veronica shakes her head violently. No. No *way* is she going to turn any of them. First, she's only read about how the change happens—what if she accidentally does it wrong and kills them? And second—this is the less noble reason, she knows, but she's okay with it—she doesn't really want them to have this.

Selfish, sure, but she likes having something separate from all of them, and she likes being New Vampire Veronica. *Vampironica.*

She rolls her eyes at herself. *Okay, joker, very funny.*

When her phone buzzes again she answers it, her voice tight. "Yes?"

"Veronica, darling."

Veronica goes cold. It's her mother's smooth voice. "Hi, Mom."

"I'll cut to the chase," Hermione says. "You're in big trouble, young lady. What you did to your father? I'm ashamed of you." She sighs. "But luckily for you, your father and I have decided not to punish you."

Veronica watches the cars pass by from where she's paused and the orange leaves on the trees waving through the air. "Wow," she says. This conversation—is it even a conversation? Can it be called a conversation when you've exchanged less than five words with the person on the other side?—is ridiculous. The way her mother's speaking as if Veronica broke curfew or failed a test rather than conspired to drug her father and break her friend out of their kidnapping clutches is *wild.* "So I'm not in trouble? Oh, thank you, Mother dearest! Thank you oh so much!"

Her mother ignores Veronica's blatant sarcasm and forges ahead. "Come home," she says. "I think if you just got to know Theodore, you'd come around to our way of thinking."

"Your way of thinking?" Veronica scoffs. *Their* way of thinking is only *Theodore's* way of thinking. "Sure, Mom. I'll get right on that."

"You should consider what I'm offering you," her mom says. "Because honestly, sweetie, it's join us or face the consequences. Understand? You're either with us or—"

"Against you," Veronica says. "Yeah, spare me the clichés. Listen,

I'm never going to get on board with your turn-everyone-and-take-over-the-town thing, so you can cut the act. I'm not coming home, and I'm not going to play the dutiful daughter anymore. Clear?"

"Veronica—"

She hangs up, jabbing at her phone angrily. No. She won't let her mother, even under mind control, manipulate her into becoming a pawn in their game. She's been that for too long already—her whole life, really.

Instead, she starts walking again, switching tracks to head to Betty's. Yes, she's a little mad at Betty and she's tired of all that's going on, but she doesn't really have the luxury of turning her back on things. The Blossoms' hotel opening gala is in two days, and they need a solid strategy for taking Theodore out once and for all.

It would help if I understood why he's doing this, she thinks. What does Theodore get out of turning everyone, besides a vampire army? What's he going to *do* with that army?

Veronica strides into the darkening evening. That's what she needs to know.

CHAPTER FORTY-TWO
DILTON

"DILLY! DO YOU want some ice cream for dessert?"

Dilton glances at the door, irritated. "No, Mom," he yells back. "I'm busy!"

He hasn't heard from Veronica since he came home yesterday evening, but that hasn't distracted him. She's probably with Betty, making it up to her after almost killing them all with that car stunt. Although Dilton didn't mind much: In the moment when he thought it was about to be all over, as the trees were speeding up to meet them, he got a flash of inspiration.

He turns back to the piece of wood in his hand and resumes whittling at it with a short, sharp knife. Something about the trees had pinged an idea deep in his brain, and when he'd come home he'd taken a look at the stakes he and Veronica had bought at the paranormal store. They were cheap and flimsy, maybe capable of inflicting *some* kind of damage, but something sturdier would be better. Pure oak or something similar would really pack a punch, he thought. And then there was the semiaccidental discovery Betty had made: the holy water as internal poison.

What if I could create some kind of reservoir inside a stake? he'd wondered. *Fill that with holy water and then add a small explosive mechanism so that, when used, the stake explodes and the holy water infiltrates their internal system?*

So that's what he's doing now. It's less for Veronica and more for himself and Archie and Betty. If they're going to counterattack at the gala on Friday, then they'll need to be prepared. Veronica can more than take care of herself, but the rest of them? Up against an as yet unknown amount of mind-controlled vampires?

Dilton slices off another strip of wood and holds the stake up to the light, eyeing the sharpness of its point before tossing it on the growing pile he's already finished. Yeah, facing off with a rabid pack of newborn vamps? They're going to need to be fully armed.

CHAPTER FORTY-THREE
CHERYL

CHERYL STANDS OUT on her balcony, surveying the scene before her.

The backyard is packed, and music thumps out. The party is in full, beautiful swing, but she hasn't gone down there yet. No, Cheryl Bombshell always makes an entrance.

She goes back into her room and admires her outfit in the mirror: short shorts, a white tee, and signature red lipstick. She's tamed her hair into tumbling waves and added a pair of gold hoops to finish off the look. Through her door she can hear the noise below, and she gives her reflection a small smile. *See? People do like me. They're here tonight, aren't they?*

Cheryl gives herself a last look and then makes her way down into the fray. She spends some time parading through the party, making sure that everybody sees her, accepting their fawning gazes and eager greetings like they're oxygen.

No sign of Veronica.

Not that she cares, Cheryl tells herself. Just because her main rival for queen bee refused to make an appearance doesn't mean she's lost her edge. Everyone else is here, and that's all that matters.

Out by the pool some of the Vixens are dancing through cheers tipsily, and Midge and Nancy are waiting for her. "Ladies!" she barks. "Fetch me a drink."

And then she turns to the group of girls hanging close behind her and throws her hands in the air. "Who wants to play seven minutes in heaven?"

CHAPTER FORTY-FOUR
REGGIE

REGGIE STARES UP at the fence that surrounds the Blossom property. He can see the top of the family's mansion looming over the fence and hear the party happening behind it.

"Can't we just go in the front?" Moose scratches at his neck, eyes red. "Seems a little dramatic to hop the fence."

"It's the element of surprise," Reggie tells him. "If we go in the front, everyone will see us and we won't be able to plan out our attack. This way, no one will know what to expect."

He licks his lips. When he heard about Cheryl's party earlier, he couldn't believe his luck. It's going to be like an all-you-can-eat buffet in there for both him and Moose.

Well. All they can eat, and then all they can *turn*.

That's Reggie plan, at least. He's been thinking about it ever since he turned Moose. What fun is it to have to creep around, hiding out from everyone, like they're monsters who need to be hidden away? And how fair is it to keep all the fun of being a vampire for himself when he could be bringing more of his friends in on this? Think about it: Veronica's already one of them. He can turn Betty, Archie and Jughead, the rest of the Bulldogs, and the Vixens, too. Cheryl—well, he has a better plan for her. But the rest of them?

Why not turn this town into one big vampire party?

Reggie takes out his phone and snaps a selfie of him and Moose, fangs out in front of the Blossom mansion, composing a message to go along with the image. *Found something better to eat than a Pop's burger. Why don't u come join us?*

He presses "Send" and then crouches, hands forming a cradle for Moose to step into. *Lay low*, Veronica had said.

Reggie grins to himself. She doesn't know what she's missing.

CHAPTER FORTY-FIVE
VERONICA

IT'S FULLY DARK by the time Veronica reaches Betty's. That's okay; she's beginning to feel more at home in the darkness.

Her phone buzzes, again, and Veronica knows it's going to be Betty, again. *I'm right here!* she wants to call out, but she takes her phone out anyway.

Above her, a window opens, and Betty leans out. "V! Oh my god, I've been texting you all day!"

"I know!" Veronica holds her phone up. "I just—"

Wait.

The name on her screen isn't Betty's but Reggie's.

Reggie. Veronica wants to smack herself in the head. She'd kind of forgotten all about him. *It's not like I didn't have a good excuse! Archie was kidnapped; I almost drove a car into the woods (again)!*

She opens the text, expecting it to be Reggie complaining about her ignoring him, but what she sees makes her stomach drop.

It's a picture of Reggie, full vamp mode engaged, and *Moose.*

Moose is a vampire? But who turned him? Did Reggie—

There's no time for figuring out all the details, Veronica realizes.

Because the picture he's sent was taken right outside Cheryl's house.

The party.

Why don't u come join us? Reggie's text says, and Veronica feels a panic begin to bloom in the depths of her stomach. *Everybody* is at Cheryl's tonight for her party. That means everybody is in danger of being attacked by Reggie and Moose.

And judging from their red eyes and bloodstained fangs, this won't be their first feeding.

"Idiot, idiot, idiot!" She gets louder with each sharp stab of the word, until Betty calls down to her.

"What's wrong?" Betty hangs farther out of her window. "V, what is it?"

Veronica looks up at her, formulating a desperate plan. "Give me your keys!" she says. "I need your car!"

CHAPTER FORTY-SIX
REGGIE

THEY LAND ON the other side of the fence with catlike finesse. There's only one person Reggie *really* wants to taste tonight, and he can see her up on the deck, spinning around with her arms in the air.

He doesn't know if there's such a thing as a vampire delicacy, but if there is, then redheaded Cheryl Blossom is probably the closest thing to it.

Reggie breaks into a run, and he can feel Moose at his back, same as they are on the football field. He was right about the element of surprise; as they break into the crowd, not hiding their vampire features, a girl screams and the air around them changes instantly.

Reggie slows, lifting his nose as he catches a sweet scent on the breeze. *Cheryl.*

She turns, her hair fanning around her, and narrows her eyes. "Excuse you," she says, and her voice is loud. Oh, she's not afraid like all the rest. Good; he's in the mood for a challenge. "This party is *exclusive*. No sloppy messes allowed. Got it?"

He skulks toward her, keeping his face in shadow.

"Hey," Cheryl says. "Are you listening? Shoo, little vermin." And then she jumps, finally seeing Moose appear out of the dark.

The crowd around them is beginning to thin out, people pushing past in their effort to get away from whatever's happening. Reggie knows what they'll be thinking, feeling—that same unease that flooded him when he woke up the morning after the crash. Knowing something's off, but not being able to pinpoint exactly what it is.

That he's the source of that unsettling feeling now fills him with pride, and he watches Cheryl as he paces closer. *Look at her*, he thinks, and he can see a little fear now. *I'm going to enjoy this.*

"Take him with you, too!" Cheryl snaps, and then she takes a few steps forward, hands on her hips. "I said, get—"

Reggie rears up, snarling as he launches himself at Cheryl, and she finally screams, a glorious sound to Reggie's ears.

"Don't worry, Cheryl," he says. "This is only going to hurt a little."

CHAPTER FORTY-SEVEN
VERONICA

VERONICA FISHTAILS TO a stop outside the Blossom mansion and stares in dismay.

People are flooding down the driveway and out of the house, the air a cacophony of panic.

I'm too late, she thinks. *Am I too late?*

She throws herself out of the car and begins running against the tide, elbowing her way through. Inside, the house is empty, and Veronica dashes through, finding her way to the yard.

There's a scream.

Veronica sprints through the open French doors, and there they are: Moose, and Reggie, hovering over Cheryl, and Cheryl on the ground scrambling backward.

She's alive, still, but she won't be for long if Veronica doesn't act.

"Get away!" she hears Cheryl yelling, her voice cracking, and Reggie looms there, a howl erupting from his fanged mouth.

Now or never.

"Hey!" Veronica's yell is loud, sharp. All eyes snap to her— Reggie, and Moose, and a terrified Cheryl on the ground.

Reggie's grin spreads wider. "So glad you could make it, Ronnie," he's saying, but she's already sprinting at him, her fist cocked back. Without slowing she reaches him, cracks her fist into his chin, and it sends his head snapping back, him stumbling. Then she drops into a crouch and kicks out low at Moose, taking his legs out from under him, and he slams to the ground. *Another big shout-out to that self-defense class.*

The hits won't take them out, of course not, but it gives her enough time to get Cheryl to safety.

"Wakey wakey, princess." Veronica grabs Cheryl's hand and yanks her to her feet.

Cheryl stares at her, bottom lip trembling. "Veronica?"

"No time," Veronica says tersely before spinning her away and pushing her toward the house. "Get in there," she says. "Lock the d—"

Veronica feels the hot, wet breath on the back of her neck a second before it's too late, and she ducks out of the way just as Moose's teeth snap shut in the air. She jumps and lands a few feet from both Reggie and Moose, crouched in attack position, drawing them away from Cheryl.

"Listen up, boys," she says, her adrenaline pumping as she shifts from side to side, their snarling faces her focus. "We can do this the easy way, or we can do it the hard way. Your choice."

For a second she and Reggie just stare at each other, a moment of stillness in the whirlwind of panic that this night has become.

And then Reggie lunges at her.

Veronica darts sideways and snaps out her fangs. "Fine," she says with a growl. "We'll do it the hard way."

The next time he lunges, she's ready—two hits to the gut and another to the face, her knuckles smacking loud against Reggie's perfect cheekbone. As he stumbles back, Veronica raises her other hand high.

Good thing Betty's car is now stocked with not only strawberry bubble gum and tampons but vampire-killing stakes, too. She grabbed one on her way in and barely had time to think about what the weight of it in her hand meant—if she was really planning on killing Reggie and Moose tonight. But she sees no other way to stop them.

If Reggie's out there attacking people and turning his friends into monsters, then he must be stopped.

Veronica flips the stake around, pointed end aimed directly at Reggie's heart, and she's about to plunge it in when—

Footsteps thunder toward her, and she glances up just in time to see Moose heading straight at her.

Nice work, Ronnie! You forgot about Moose. Get it together, god.

He's coming so fast that she doesn't have time to dodge or duck or do anything but take the tackle. Moose brings down not only her but Reggie, too, and all three of them fly through the air in a tangle of limbs and crash into the pool.

Veronica holds her breath as they go under, and through the water filling her ears she could swear she hears Cheryl scream her name.

But again—no time.

The water slows things, but Veronica's always been a good swimmer. And most important: She still has hold of the stake.

Her lungs are beginning to burn already, but she pushes herself deeper in the water, kicking and thrashing her arms to send up a storm of bubbles. Enough so that she can no longer tell which way is up or down—but neither can Reggie or Moose.

They're grabbing for her through the water, meaty Bulldog hands trying to catch her clothes, an arm, an ankle, but Veronica's distraction proves useful, and they can't get to her.

She spins around behind Moose. *Aim right*, she tells herself. *One shot*.

Veronica moves as fast as she can and slices down through the water. She connects, and Moose's flesh has a strange soft give kind of like Jell-O as the stake slides into his heart, and when she rips it back out a trail of blood follows.

She doesn't have time to admire the almost pretty shapes the blood forms in the water; she still has Reggie to deal with.

The bubbles are beginning to clear now and Reggie's in front of her. Fast as the first time, she jabs—and misses.

Her lungs are on fire now but she can't stop, not until Reggie *is* stopped.

Veronica pulls back again but Reggie's ready this time, and he grabs her wrist, squeezing hard.

She watches in desperation as her fingers start to let go of the stake without her meaning to. If she drops it, she's dead. For *real* dead this time.

With no time to think, she pulls the same old move as she did on Theodore, and kicks Reggie as hard as she can between his legs.

His faces twists in surprised pain, and he releases her wrist. Veronica wastes no more time; she tightens her grip on the stake and stabs again, and this time she gets him right in the neck.

Reggie gasps, opening his mouth to let a stream of air spread through the water, the last oxygen in his lungs leaving him, and he begins to float to the surface.

Through the heart, Veronica thinks. *It has to be through the heart.* If he gets up there and takes a breath, that neck wound will start to heal and she'll be back in danger.

Cheryl will be in danger.

With her vision darkening at the edges, Veronica grasps for Reggie. She catches his ankle and pulls him down, and places the stake over his heart.

He's watching her, and Veronica meets his eyes for a split second. This is Reggie. She's about to kill Reggie. Is she really going to kill Reggie?

I'm sorry, she thinks. *We had fun, you and me, most of the time. You weren't a bad guy. Maybe I could have treated you better, and maybe you could have treated all those other girls you screwed around with better, too. But you weren't rotten, at your core. Only now you are, Reggie, and you get it, right? I can't let you run around out of control like this. I'm sorry it had to come to this but—this is how it has to end.*

She punches the stake through his chest. It feels just like it did with Moose, his flesh surprisingly soft and then his blood flooding out around her hands, warm. She watches as long as she can, as long as she can keep that breath held, as Reggie's red eyes empty and he's left floating there, a normal boy. The Reggie she used to know.

Veronica takes hold of Moose's body then, Reggie's in the other hand, and uses her last bit of energy to propel herself to the surface, to air.

The water seems to crack as she bursts through, and Veronica gulps in a greedy lungful of oxygen.

Congratulations, Vampire Slayer, she thinks. *Add two to the body count.*

"Oh my *god*."

CHAPTER FORTY-EIGHT
CHERYL

CHERYL'S WATCHING THE water. *Go inside,* Veronica told her, but what was she supposed to do? Leave her out here alone to face those—those *monsters*?

Only now Veronica's in the water with them, the surface still and steaming, and Cheryl doesn't know what to do. Go in after her? Call the sheriff?

What would she even say? *Hi, Sheriff Keller, there's a couple of vampires in my backyard, could you swing by real quick?*

Sure! That won't get filed under "Cheryl Blossom's being dramatic again" at all!

She shivers, wrapping her arms around herself, and then she sees it.

A swirl of red, bubbling to the surface and then beginning to spread.

A scarlet slick that takes over the placid blue, until the pool is more blood than water.

And then, like Venus herself, Veronica erupts from the deep.

Her black hair is plastered to her face, and bloody water slides down her neck, but she's victorious because with each hand she's dragging a body, like a cat come to drop her prey at the feet of her mistress.

"Oh my *god*," Cheryl says, a quiet shock, eyeing the dead bodies. Because that's Reggie, and that's Moose, and they're *dead*, and Veronica's holding their bodies, and she's covered in blood, and they're dead, *they died*, at her house, in her pool— "Oh my god, oh my god, Veronica—"

Veronica tosses her head back, and Cheryl wants to scream but she can't find the sound.

For a moment she thinks it's the boys' blood turning Veronica's eyes red, but that doesn't explain her mouth. The fangs.

Veronica is a *vampire*?

She drops the bodies at the edge of the pool, panting. "Sorry about the mess," she says. "God, they would not play the easy way."

Cheryl feels it coming, and she tries to hold it in but it's no good, she can't, and then—

She folds in half and vomits at Veronica's feet.

CHAPTER FORTY-NINE
VERONICA

THE MOON SHINES down through the trees, illuminating the ragged hole Veronica's standing in.

She leans on the shovel for a second, breathing hard, and looks toward Cheryl. "Hey," she says. "Hey! Look at me."

Cheryl's staring at the bodies by her feet, like she's unable to look anywhere else. And Veronica gets it. She's had to force herself to look away and focus on the job before her multiple times.

Those were her friends. That was Moose, the most genuinely good guy Veronica's ever known, and that was Reggie, the boy she maybe used more than he deserved, and now they're both dead. Because of her, they're dead.

She shakes her head as she resumes digging. *No. Not because of me. I didn't turn Reggie. I didn't turn Moose. That's not on me, and their actions aren't on me, but I had to kill them; I had to stop them before they could do any more damage. Before they could hurt me. Hurt Cheryl.*

I did what had to be done.

When the shoulder-deep ditch is wide enough, Veronica climbs out. "Help me with this," she says to Cheryl, and even though

Cheryl looks completely shell-shocked, she bends down and picks up Reggie's arms.

Veronica takes his feet, and together they swing once, twice, three times to build momentum and then toss him down into the hole.

His body makes a dull thud when it hits the ground, and Veronica feels it deep down in her stomach.

They do the same with Moose, and it's funny, how familiar the motion is in the moment. Her and Cheryl lifting a body between them, synchronized. The only difference is it's usually a Vixen they're tossing through the air, not a dead vampire.

Veronica wipes a hand across her brow, leaving a streak of mud through the redness that's already there, and she watches as Cheryl steps up to the edge of the hurried grave and looks down.

She's barely said anything since Veronica emerged from the pool with the boys' bodies. Didn't protest when Veronica wiped away the vomit from around her mouth; nodded when Veronica told her they had to get rid of the bodies; pointed when V asked where she could find a shovel. It's extremely unlike Cheryl to be this quiet, this compliant, and it's making Veronica uneasy. At some point Cheryl's going to ask, she knows: She's going to ask what Veronica is and why their friends are dead and what the hell is happening, and Veronica's going to have to tell her.

Yet another person she's going to have to convince that she's not a complete monster. And what's she supposed to say this time? *Reggie and Moose were vampires on a rampage, so I had to kill them. Oh, me? I mean, yeah, I'm a vampire, too, but I'm, like, a good vampire. Sure, yes, I get how me having just killed two people probably makes me look like a* bad *vampire, but it's really more complicated than you think, I swear.*

Veronica moves up to stand beside Cheryl. "Almost done," she says. "I just have to—"

"I'll do it."

Veronica raises her eyebrows, both at Cheryl finally speaking and what she's implying. "You want to fill it in?"

"You did the hard part." Cheryl doesn't look at Veronica as she talks, her eyes locked on the bodies still. The moonlight hits her, running a pale gleam through her red hair, over her smudged-makeup face. "I got this."

"Okay," Veronica says, although it goes against her better judgment, and hands over the shovel.

Cheryl begins heaping dirt down into the grave, and Veronica watches as slowly, slowly, slowly, the moonlit bodies disappear.

CHAPTER FIFTY
VERONICA

THEY TRUDGE BACK up to the house when it's done.

Bypass the pool full of tainted water, the small pile of vomit from Cheryl, the mess of plastic cups and bottles, and a single shoe abandoned in the earlier rush to escape.

Cheryl leads Veronica upstairs and shows her to an opulent bathroom before leaving her.

Once inside, Veronica locks the door and turns the shower on, running the water as hot as she can bear. She strips off her wet clothes and steps under the water, watching as it snakes clean rivulets through the dirt streaking her hands, her legs, the top of her chest. Blood and soil swirls around the drain, and she watches it spiral.

What am I doing?

What have I become?

Heat pricks at her eyes, but she tips her face up to the water and refuses to let any tears fall. Feeling sorry for herself is not going to fix anything. So, she killed them. She's going to kill Theodore, too. And maybe before, back in her own home, she would have killed her father, if he'd given her the chance. It's not so much that she's a monster now as it is that being a vampire has released the strength within her.

Sometimes bad things must be done, in the name of protection, in the name of justice.

The water stings as it hits her face, but Veronica welcomes it. She uses an obscene amount of shampoo and conditioner, trying to get every ounce of chlorine and blood from her dark hair, and then scrubs herself all over until she feels raw but clean.

There's a terry-cloth robe hanging on the back of the bathroom door, so she puts it on and then ventures out. She's been to Cheryl's house plenty of times but usually for parties where she and Betty and the boys stay down in the vast kitchen, or out on the deck. Only once has she actually been in Cheryl's bedroom, and that was years ago, when they were little kids and forced to go to each other's birthday sleepovers even though they didn't really want to.

Veronica steps lightly through the corridors, trying to find her way to Cheryl's room, and eventually she sees a soft pink light emanating from a crack in a door. She knocks and then pushes it open. "Cheryl?"

Cheryl looks up, sitting in the middle of a huge bed. Her hair's wet, too, and she's wearing a robe, but hers is silk. "Hey," she says with a small, tired smile. "Feel better?"

"Cleaner, at least." Veronica comes in and then hovers. Cheryl's bedroom is kind of like Betty's but on steroids and with an altogether darker undertone. Betty's bedroom is like a cotton candy cloud; Cheryl's is the Moulin Rouge, all pink and red satin, frothy tulle curtains, pink bulbs in the lights dotted across the ceiling so everything seems to glow.

"Sit," Cheryl says, patting the bed, but when she moves she makes a pained face.

Veronica moves over and crouches by the bed, peering at Cheryl as she inspects her for any sign of injury, any damage that Reggie might have inflicted on her. "Did he get you at all?" she asks. "I tried to get here as fast as I could, but—"

"I'm fine," Cheryl says, shaking her head. "I almost wasn't, but—" She stares down at Veronica with her gleaming brown eyes. "You saved my life."

The way Cheryl's looking at her makes Veronica feel uneasy, a swoop in the space behind her ribs, and suddenly she feels more responsible than she cares for. "It's— I mean, I only—"

"Why?" Cheryl's eyebrows slope together now as she cuts off Veronica's babbling, a frown of confusion. "That's all I can think about now. Why did you come here—why did you help me—when you hate me?"

"What?" Veronica inches back and then sits on the floor, the ivory carpet like a cloud beneath her. "Cheryl, I don't *hate* you. Why would even think that?"

Cheryl gets up and begins walking around her bedroom, idly touching trinkets that she passes. "Because it's true," she says. "Or— okay, fine, maybe you don't *hate* me, but you don't like me. Nobody *really* likes me."

"Um, hello? Didn't you just have practically everybody from school partying at your house on a Wednesday night?" Veronica holds up her hands. "Who else could get people to do that?"

Cheryl turns, leans on her dresser, and gives Veronica a look like she's being deliberately obtuse. "They came for a party," she says flatly. "Not for me."

"But they—"

"See how fast they all left?" Cheryl says, cutting Veronica off again. "See how they all ran out of here and not one person, not a single one, not even Midge and Nancy, who are supposed to be my *friends*, stopped to make sure I was okay?" And then she shakes her head again and looks to the ceiling. "It's fine. I don't expect you to understand. You have Betty; she's your best friend. And then you have everybody else, all those people who actually *like* you, who want to be around you even when you're not giving them anything. You wouldn't get it."

Veronica rakes a hand through her damp hair. "Cheryl—" She exhales. She's never known Cheryl feels this way. She's the most popular girl in school, the one everyone's equal parts in awe and afraid of. Never shies away from an argument, always ready with a snappy barb or the kind of up-and-down look that lets you know exactly how little Cheryl cares about meaningless you.

But Veronica looks at the girl in front of her, barefaced and vulnerable, and it's obvious.

God, it's so obvious she feels like an idiot for not seeing it before this second.

It's a shield. Cheryl's acting, too.

Veronica knows all too well what that feels like. "I don't hate you," she says, softly now, almost like the pink light and the delicate surroundings demand it. "Actually, I think we have a lot in common. More than anyone would think, probably, and not just the surface stuff. Not the Vixens, or our legacies."

But Cheryl's shaking her head. "I knew you wouldn't get it," she says again. "It's like—who would you call, right now, to pick you up? Betty, right? And she'd be here in a heartbeat, because that's what best friends do. You have someone to rely on who knows you inside and out, and all I have is a bunch of people who like me for my parties and a group of girls who like me enough to have me on their team but never invite me to hang after practice, never ask me to stay over the night before competitions or games. Look at me." She gestures dramatically at herself. "None of them would want *this* version of me. I have to be Cheryl Bombshell all the time, and I'm exhausted."

Veronica crosses her legs, holding on to her ankles. "Cheryl." She looks up at her. "You think you're the only one putting on a show?"

Cheryl says nothing, but her eyes widen a little.

"I'm *Veronica Lodge*," Veronica says, the emphasis apparent. "There are days I wish I didn't have to be me, because then I could do whatever I wanted without worrying that it's somehow going to get back to my father and give him another reason to dismiss me. There are days I wish I didn't have to be me, because then I wouldn't have to watch my best friend get the boy she likes while I sit on the sidelines waiting for whatever scraps he'll give me. And then there are times when I wonder—do I even *like* that boy, or am I just stuck in this pattern of doing only the things that I think *Veronica Lodge* would?" She swivels to kneel, a little like prayer position. "Sure, people like me. But they don't *know* me. They like the Veronica I give them, and if I ever try to step outside of that?" She laughs a little. "I spend a couple days wearing something that's not pristine-preppy-perfect style and Betty can't bear it. I come here for you, and even you think I'm doing something wrong or weird."

Cheryl is looking at her own reflection, and when she turns back to Veronica, her face has gone carefully blank. "Oh, boo-hoo," Cheryl says. "You want me to clap for you?"

Veronica laughs again. "Oh my god," she says, half of her surprised and the other half not at all to see Cheryl's wall snapping back up so fast. "You can't help yourself, can you? I'm trying to tell you that I *do* get it. Maybe we don't have the exact same problems, but I—I'm not somebody you should be jealous of. I'm just a person, like you."

And then Cheryl catches her gaze, the blankness dropping and the question apparent in her eyes. "You're not, though, are you?" she says.

Veronica swallows, hard.

"You're not a person at all. Right?" Cheryl moves suddenly, fast enough that she's right in front of Veronica in a second. Close enough now that Veronica can see the light freckles scattered over the bridge of Cheryl's nose, smell the dark amber of her shampoo or lotion or perfume, maybe. "So what *are* you, Veronica Lodge?"

CHAPTER FIFTY-ONE
BETTY

"**PICK UP, PICK** up, pick up." Betty chews on her thumbnail as she paces her bedroom, wearing a path in the carpet between the door and the window. "V, come *on*."

It's been almost two hours since Veronica took her car and raced off to whatever crisis was in progress, and Betty's been trying to reach her ever since. She has a bad feeling in her bones, worsening since she saw the news flying over social media: some kind of incident at Cheryl Blossom's party, something about two crashers freaking out and attacking, like they were high or something.

High on blood, Betty thinks. *Or being controlled by a malevolent vampire puppeteer, maybe.*

The call goes to voicemail again and Betty throws her phone down, letting out a little yell of frustration. She has no car, since Veronica took hers. Walking all the way to Cheryl's will take too long.

She picks her phone back up and tries Archie first: nothing. Then Dilton: similarly, no answer. In her desperation she even calls

Cheryl, but as it rings and rings, she's already given up.

In the end she settles for a text to both boys: *Have you talked to V? I think she might be in trouble. Let me know if you hear from her.*

Betty falls asleep fully dressed, phone clutched in her hand, and dreams of bloodied fangs.

CHAPTER FIFTY-TWO
VERONICA

VERONICA'S HEART IS pounding. She can feel her chest lifting and falling, almost in sync with Cheryl's.

Fine. *She wants to know, then she deserves the truth. She did just help me bury a body.*

Or two.

"It would be easier if I . . . showed you."

"Showed me?" Cheryl repeats.

"Like this—" Veronica opens her mouth wide and flicks out her fangs to show Cheryl. At first they were uncomfortable in her mouth, but she's quickly gotten used to them. Her own personal weapons.

Cheryl stares, but the look in her eyes isn't one of fright. It's pure curiosity.

She lifts a hand. "Can I?"

Veronica nods.

Cheryl touches her middle finger to one of Veronica's fangs, and it takes absolutely every ounce of Veronica's willpower not to shift lightning fast and sink her teeth into Cheryl's wrist.

Human blood. It's the one thing she really wants, and that's why she can't let herself have it. She doesn't want to end up like Reggie, drunk on it. She can't let herself go that far.

When she feels the sharp edge of her tooth pierce Cheryl's soft flesh, Veronica darts backward. "See?" she says. "I'm a vampire. There's your proof."

"Ow," Cheryl says without anything behind it, and she sucks the drop of blood on her fingertip away.

Veronica smothers the flash of jealousy she feels. What she would give to have that drop of blood for herself.

"Huh," Cheryl says after a moment. "So. Monsters are real."

Veronica's sharp when she answers. "Is that what you think?" she asks. "That I'm a monster?"

Cheryl shrugs as she steps away, walks over to the bed. "I mean, aren't you?" she says. "*Vampires*. Who would have thought?"

Not me before this week, Veronica thinks. She moves to sit on the bed, too, Cheryl at the head and her at the foot. "It's kind of a messy story," she says.

That only makes Cheryl smile. "I want to hear it all," she says. "Spare no detail."

So Veronica tells her, haltingly at first as she tries to sort the blur of the last five days into separate events, doubling back to explain herself when Cheryl says things like *A strig-what?* and *Wait, wait, Dilton Doiley did* what?

And then Veronica has to tell Cheryl the worst part—for Cheryl, at least. "So I know where Theodore's going to try to do this thing," she says slowly. "That gala your parents are throwing on Friday."

Cheryl's mouth drops open. "No," she says, outrage saturating the word. "Excuse me, but *no*. I have been working on this event for *months* now. I am not going to have it ruined by a bunch of vampires coming in and trying to make their stupid little vampire gang. No *freakin'* way."

Veronica almost laughs at Cheryl's indignation. Almost, but not quite. "Don't worry," she says, even though that's mostly what she does now, when she's not distracting herself with new clothes and new personas. "Now that we know, we're going to figure out how to stop them."

"What's to figure out?" Cheryl repeats. "Don't you already know? Isn't it just like with . . ." She swallows, lowering her voice. "Reggie and Moose? Doesn't stopping them mean *killing* them?"

Veronica takes a deep breath. "In theory, sure. But it won't fix things. If I killed my parents—" She swallows hard at the thought of it. "It wouldn't stop anybody else. And as pissed as I am at my father right now, I'm not sure I want him *dead* dead. No, killing him wouldn't take care of the real problem. As long as Theodore Finch is still alive—"

Cheryl startles. "What did you say?"

"As long as the strigoi who turned everybody's alive—"

"No." Cheryl leans forward. "His name. Did you say Theodore Finch?"

Veronica nods slowly. "Yeah," she says. "Why? Have you heard of him? Because Dilton and I did some research, and it seems like he belonged to a founding family, but I've never even heard of the Finches."

"Heard of them?" Cheryl widens her eyes. "Of course I've heard of them. They weren't just a founding family, you know—they were the *first* founding family."

"First?" Veronica leans back, trying to grasp at a connection she knows is somewhere there.

Oh, she knows this has to be more than just a power grab. And if once upon a time Theodore Finch's family started this whole town, if they were even more powerful and influential than the Blossoms and the Lodges—well. Where are the Finches now?

"Do you know anything else about them?" she asks Cheryl. "It's been nagging at me this whole time. I know there must be something else to his plan that I haven't figured out yet. Maybe it's connected to his history here, I don't know."

"I don't know, either, but . . ." Cheryl gets up and goes to her dresser, rifling through the third drawer down. She turns and throws a pair of black pajamas in Veronica's direction. "Get dressed," she says. "We're going on a mission."

CHAPTER FIFTY-THREE
CHERYL

MAYBE "MISSION" IS a grandiose way of saying *to the library on the second floor of my house*, but Cheryl doesn't care.

She takes Veronica to the imposing room, the heavy door clanking shut behind them. "The book should be in here somewhere," she says. "It's, like, an entire record of early Riverdale history, starting from the founding and going up to around the fifties. Whatever we need to know, I think it'll be in there."

Veronica puts her shoulders back. "Then let's start looking."

They begin searching the stacks for the old leather-bound book, and Cheryl somewhat absentmindedly wonders what this chapter of Riverdale history will say when people in the future look back: *During the Great Vampire Invasion, many figures from the town were transformed into mind-controlled zombie vampires. However, some escaped the mind-control aspect and got to retain their free will. One of those was Veronica Lodge, last in the line of the founding Lodge family. (N.B. As she is immortal, the Lodge family line technically has not ended.)*

Cheryl shakes her head, clearing the thought, and glances over at Veronica working her way through the *E* section.

A vampire. Veronica Lodge, Frenemy Number One, is a real-life, actual *vampire*.

Cheryl wouldn't have believed it so quickly if she hadn't seen it all with her own eyes, hadn't seen the red film over Reggie's pupils and those fangs of his ready to rip her throat out. Until Veronica saved her.

Veronica *did* save her. *And then of course I had to go off on her about how jealous I am of her and Betty, how nobody likes me, how I'm, deep down, just a loser.* If there's one way *not* to convince somebody to be your friend, then it's probably by complaining about how few friends you have.

But she's here, still, a part of her thinks. *She could have left and gone back to Betty, or Archie, or apparently even Dilton Doiley, which is* beyond weird—

Cheryl stops herself. No. Why is it weird that Dilton and Veronica might really be friends? Isn't she just doing exactly what she hates everybody else for doing to her: judging him for the person she *thinks* he is when she's never really spoken to him at all?

Veronica glances over, catches Cheryl watching her. "What?" she says. "Did you find it?"

Cheryl shakes her head. "I feel like I didn't properly thank you," she says. "You know, Reggie really would have killed me. I would be dead right now, if it wasn't for you. So—thank you."

"Cheryl." Veronica smiles at her. "You don't have to keep thanking me. Friends save friends' lives, right? It's no big deal."

Friends.

The idea of it is warm, wondrous, and Cheryl doesn't know what to do with that feeling because it's been so long since she felt it. Friends. She and Veronica are friends.

"Oh!" Veronica tugs a book off the shelf. "Is this it?"

Cheryl goes over and takes the book from Veronica, running her hands over the gold embossing. *From Ice to Industry: How Riverdale Became a Town of Success* by R. M. Eames. "Yes," she breathes, and takes it over to the mahogany table by the window, curtains open to the dark outside that the glow of wall sconces is keeping somewhat at bay. Cheryl lays the book out and begins flipping through it until she passes the boring introduction and comes to the section titled "Founding Families: An Alliance and a Betrayal."

"Betrayal?" Veronica reads over her shoulder. "Well. Might explain why we don't talk about the Finches anymore."

Cheryl turns the pages. "Only one way to find out," she says, and they begin to read.

CHAPTER FIFTY-FOUR
ARCHIE

ARCHIE WAKES WITH a start, groaning at the noise that pulled him from sleep.

His phone is ringing, and he throws a hand out to find it while he sticks his head under a pillow. Eventually he grabs it and brings it to his ear, not opening his eyes to see who it is. He doesn't really have the energy to open his eyes.

Turns out, being held hostage with no food or water for two days really takes it out of you.

"Hello?" he answers blearily.

"Archie! Don't you text people back anymore?"

"Betty?" Archie groans again. "God, what time is it?"

"Time to get up and get over here," Betty says. She sounds obscenely awake and energized. "V needs us. You, me, and Dilton. So wake up, I'll call Dilton, and then you can drive us all over there."

"Over where?"

"To Cheryl's."

Now Archie's awake. "Wait," he says. "Cheryl Blossom's in on this now?"

Betty makes an irritated sound. "Just get dressed and meet me in ten," she says. "Chop, chop."

CHAPTER FIFTY-FIVE
VERONICA

IT'S ALMOST DAWN when the others arrive at Cheryl's.

Cheryl brings them up to the library, and Veronica would laugh at the range of expressions on their faces—Dilton confused, Betty worried, Archie yawning wide—if she wasn't dreading telling them about Reggie and Moose.

"First things first, let's get this out of the way," Veronica says, standing in front of her friends. "Cheryl is now fully caught up on the current Riverdale vampire saga, and since her family's hotel is going to be the staging ground for our Big Bad final battle, she's now part of the team."

The boys sit, but Betty stays standing, her eyes narrowed at Cheryl. "I thought you didn't care about what was going on," she says. "I mean, that's what you said the other day when I told you I was worried about V."

Cheryl waves a manicured hand. "That was so long ago," she says.

"Um, three days!"

"Three days, a lifetime, whatever," Cheryl says. "Didn't you hear what Veronica said? I'm on the team. Deal with it."

Veronica elbows her but only gently. "Play nice," the move says, and then Veronica nods at Betty. "Trust me, B. She's on our side."

Betty folds her arms and nods. "Fine."

Veronica takes a deep breath. *Now for the hard part.* "Something else you need to know: Reggie and Moose are dead."

"What?" Archie snaps to attention. "Ronnie, *what?*"

"Reggie and Moose are . . . dead?" Betty repeats, her eyes wide with shock. "Are you—I mean—*dead* dead?"

Veronica wrings her hands and tries her hardest not to look away from her friends. They deserve to know what happened—the truth, and not some story that might make Veronica look better than she really is.

She killed them. That's what happened.

"The thing is—"

"They were going to kill me." Cheryl's voice is loud, and she holds herself tall, even though Veronica can see her hands shaking from here. "Reggie and Moose were attacking me, and if Veronica hadn't gotten here in time, I'd probably be dead. Or turned. And if she hadn't killed them—" Cheryl throws her shaking hands up. "Who knows who else they'd have killed by now."

Dilton looks up at Veronica. "They were *both* attacking?" he asks. "So—Moose was . . ."

Veronica nods. "Reggie must have turned him. It all happened so fast, and if there was any way I could have ended it without killing them, I would have, but they weren't going to let that happen." She takes another deep breath. "I did what I had to do."

The room is silent for a long minute, and Veronica isn't sure whether they believe what she's just said. Whether they think she's a murderer or a hero.

What am I? she thinks. *Something between the two?*

Archie is the first to break the silence. "Well. I guess this is the world we live in now." He looks at Veronica. "Reggie and Moose made their choices. You did what you had to," he says, an echo of her own words. "No one can blame you for that, Ronnie."

Dilton nods, and Betty, too. "If it was a choice between letting them rampage through town or saving everyone, then you made the right choice," Betty says.

Veronica exhales slowly. "Yeah," she says. "Yeah, I know."

"So," Dilton says, with a clap of his hands that breaks the tension somewhat. "You stopped one potential crisis. What about the other, bigger, crisis? What are we going to do about that?"

"That's where I come in," Cheryl says. "I know every inch of the new hotel, and every single part of the plans for the opening on Friday."

"That's not all." Veronica picks up the large, heavy book she and Cheryl have spent all night poring over. Inside is the story of how Riverdale came to be—and more, besides. "Cheryl showed me this. You know what's in here?"

"Something boring that you're about to summarize for us?" Archie says, hopeful.

Veronica makes a face. "Well. Yes," she says. "But it's not boring. You want to know how Theodore Finch really connects to our town?"

"He's a founder," Dilton says. "Or, his family were founders. That's what my research said."

Veronica drags a wingback chair over to the table and sits, like she's ready for story time. "Sure," she says, settling in. "But it's not quite as simple as that."

The Finches were, as they had originally thought, one of the families who'd been instrumental in turning Riverdale from the small mill settlement it had begun as into a thriving town of entrepreneurs, socialites, and chancers, back in the early 1900s. The *first* family to pour money into the town and make it their own. They built properties and ran businesses up and down what became the Main Street of Riverdale. And they brought power and more money to the town through their connections with New York tycoons and their young families wishing for a quieter life in a smaller pond.

The three families—Lodge and Blossom and Finch—worked side by side, an uneasy alliance, according to the book's author. There was much sniping back and forth, deals poached from one another, and boundaries crossed, but the town's success in the beginning depended on all three families bringing their best and combining it. So after a while, things settled down: no more double-crossing, no more shady deals. Everyone was in alignment and kept the town thriving.

"Okay," Dilton says after Veronica's told them this. "So what happened to the Finches?"

Veronica flips to a section of photographs. "Get this. Their entire estate burned down," she says. "They all died, and that was it—the end of the Finch line. It says the fire started in the early hours of the morning and burned for a while before the nearest neighbors saw and brought help. By the time they were able to put the fire out and it was safe to go inside, there was barely anything to go inside of."

"They assumed all of the family had died," Cheryl says, pulling her hair over one shoulder. "Theodore; his mother, Jeanne; his father, Patrick; and his sister, Odette."

"But," Veronica says, "as we all know—Theodore is not dead."

"So what happened?" Betty finally sits, crossing her legs, her foot tapping the air. "He escapes from the fire and then becomes a vampire and hides out for a hundred-some years? Or—was he a vampire before he died? I mean—" She pauses, her face thoughtful. "Before he supposedly died. Before the fire."

"I don't know." Veronica looks at the family portrait in the book before her. It's a formal picture, the four Finches posed in front of their family home. Theodore looks exactly the same, not one more line on his face or a hint of age in his eyes to separate him from the young man in the picture. But it's his sister Veronica can't stop looking at.

A girl just like her—daughter of a founding family, heir to a legacy. In the photo she's smiling, a knowing smile, dark hair like Veronica's set in long waves that spill down a pale silk dress. According to the information given, she would have been only a few years older in this picture than Veronica is right now: early twenties, maybe.

Betty's gotten up and come to stand at Veronica's side, examining the picture, too. "She's pretty," Betty says, pointing at Odette.

"Wonder what she was like," Veronica says. "Isn't it weird to think of her, burning to death, trapped in that house?"

"God, I can't imagine," Betty says, and she takes the book from Veronica so she can look closer.

Veronica turns back to the others. "So we know who Theodore is and where he came from," she says. "But it doesn't really change anything. We still need to know exactly how we're going to handle things on Friday. We've tried attacking him before, and it didn't work, because we weren't really prepared. This time—"

"Hold on," Betty interrupts, and comes forward with the book flipped to a new page, a new photo. "Look at their house."

"What about it?" Veronica says. "I'm trying to focus on—"

"*Look*, here," Betty says, jabbing at a grainy black-and-white photo with a pink-painted nail. "See this old road sign here? And the church spire way in the background?"

Veronica squints. The house isn't like any she's seen in town before, but of course it wouldn't be; it doesn't exist anymore. Hasn't existed for close to a century. "Yeah, the sign, the spire," she says. "So?"

"So this place, their estate, it was on the west side," Betty says, pointing again. "See the angle of the spire? That's the angle you see when you come down over the hill and that land opens out in front of you." She stops, and looks up at Cheryl. "Or, it used to. Until the Blossoms started building there."

And like that, it all slips perfectly into place. Veronica looks at Cheryl, too, sitting there with her mouth half-open like she's just catching up to what Veronica and Betty already understand.

"Your family's new hotel is built on Theodore's family's estate," Betty says. "His takeover isn't just about power."

No. No, it's not that at all.

Veronica flicks her fangs out and runs her tongue over their sharp points. "It's about revenge."

CHAPTER FIFTY-SIX
VERONICA

AFTER THE REVELATIONS, the day must go on.

While the others go to school—*keep the everything's-completely-fine-and-normal charade going,* Dilton said—Veronica heads upstairs to take a blissful rest in Cheryl's bed. Cheryl's parents won't be back until evening, and Veronica desperately needs to sleep.

She falls asleep almost as soon as her head hits the silk pillow, all daylight blocked with thick curtains.

And she dreams about the room burning down around her. Flames eating up the curtains and heat swelling around her, and her body pinned to the bed by some invisible weight, no way to move, nowhere to escape. She can only lie there as the blaze creeps closer and closer still, until it catches hold of her and her skin begins to burn and blister, glowing deep dark red, any scream of pain caught inside her throat by the smoke that's choking her.

Then the dream morphs and shifts, becomes Veronica back out in the woods digging an endless hole while Reggie and Moose taunt her from the dirt surrounding her. *Murderer,* they sing, over and over. *Murderer, murderer, murderer!*

When she wakes it's in a panic, sweat beaded on her forehead and a hand to her pounding heart. "It's not real," she whispers to herself. "It's not real, that's not you. It's not real."

She cannot shake the dreams, but she tries, anyway. She spends some time sketching out a plan of attack for tomorrow, using the blueprints Cheryl gave her before she left for school. The first time she tried to kill Theodore, she'd been surprised by her parents. During their escape with Archie, Veronica had let herself be surprised again, by Theodore himself.

This time around she doesn't want anything unexpected to happen, nothing that might rock her focus or endanger the plan's success—and, in turn, her friends' lives.

I have to kill Theodore, she thinks. *That's the only way to end this. If I don't, he or his minions could turn Betty and Archie and Dilton, and they won't be like me—they won't be free, making their own choices, picking their own battles. They'll be more of Theodore's mind-controlled zombies.*

And Cheryl will be right in their crosshairs.

The Veronica of a week ago would be amazed by the loyalty and protectiveness she now feels toward Cheryl, but it's there. That night they went through together, the things they had to do—they're bonded now. And if Theodore wants to kill Cheryl, he's going to have to kill Veronica first.

She focuses on the blueprints again, mapping several routes in and out of the building. They're going to need to be fully stocked up on weaponry, and Veronica's going to need to feed before they fight.

Her phone buzzes, and she sees Betty's text: *On our way to pick you up!*

Veronica smiles and pushes the blueprints away and her dreams aside. "Fully prepped" includes being ready for the gala itself, and that means shopping for all of Veronica's favorite things. *Gowns and heels and jewels*, she thinks. *Oh freakin' my.*

CHAPTER FIFTY-SEVEN
VERONICA

VERONICA FLINGS BACK the curtain and steps out, bare feet on the dressing room's plush carpet. "I think this is the one."

Cheryl claps excitedly, and Betty gestures for her to spin. Veronica does, the narrow-cut black gown shimmering under the lights as she turns. In the dressing room behind her are all the gowns she's already tried on and rejected: red tulle was too dramatic, navy fifties-style too costumey, and the rest were just a combination of too small or too Old Veronica.

But this one, a sleek dress that clings and gleams, razor-thin straps crisscrossing Veronica's back and shoulders, is perfection.

She turns back to the mirror and drops one hip, hitching her knee out through the high slit in the skirt. Around her thigh is a holster, of course meant for guns, but Veronica's not a fan of firearms. No; it's a perfect fit for her stakes, though. "See?" she says. "Easy access to weaponry while still being extremely *Bonjour, oui, delighted to be at your event, merci beaucoup pour l'invitation.*"

Another bonus about this dress: It makes Veronica look startlingly like her favorite ancestor, Mirabelle Luna Lodge, a wild child from way back in the Lodge family line. Mirabelle's skin was a deeper brown, her hair intense curls, but it's the determination behind Veronica's eyes that really brings to mind the image of her relative. In the few pictures they have of Mirabelle, she's dressed to kill, and the story goes that she was always in the center of some storm or another, causing havoc both on the island she called home and in Riverdale, when she arrived.

She watches in the reflection as Betty stands behind her and picks up the dangling ends of the straps, ties them into a swooping bow. "You're only going to carry the stakes?"

"What else can I have?" Veronica says. "It's not like I can take the crosses, or the garlic, or the holy water. I'm trying to kill Theodore, not myself."

Cheryl kneels and lifts the hem on the non-slit side. "You could always wear one on this ankle, too," she says. "It won't show, if you put it in the right place."

Veronica runs her hands over her hips. "Excellent," she says, and gives herself a fanged smile. "Now let's get you two done."

When they leave the department store, it's with an armful of bags each and Veronica's credit card burning in her back pocket. She bought Betty's pale lavender dress and the gold strappy sandals to match, plus two sharp, slim knives from the homewares section. *Silver*, she'd said as the sales assistant handed the bag to Betty. *You need to protect yourself, B.*

Cheryl already has a dress, she says, but she's bought herself a beautiful new necklace: three long, interwoven delicate chains dotted with a rainbow of jewels. *Pure silver*, the sales assistant had said as

Cheryl admired herself in the handheld mirror, *2.5 carats throughout.* And Cheryl had laid down her black card without even asking the price.

Veronica swings the bag containing her gown, carefully wrapped up in soft tissue paper. "You know what we need?" she says. "One of those, like, fancy hidden labs. You know how in a movie, at this point they go get all their spy gadgets from the unassuming spymaster who they, up until that moment, just thought was the barista at their local coffee shop? We need that."

"Isn't that Dilton?" Cheryl says. "You just described exactly Dilton."

"Sure, but he doesn't have a lab," Veronica says. "He has a smelly boy's bedroom and that's about it." She glances at Betty, walking beside her silently. "B? You okay?"

Betty snaps back to the moment. "What? Oh, yeah." She shakes her head as they serpentine through the parking lot toward Cheryl's shiny red Mustang. "I just can't stop thinking about the fire that destroyed the Finches' estate. How horrible it must have been for them to be trapped inside, surrounded by the flames, knowing there was no way of getting out of there alive."

"Except for Theodore," Cheryl says darkly.

Veronica keeps quiet. It's been bothering her, too. She remembers a story she once read, about another house that burned down back in the 1930s, killing the entire family inside—and theirs wasn't a small one. They had something like seven or eight kids, plus the parents. Except that afterward, searching the scorched rubble for human remains, the authorities found nothing.

Did the old Riverdale fire department even search for the bodies of the

Finches? she wonders. *Or did they just assume there could be no survivors? How did Theodore make it out of there alive—and was it really an accident, like the history book described it, or did something more sinister happen?*

Veronica throws her bags into the trunk when they reach Cheryl's car and then slides into the passenger seat. She squeezes her eyes shut, trying to erase the film of fire she's seeing over everything. No time for that: They have less than twenty-four hours until the gala now, and the pressure is beginning to weigh on Veronica. It's odd, but part of her wants to talk to her parents—she's never gone this long without seeing them before, and their lifelong connection is threatening to override her clear focus. Her parents are not her parents anymore, she knows. Or—maybe they are. Just as the vampirism has brought out parts of Veronica she's always repressed, maybe her parents in moroi form are only the purest versions of their selfish selves.

Not maybe, she thinks. *God, why am I so hell-bent on giving them the benefit of the doubt? Daddy threatened to kill Archie. Mom wants me to be on their side. There's nothing good left in them, not really. Not while Theodore has them in his grasp.*

"Veronica?" A hand waves in front of her eyes. "Hello?"

"What?" Veronica glances at Cheryl, looking at her expectantly, one hand on the steering wheel.

Cheryl arches her brows. "I said, where to now?"

Veronica tries to forget about her parents or, more specifically, how she has been slowly trying to convince herself that killing her parents is something she's okay with. *Home*, she wants to say, but she can't.

She misses her bed and her bathtub and the quiet that surrounds her at night. But home is only another trap now. "Back to yours, I guess," she says. That's where the blueprints are; that's where they will solidify tomorrow's plan of attack.

Her stomach folds in on itself, a sharp bite of hunger. Veronica winces and puts a hand right where the waist of her jeans cuts into her soft belly. "On second thought," she says as Cheryl begins to reverse, "let's go to school. I need to pick something up real quick."

CHAPTER FIFTY-EIGHT
DILTON

DILTON CHECKS his watch.

One hour until the event's official start time.

One hour until they need to be in position.

"Dilton, c'mere." Veronica adjusts his tie, sighing as she fixes the knot. "Honestly, what would you do without me?"

"Look like a mess?" he says. He means it as a joke but as soon as he speaks, it's obvious how nervous he is.

Veronica lays her hands on his shoulders and catches his eye. "Hey," she says. "It's going to be okay. It's not your first rodeo, remember?"

"Feels like there's a lot more riding on it this time." Dilton swallows. He hasn't told Veronica, hasn't told any of them, but he's spent the last day and a half tracking Mr. Lodge. From a distance, cautiously, of course cautiously, but—

Hiram Lodge has made visits to every power player in town. Sheriff Keller, the mayor, every wealthy business owner in the area. Once, Dilton tried to sneak into Mr. Lodge's office, to get up close to the door they were shut behind and listen in on what

Hiram was saying, but all he could make out were muffled voices.

There's something about the meetings that have put him on edge. For a while he thought maybe they'd gotten it all wrong—maybe Hiram wasn't going to wait to turn them, maybe he was doing it one by one instead. But Dilton had waited outside of the mayor's office after Mr. Lodge left. He saw the mayor come out only five or ten minutes later and get in her car, and then Dilton had followed her home. He sat outside watching through the window as she sat down to dinner with her family, and then went upstairs to continue working, he guessed. No sign of her turning, and no time for it to happen, either, really.

But if he wasn't turning them, then what was he doing? A preemptive strike for his plan? Sowing the seeds?

"Dilton."

When he snaps out of his thinking, Archie's there with a stake in his hand. Not one of the crappy ones Dilton and Veronica bought, but one of Dilton's new creations. "So how does this work, exactly?"

Dilton clears his throat and focuses on the weapons. This is his job now; it feels good to be a vital part of the team. "It's just like a regular stake," he says. "Through the heart, it'll kill a vampire instantly. Moroi *or* strigoi. But if you can't manage to get the right shot, with my modifications it should still incapacitate them." Dilton takes the stake from Archie and draws his finger along the wood. "See, inside is a reservoir filled with holy water. Then there's a mechanism kind of like—you know those annoying firecrackers people always bring to school on the last day?"

Archie nods, and Betty, who's come to watch, does, too.

"It works kind of like that," Dilton says. "But with more power. Two strips of paper laced with potassium nitrate and sulfur. The impact of you striking a target causes movement within the reservoir, and the friction sets off the reaction. Causes a buildup of pressure and then—" He pulls his hands apart, blowing his cheeks out. "Explosion."

"And the holy water infects the wound," Betty says. "Goes into their internal system? Huh." She nods again and gives him a measured look. "Nice work, Dilton."

"Thanks," Dilton says, a bubble of pride warming him. "Get equipped. And don't forget the crosses. They might seem cliché and old-fashioned, but if that's what the folktales say works, then we're going to use them."

He turns to Veronica and points at the set of stakes he's constructed just for her, no holy water reservoir, just sharp, reliable wood. "For you," he says, watching Veronica pick the first one up. She starts to slide it into her holster, and Dilton stops her. "Wait. Look on the end."

Veronica gives him a curious glance and then brings the stake's flat end toward her face, peering at the wood. Dilton knows she's seen it when he face changes and she smiles so wide her fangs slip out. "Oh, shut *up*. I love it!"

On the end of each stake he carved for Veronica, Dilton has burned a small message into the wood. A monogram—*V.L.* in ornate script. "What is it you always say?" he asks. "Oh, yeah— image is important. You control the narrative. With these, everyone will know *exactly* who killed Theodore Finch."

Veronica grins and slips a stake into each of the holsters on her thighs, then another down at her ankle. "Well, vamp army, if you didn't know my name before tonight," she says, almost glowing, "then you sure as hell will when I'm done."

CHAPTER FIFTY-NINE
CHERYL

THE HOTEL IS everything Cheryl dreamed.

High ceilings throughout the first floor: in the restaurant and the ballroom and the lobby with its two-story chandelier. The rooms decadent and impeccably styled, with four-poster beds and perfectly patterned tiles in the bathrooms. And the grounds—beautifully landscaped, hedges sculpted like artwork, and wild rosebushes bordering the vast pool area.

Cheryl walks around this building that her parents have been planning for so long, filled with all the décor and finishing touches of the celebratory opening gala. All that planning and all that effort, but she knows that the work was worth it. It's perfect.

And built on bloodied, cursed land, possibly. But who's keeping track?

She checks her phone: no messages. Cheryl chews her lip as she makes her way to the ballroom. Veronica, Betty, Archie, and Dilton are back at her house, getting ready for the action. Cheryl had to be here, to keep the illusion of normality running. She begged and pleaded and tantrumed so hard to be allowed to head up the party tonight that not showing up to run it would have set her parents off on a stratospheric level.

Cheryl swishes down a back hallway, the train of her dress trailing along the gold carpeting. Her being here works out well for them, though.

She passes the kitchen, full of the noise of the chefs preparing canapés and decadent desserts. At the end of the hallway is a fire door, and Cheryl leans on the bar to open it, then wedges a doorstop just so, angled in a way that the door remains open but not obviously so. This will be their emergency escape route, if things get truly out of hand.

On her way back to the main lobby she ducks into the bathroom. It might sound weird, but the bathrooms are her favorite part of the entire hotel. The sinks are deep pearlescent bowls set on top of dark wood, and each bathroom has two chaise longues perfect for guests to sit on while they pretend like their heels don't hurt at *all* and they can *totally* stand up again whenever they want to, but they're just going to keep sitting here for a minute, while they redo their makeup that does not need to be touched up.

It's an ordeal to pee in this full-skirted dress but Cheryl manages, and she's washing her hands when she notices the closed door at the end of the row and the telltale Ferragamo shoes peeking out from under it. "Mom?" she says loudly. "I didn't even know you were here yet. Why didn't you come find me?"

Cheryl dries her hands on an organic cotton hand towel and drops it into the linen basket. She gets out her lipstick and fills in the gaps that she's worn with her worried chewing on her lip. "Mom?"

There's no answer, and Cheryl caps her lipstick, turning. *Hmm.*

"Mother," she calls, singsong. "Please don't ignore me. You know it irritates me so."

The lights cut out.

Cheryl groans. This is the only part about these bathrooms she hates: these stupid motion-sensor lights her father insisted they have installed, even though they frequently cut out like this and take an annoying amount of effort to activate again.

She reaches up as high as she can and waves her hand through the sensor's beam, and it takes almost fifteen seconds for her movement to register and the lights to flash back on.

When they do, the last stall door is open. Cheryl blinks. "Mom?"

Bony fingers grab her from behind, and Cheryl jumps, an involuntary scream escaping her. "Mom!"

She is pulled, panicked, to face her assailant. But the woman in front of her isn't Cheryl's mother—not as she knows her.

It's clear in an instant. She looks almost like normal—an older Cheryl, her hair a shade or two darker and twisted into an elegant chignon, lines around her heavily mascaraed eyes.

Her *red* eyes.

"Cheryl, *mon amour*." Her mother smiles, her eyes almost but not quite focused on her daughter's face. "I've been waiting for you. Join me, won't you? Join me, Cheryl."

Her grip is so strong that Cheryl isn't sure she'll be able to pull herself out of her mother's grasp. It's started, she realizes. There, on her mom's neck, are two deep red bloody smears, and her mother's eyes, the teeth that seem to be growing, elongating, right before Cheryl's eyes—

It's already happening.

Cheryl's fight-or-flight response kicks in. *I have to let Veronica know* is all she can think. *They won't be prepared for this. I have to let her know, or else—*

Her mother's teeth gnash dangerously close to Cheryl's face, and she pulls away while at the same time she's searching among the folds of her dress for the weapon she's brought for this exact occasion. She finds it, pulls it free, but her mother yanks her forward and the stake slips from her hand.

"The world is not what you think," her mother hisses. "Come with me and I can show you, Cheryl."

"Come with you? In your *nightmares*, maybe." Cheryl wrenches herself backward, freeing herself, and *where is it, where is it—*

She spots the stake underneath the chaise longue. Cheryl throws herself on the floor, stretching an arm beneath the stuffed lounger, and she gasps in pain as nails rip at her ankle.

A little farther, she thinks, reaching, reaching. *Just a little farther—*

And then the lights cut out.

CHAPTER SIXTY
VERONICA

THEY PULL UP to the hotel in Betty's car.

The parking lot is almost full, and the hotel is lit like a beacon in the night.

"Okay." Veronica looks to Betty, to Dilton, to Archie, all watching her somewhat reverently.

She gets that feeling like she had before, when Cheryl kept saying Veronica had saved her life. Like there's too much responsibility weighing on her and she's not sure she's equipped to carry it.

But she forges on, regardless. "We got this," she says, keeping her voice steady. "No surprises, no mistakes. My father's going to be in there, and Theodore won't be far. So all we have to do is find him without my parents seeing us and letting Theodore know we're here." She grits her teeth. "I've tried to get him twice and failed both times. I'm not failing again. Everybody in?"

Her friends nod, even Betty, although she looks worried, and Veronica lets out a slow, steadying exhale.

It's Kill-Theodore-O'Clock.

They exit the car, slamming the doors in synchronized symphony.

Veronica leads the pack, striding up to the hotel entrance.

As she passes under the floral arch, something in the air changes. She feels it, like a physical shift around her. What—

"Whoa." Betty comes to a stop, holding her hands out. "Do you feel that?"

Veronica looks at her feet. No: at the ground beneath them.

It's vibrating.

A hum of energy.

"What is that?" She looks up, over at Dilton. "Is it some kind of power source, or surge, or something?"

Out of the corner of her eye she sees Archie shift his weight, dropping back like he does when he's about to throw a Hail Mary pass. "Not a power surge," he says grimly, and Veronica whips around to follow his gaze, looking back through the hotel.

Her mouth opens wide. *"Holy—"*

Because there, up ahead, is a tidal wave of people running through the lobby. Gowns are flying, ties are ripped free, and the panic is palpable. "We're too—"

Veronica stops. *We're too late*, she was going to say. Her father and Theodore have already started, and this is the fear frenzy pushing people to escape.

But something about them makes her pause. They're running, yes, but it sounds wrong. Too—even, somehow.

And they're panicking, but the only noise is the pounding of their feet. No screams, no yells.

On second look, she sees it.

Those gowns, those fancy suits, they're streaked and stained with red.

Yes, they are too late. Much, *much* too late.

Veronica takes this all in in a split second, and then she rips a stake from the holster at her thigh. "Ever faced down a raging vampire mob?" she says, as if it's anything but a stupid rhetorical question. "Well! Today's your *lucky* day!"

Then Veronica darts forward, into the fray.

CHAPTER SIXTY-ONE
BETTY

DON'T PANIC, DON'T panic, don't panic.

That's all Betty can think as she watches Veronica sprint into the melee. But she can't move, even though she knows she should go after her.

It's not until Archie yanks at her that Betty unfreezes. "Come on!" he yells. "We need to stick with her."

Archie begins to run and Betty follows, Dilton just ahead of them. Veronica's farther away, but when the first of the turned gala guests near her, she slows.

"We gotta catch up to her!" Dilton calls over his shoulder. "We can't stop her dad turning people now, so we need to focus on getting to Theodore. She has to kill him; it's the only way we'll get out of this alive!"

And it's the only way Veronica can get her humanity back, too, Betty knows.

She puts on a burst of speed and passes Dilton, skids to a stop beside Veronica. "V!"

Then Dilton jumps in front of them, and not a second too soon, because the first of the pack is on them. Dilton flings something out—holy water, Betty realizes as she watches it arc through the air and land on the vampires, who howl in pain.

"We'll make a shield!" he says. "Carve a path for Veronica through all of this."

"Put your cross up, Betty." Archie thrusts a piece of the heavy silver into her hands, and when Betty lifts it, the vampire closest to her shrinks back. Then they begin to move as one, a protective barrier making their way through the mess.

"This is bad, Betty," Veronica says. She's gripping a stake in her left hand and staring dead ahead at the vampires as they move. "He knows we're here. He's sending them after us to slow us down, to stop us."

"We're gonna get you through," Betty says, brandishing her cross again. Another vampire falls back, but this one doesn't take its eyes off Betty.

It's Mayor McCoy, Betty realizes as Dilton calls back.

"Keep around Veronica," he orders. "It's working! They won't get too close, as long as we keep moving."

Veronica points ahead. "The ballroom," she says. "Let's go."

Betty swallows, her eyes following Mayor McCoy's red ones as the four of them set into a run now, albeit a slow one. There must be at least two hundred people here, maybe two fifty. *No, not people*, Betty thinks. *Vampires*.

Mayor McCoy's usually pleasant smile twisted into a snarl is imprinted on Betty's eyes, but she follows behind Veronica, her best friend powering forward in her vertiginous heels. For the most part, their three-point shield works; when the moroi see the silver of the crosses, they hiss and turn away, their anger palpable. But some of them push through anyway, grabbing for Veronica, or yanking on Betty's ponytail, snatching at Dilton at the head of them.

Archie darts around, knocking hands back, punching the fighters away.

When a foot trips Betty, she yelps, but Archie's busy defending Dilton, and Betty's on her own. She flips onto her back, staring up at the mouth gaping wide above her. She brandishes the cross, but the moroi barely flinches. *Stake*, she thinks, *hit them right in the heart*.

But when she reaches for her weapon, her hand knocks against more cold metal.

Her knives.

Betty had almost forgotten them, her gifts from Veronica, now tucked inside the lining of her dress.

No time to think; she slips her hand inside her dress and pulls out one of the knives, driving it upward right as the vampire before her lunges for her throat.

The blade explodes up into the vampire's soft palate, and Betty gags. The knife sticks there, and she scrambles to her feet as the vampire grapples for the invading foreign object, blood pouring down its chin.

"Sorry," Betty pants, but not to this vampire. To Veronica, really, because she's pretty sure she's not getting that knife back.

"Almost there!" When Veronica calls, Betty looks, and she sees them ahead of her, almost to the ballroom. She breaks into a run and catches up to them just as Dilton bursts through the double-height doors.

"We've gotta close them!" Betty says as she slides through, the last of them. "We need a barricade, something, just—"

The boys are already on it, and Betty begins to stack the chairs they're sliding in her direction up against the doors. "We can hold them off," Betty says. "Then we'll—"

A single, gunshot-loud clap cuts her off.

Betty's head snaps in the direction of the sound, as do the others'.

In the center of the ballroom, on the black-and-white-patterned dance floor, is Hiram Lodge.

Veronica stands tall, stake in her hand. "Daddy?"

CHAPTER SIXTY-TWO
VERONICA

"DADDY?"

He barely raises his head when Veronica calls to him. When his eyes focus on her—well, they don't. They stare right through her, like she's not even there.

"Daddy," she says, taking a step forward. He's holding on to something, someone—a woman Veronica recognizes from various Lodge Enterprises events. The woman's eyes are rolled so far back in her head that only white is visible, and the way she drapes across her father's arm—

She's dead.

But soon to be spectacularly undead, Veronica thinks.

She takes another step forward, her heels loud on the hardwood floor. *"Daddy,"* she says, a third time, like it might get through to him now. "Where's Mom? You can stop this, now. Stop."

"He can't."

The voice comes from all around, fills every spare inch of air around Veronica.

She squeezes her eyes shut. That's not possible, she knows, but that's how it seems. The words echo down and up and from behind. *He can't he can't he can't.*

She knows that voice now, the sickening slickness of it. "Theodore!" Veronica throws her head back. "Show yourself, you *coward*."

"You're far too late." Theodore's voice echoes again, followed by a cruel laugh. "It's over, Veronica. And to think—you could have been with me through all of this. You could have been part of this and lived the rest of your life as the powerful being you are, but you chose to fight me instead."

Veronica's turning in slow circles, trying to pinpoint where Theodore's voice is really coming from, knowing this is just another trick—like the vanishing act on the road through the woods, and the mind control he's clearly exerting on her father right now. "You turned my parents," she yells. "You turned me. Without my *consent*! You have to ask permission first, you jerk!"

There's a swirl of black in the corners of her eyes, and then Veronica sees him, watches as he steps out in front of the plate-glass floor-to-ceiling windows. There's no moon, only the light of the night. "You chose weakness," he says, his voice softer now, a slither through the air to Veronica's ears. "So you have chosen, and so you have doomed yourself." He dips his chin, handsome face turned ugly by his venom. "Farewell, Miss Lodge. We could have had such fun together."

He flicks his hand in the direction of her father. "Hiram," he calls. "Finish the job." And then he cracks his fist against the window before him. It splinters, one crack turning to a dozen turning to a hundred, all racing across the glass before it shatters and crashes down around him, a rain of sharp pieces, and Theodore steps forward into the outside world.

"V!"

Veronica turns at Betty's call and understands the panic in her best friend's voice.

Her father is headed straight for her—straight for her friends. Now he's focused; now he sees.

He's going to kill them, she thinks, and looks after Theodore. *But I have to kill* him.

She only has a second to decide, she knows—if she doesn't follow Theodore now, it'll be too late. There's no way she'll be able to get to him after tonight, not when he has this many newly made moroi to operate at his will. But if she leaves her friends here with her father—

"Go!" It's Dilton who says it, and he's wielding one of his doctored stakes. "We'll handle this."

What does "handle this" mean? *Kill?*

Maybe, she knows. But isn't this just like when she killed Reggie and Moose? She made a choice, and Dilton and her friends will make theirs, if they have to.

This is all because of you, Theodore.

She swallows her hesitation and runs at the now-empty window, leaping over the shards of destruction and landing gracefully, powerfully.

The air outside is chilly, but Veronica doesn't feel it. She only feels adrenaline and the heft of the wood in her palm. She has left Betty and Dilton and Archie behind. Maybe left them to die.

Cheryl, she thinks. *Where are you?* Safe, hopefully, like they had planned.

"Planned?" A small laugh echoes in her mind. *"How well has your plan gone tonight, Ronnie?"*

It's Reggie's voice in her head as she spies Theodore, standing at the edge of the icy-blue pool. His stupid taunting grin is still on his face, and Veronica wants to smack it right off, claw the glee out of his eyes.

"What, Ronnie? Gonna kill him like you killed me?"

She shakes her head as she stands, chest rising and falling rapidly, staring at Theodore. That voice in her head is not real.

Powers of persuasion, she remembers. *Mind tricks.* "I know what you're doing!"

"Me?" Theodore holds his hands out, oh so innocent. "Enlighten me."

Veronica only steps toward him. "I'm going to kill you," she says. "I'm going to undo everything you did to this town."

Theodore tips his head to the side, red eyes wondering. "You really are very beautiful," he says. "It's a shame to waste that pretty face, but—"

It happens so fast Veronica can't process it. One second he's at the edge of the pool, and the next he's an inch away from her. "What has to be done must be done," he says, and now *he's* holding a stake, and when Veronica looks down her hand is empty. "Truly, I am sorry."

He raises the stake and Veronica would scream if every inch of her wasn't frozen.

Then she feels it.

Not the point to her chest, as she's expecting, but a quick rush of air past her ear, accompanied by a harsh *zzzzup*.

"Hey, creep!" Cheryl's voice rings out. "Get your nasty hands off my friend!"

CHAPTER SIXTY-THREE
VERONICA

VERONICA LOOKS UP, and there, on the roof of the ornamental greenhouse, is Cheryl. She's bloodied and bruised, but she's also holding a crossbow.

When Veronica looks back at Theodore he's tripping backward, fingers grasping at the bolt protruding from his stomach. "Wha . . ."

"Now, V!"

Veronica glances over her shoulder to see Betty scrambling toward her, a crowd of vampires at her back. The barricade; it's destroyed.

She whips into motion, snatching her monogrammed stake right back from Theodore, that second of disconcertion all she needs. "You know, you really are kind of hot," she says, tossing the stake into her right hand. "It's a shame to waste such a pretty face. Oh, wait—"

Veronica lunges, decisive and clean, and she arcs the stake through the air directly toward Theodore's heart, and it lands perfectly. Slick and fast, right into his chest. "Just kidding," she says as

249

Theodore erupts into a howl. "Time for you to go! Bye-bye."

She spins and kicks him, full force of her sharp stiletto right in his stomach, and it sends him teetering back, back, and crashing into the water.

The water that, if all went according to plan, Cheryl should have laced with plenty of holy water.

Veronica rushes to the edge, barely hearing Cheryl calling out to her. "Is he dead? Did it work?"

Stake through the heart, Veronica thinks. The laced pool water was just a precaution.

But—

At first she thinks it's her stake, floating up to the surface. But when she leans closer, she can see: It's bone.

Cheryl reaches her then, tossing her crossbow on the ground. "Is he—ew!"

More bones are floating to the surface, and as they watch together, Theodore's flesh dissolves before them, steaming and fetid as it melts from his skeleton.

"It worked," Veronica breathes. She twists to look at Cheryl. "It worked. He's dead." And then she holds her hands out, staring at her palms, the veins running up her wrists.

Theodore is dead.

But she feels no different.

It should be working, shouldn't it? It should be happening now, she should be feeling something, some kind of change pushing her back toward her humanity—except nothing at all about this feels different.

"It worked," Cheryl echoes, but there's a lift to her words, turning it into a question. *It worked?* "So you—you should be changing back now, right?"

"I should be," Veronica says, and she clenches her hands into fists. "But I'm not. So that must mean—"

She whips around and there they are, Riverdale's best and brightest in raging vampire form, still coming after her friends, still coming straight for her.

If Theodore turned her father, and her father turned all these vampires, then they should be reverting. That's how it works: Kill the strigoi sire, and the bloodline turns back.

But they're still vampires, Veronica thinks, and the meaning of that hits her like a punch to the face.

It's not him. "Theodore wasn't the sire," Veronica says, and she springs to her feet.

This isn't over.

"What?" Cheryl stares up at her. "Then who is? What do we do?"

Veronica's about to say *I don't know* but then suddenly she does. A feeling kicking deep in her gut, a memory.

A coffin and a symbol etched into it. The kind of coffin where a vampire might make their bed.

"I have to go," she says to Cheryl, backing away. "Hold them off as long as you can. I think the real master's back at my house—I have to go! I have to finish this."

"Go!" Cheryl says, but Veronica's already sprinting off, toward the parking lot, and she spots the perfect ride instantly.

She pulls the skirt of her dress up, gathering the silky fabric so she can tie it into a knot up and out of the way. Then she climbs on the inky-black motorcycle and kicks it into action, a loud engine rip through the noise behind her, and Veronica guns it. She rides off, leaving her friends behind and heading toward her own home.

Watch out, watch out, wherever you are, Veronica thinks as she speeds along the rain-slick roads. *I'm going to find you.*

CHAPTER SIXTY-FOUR
CHERYL

"GO!" CHERYL YELLS at Veronica, no time for explanations or planning now. It's all action, only.

Cheryl's still running on the adrenaline that first shot through her in the bathroom, as she was clawing at her transformed mother. For a moment she had thought that this was going to be the end for her: killed at the hands of her own mom, a monster now, and she'd let Veronica and the rest down by not fulfilling her part of the plan.

It was the thought of that, the thought of letting Veronica down, that gave Cheryl the burst of fire she needed to grab the stake out of the darkness and aim it at her mother. Not her heart—Cheryl was not sure she wanted to kill her mom, not just yet—but deep in her thigh, with an almighty crack.

The mechanism Dilton had rigged up exploded, sending wooden shards and holy water into her mom's flesh. Enough to cause her mom to howl, and to distract her for long enough that Cheryl could escape.

By the time she made it out of the bathroom, she could sense she was way too late. Hear it—the baying of hundreds of people, desperate for fresh, hot, human blood.

The plan, she'd thought. *Stick to the plan.*

So she'd run outside, away from the noise, and found the stack of bottles of holy water that she'd stashed behind the outdoor bar earlier. She worked as fast as she could, ripping their caps off and emptying the contents into the pool, until her fingers were criss-crossed with tiny cuts but the cool blue water was sufficiently tainted.

Then she'd run back to rescue her crossbow from its hiding place, and as she'd cradled it in her arms, that's when she'd heard the painful screeching of the plate-glass window shattering. She climbed up on the greenhouse roof and watched as first Theodore Finch came out, and then Veronica after him. She'd watched in horror as Theodore had grabbed Veronica, a stake in his hand and a fear in Veronica's eyes that Cheryl could see even from this distance.

Cheryl knew she had only one shot at delaying him. She'd brought her crossbow up and aimed, steady, a lifetime of practice coming through, as she let the bolt fly; it thrummed through the air and landed true, piercing Theodore right in the stomach.

But now Veronica's running away before Cheryl can even finish telling her to get out of there, and when Cheryl looks back she sees Betty running toward her. She can't see Dilton or Archie, or Mr. Lodge, not in the fray following at Betty's heels.

"Cheryl!" Betty calls out to her, her eyes wide and full of fear. "What do we do?"

A bone floats by, catching Cheryl's eye, and she knows. "In

here!" she yells to Betty. "It's laced with holy water—they can't follow us in!"

Without waiting to see if Betty understands, Cheryl twists to
grab her crossbow before throwing herself and it into the water. She
keeps her eyes open underwater, and there's more of Theodore's
remains, and then a splash as another body falls through the water.
It's Betty; she opens her eyes under there, too, and holds Cheryl's
gaze.

They swim up and break the surface together, taking gasping
breaths in unison. It's then that Cheryl sees the boys, back-to-back,
fighting their way through the tangle of people who used to be their
neighbors, friends, authority figures. "Archie! Dilton!" Cheryl yells.
"Get in here!"

Dilton hears her first and grabs Archie by the collar of his for-
merly pristine white button-down, now torn and stained. Dilton
runs at them and slip-slides his way into the water, clumsily, and
Archie throws himself into a kind of dive, cracking down on the
surface.

Cheryl scrapes her wet hair out of her eyes. "Everybody okay?"

The boys come up for air, and Betty grabs on to Archie. "I think
so," she says, gulping oxygen. "What now?"

"Where's Veronica?" Archie interrupts.

"They should have turned back," Dilton says. He's watching the
vampires heading toward them. "Why didn't they turn back?
Unless—"

Cheryl treads water, some of it lapping up and over her chin, trying to keep herself afloat. She's never been a big swimmer—more
interested in lazing in the shallows showing off her vast bikini

collection than the actual functional act of swimming—which is annoying now. And doubly so, because her gala dress is *completely* ruined.

Unless dry cleaners know how to remove chlorine and holy water *and* the rotting remains of a vampire corpse.

"She's going home," Cheryl says, legs kicking frantically beneath the surface. "She said Theodore wasn't the sire. There's another one out there and she thinks—"

Dilton's eyes light up. "The coffin," he says. "Of course!"

"Coffin?" Betty says.

"So what do we do?" Archie interrupts again.

It's quiet.

It happens suddenly, one moment the night filled with sound, and the next so still that her own breathing sounds like a hurricane.

A chill jackknifes up her spine, and Cheryl looks up.

The vampires have stopped dead. Some look at the bones drifting around, some look at their prey in the pool, but all of them are still and staring. *They can look all they want*, Cheryl thinks. *But they can't touch.*

She's beginning to shiver, but it's not from the pool, heated to the perfect last-gasp-of-summer temperature. "Where are we with weapons?" Cheryl says through gritted teeth.

"I have stakes," Archie says.

Betty moves back, toward the center of the pool, the farthest spot from the watching vampires. "I have one knife and a stake and some silver."

"Dilton?"

He looks ashamed. "I lost them," he says. "I don't have anything."

Cheryl nods. "Well, we have *some* stuff, at least," she says. "And I have this." She shifts her crossbow, slow through the water. Maybe if she weren't holding it she'd have an easier time staying afloat, but she feels more comfortable with it in her hands. Letting them know that she's not completely vulnerable. "They can't get in here. So, if Veronica's right, we just have to trust that she can kill the true sire."

"And until then?" Archie says.

Suddenly Cheryl can feel someone watching her, the intensity of a gaze drilling into her. She looks up and there's her mother. Her fur stole hangs off one shoulder, and her chandelier earrings glimmer, just like the crystals stitched into the straps of her diaphanous green gown. And there's a long streak of blood on one thigh where Cheryl had staked her, the wound itself now healed.

Her mother's red eyes are locked on her. *I see you*, they seem to say. *You can't escape me.*

Cheryl swallows her fear. "Until then," she says, "we wait."

CHAPTER SIXTY-FIVE
VERONICA

VERONICA DITCHES THE stolen motorcycle outside her house and marches up to the front door.

She pauses, hand on the doorknob, and checks herself. One stake still wrapped around her thigh, and another on her ankle? Check. Fangs out? Check. Fists ready to punch the stupid strigoi in the face for, one, turning her town into a vampire haven and, two, making her sweat in this perfect dress? Oh, check and *check*.

If there's another strigoi, they must *be in that coffin, Veronica thinks. Must have been hiding out here all along. So all I have to do now is get down there and kill them.*

Easy.

She takes a deep breath and pushes the door open. It creaks, so loud in the silence of the dark and empty house that Veronica winces. She can't let the strigoi know she's here, can't give any sign at all that she's figured out their true plan.

Veronica slips inside and shuts the door behind her.

It's only been a few days since she was here last, but this house doesn't feel like her home anymore. No; now it's the place where her parents turned from flawed humans to broken monsters. The place where she thought she was going to die at the hands of Theodore.

But Theodore's dead now, she thinks, a sheen of pride on the words. I *did that. I killed him, and okay, it might not have had the exact outcome I was planning, but I still did it. He can't touch me again, and now you— whoever you are and wherever you're hiding—you're next.*

She only takes two steps into the foyer when something appears on the stairs, as if out of nowhere: a monstrous, gargantuan spider.

The horrified noise Veronica makes is involuntary, and she slaps a hand over her mouth to keep it inside, shaking as the creature— twice as tall as Veronica, thick hairy legs skittering and huge, multi-faceted eyes searching—rears over her. It's no normal spider. (*Well, no normal supersized spider*, she thinks.) No, this one's eyes are just as red as Veronica's, its grossly enlarged mouth flashing fangs like Veronica's.

"Giant vampire spider?" she says aloud, her nerves still on edge. "Oh, come *on*—"

Its head lowers so fast Veronica only has time to drop to the ground, just beyond the grasp of its teeth snapping shut on air. She rolls to one side and hits something; when she puts her hand out, she feels sharp bristles and gags as she realizes it's one of this monster's many, too many, legs.

"Gross, gross, gross!"

It lowers its head and gnashes those teeth again, and Veronica army-crawls away, sliding over the polished tile. *How do you kill a vampire spider?* Usually she doesn't kill spiders at all; she calls some-one else to do it for her.

You're on your own now, kid, she thinks, and flips to her feet.

But when she lands, crouched and ready to attack, the foyer is empty.

It's just her. No spider to be seen. Veronica whips her head around, left, and right, and above her. *Please don't be above me.*

There's nothing there.

She creeps toward the stairs. Wherever it went, it doesn't matter, as long as it's not here now. All she has to do is get to the basement—

"Crap!" A leg lands in front of her, blocking her path, and Veronica falls hard on her hip. She scrambles backward as the spider moves closer, its legs making a *tick-tick-tick* noise as it crawls toward her, hovers above her.

It lowers its head and those red eyes, eyes within eyes, like the surface of a polished ruby gone wrong, all bulbous and leaking, watch her. *They're actually watching me,* she thinks, pushing herself back until she can go no farther and smacks into the wall. "What do you want?" She yells it, as loud and harsh as she can, throwing away any attempt to be quiet and not alert the strigoi to her presence. She uses her hands to climb the wall, raise herself to her full height, and stand tall. "What do you want from me, huh? Come on! Do your worst!"

The spider opens its mouth, and for a long endless second Veronica can see straight inside it. The raw, glowing red of the cavernous opening, dripping with viscous white liquid, and oozing blood from between its sharp teeth.

It's only when she feels something wrapping tight and sticky around her left ankle that she manages to force her gaze away. Down to her leg, where there's a white ribbon twisting around her skin, trailing up and away to the beast's underbelly.

Silk.

Spider silk, she realizes, and oh crap, she's about to be trapped in its web. Trussed up like a delicacy, ready to be consumed.

Veronica feels the tug at her ankle as the silk tightens and the spider begins to reel her in, and she begins to slide across the shiny floor. "No, no, *no*," she says, and she tries to grab on to the wall, her nails ripping through the obscenely expensive wallpaper and then catching on the antique baroque picture frame that hangs in the entrance.

Picture frame.

She digs her nails into the frame and wrenches it off the wall. *Sorry, ancestors*, she thinks as she flips the family portrait over and braces herself. She just about still has traction on the floor, and with her unbound foot she pushes off and up, bringing the painting down on the creature's head.

She expects the sound of the canvas ripping, tearing, and she expects the jarring impact of it hitting the spider, and she expects to be yanked back by the tether at her ankle but—

None of it comes.

Veronica brings the painting down and it keeps coming down, smashing onto the floor, the frame splitting in two as she falls flat on her front this time, her chin cracking on the tile.

"Ah!" She gasps as one of her fangs slices right through her bottom lip, the heat of it searing, and in a panic she turns over, throwing her hand out for a shard of the picture frame, a weapon against the creature.

But it's gone, again, and Veronica lets her arm fall to the floor as she breathes heavily. It's not real, she thinks, and it's just something she's telling herself—but then it snaps into place and she stares, wide-eyed, at the gilded ceiling above her. "It's not real," she says out loud, and smacks the floor, making a sound somewhere between a laugh and a cry. "It's not *real*."

These strigoi and their dizzying mind tricks.

Veronica's just spent too much time and too much energy fighting a phantom vampire spider, an absolute figment of her imagination.

She groans and rolls over, gets to her feet. No spider silk clinging hot and wet to her ankle; no creature barring her way.

A wipe to her face leaves a slash of scarlet across her forearm, and Veronica swallows her own blood and the sour taste of bile as she rolls her shoulders back. *You're gonna need to try harder than that,* she thinks, and marches up the stairs.

CHAPTER SIXTY-SIX
VERONICA

VERONICA SLIPS INTO her father's study, clicking the door shut behind her. She pauses for a second, eyes closed as she leans against the weathered wood and breathes.

"Veronica."

Her eyes snap open.

No *effin'* way. "Daddy?"

Her father's sitting behind his desk, swirling something clear in one of his heavy crystal tumblers. He sighs, a hand rubbing at his temples. "Good lord," he says. "What are you wearing?"

"Daddy," Veronica says, moving forward. "I don't under—"

"You look a complete mess," he says sharply. "For god's sake, with all the time you spend running around and flashing my credit cards, couldn't you have found something a little classier to wear? You're a *Lodge*, after all. I have to be seen in public with you. I can't have you dressing like this. People will talk."

Veronica looks down at her black dress, a little worse for wear after the beginning of the night's activities but still just a dress, like a dozen others she's worn to formal events. "I don't know what you're talking about. One, this is a perfectly fine dress, and two—I'll wear what I want!"

Her father shakes his head as he rises to his feet. "That's your problem, Veronica," he says. "You always want to do what *you* want. Wear what you want, talk how you want, hang out with whomever you want. It's really very unbecoming."

"Unbecoming?" Veronica's mouth hangs open. "Are you kidding me?"

"Oh, I'm sorry," her father says, slapping a hand to his forehead. "I forgot that word might be too complex for you. Here, let me say it in a simple way that you might understand: *You are a pain in the ass*."

"Oh, don't I know it," a voice says, and Archie melts out of the shadows.

Veronica scrubs at her eyes. "You're not here," she says to Archie. "You're back at the hotel, you're not here, this isn't real."

Archie and her father exchange glances, and then break into loud, cruel laughter. Archie wipes a tear from his eye. "Ronnie," he says. "You really *are* incapable of seeing the truth even when it's right in front of you, aren't you?"

"Thank you for bringing her to me," Hiram says. He pulls a wad of cash from his pants pocket and licks his thumb, then begins counting it out. "Your payment, for your very last job."

Archie strolls over to collect the money. "You're lucky," he says. "I was about to raise my prices. Spending all that time with *her*?" He whistles. "Should've started charging you double months ago."

Veronica watches as her father passes the stack of cash to Archie. "I don't understand," she says. In her head, a voice reminds her: *This isn't real. This is a trick, an illusion. This isn't real.*

But it feels real enough, and when she stumbles forward to rip the money out of Archie's hand, it's real enough: the slip of the notes, the warmth of Archie's fingers as they brush hers.

"Stop it," she says. "What are you doing?"

Her father's eyes narrow. "I'm paying the boy for his services," he says. "Like I have to pay every single one of your so-called friends. What? Did you think they were hanging out with you because they truly *liked* you?" He leans over the desk, cold eyes fixed on his daughter. "Pathetic. Who could ever like you, Veronica? You're a self-obsessed, spoiled, stupid little brat."

It's not real it's not real it's not—

Her father's words—the illusion's words, whatever—slice deep into her and lodge themselves inside her bones. Stupid and spoiled and self-obsessed, yes: That's what she's always feared she is.

"—you going to cry now?" Archie's taunt reaches her ears. "That's what you always do, isn't it, Ronnie? Turn on the tears when you don't get your way, or when someone says something you don't want to hear. God, you're a sad excuse for a girl."

"And to think she believed you wanted to date her," her father says.

Veronica presses her hands over her ears, so she can only hear every other word they're saying. *Stupid—worthless—immature— vapid—ugly—*

"Look at you," Archie says. "Who would ever love you?"

"As if anyone ever could love you," her father says.

Veronica is crying, she can feel the hot tears streaking down her face, but she won't give them the satisfaction of wiping her face clean. Instead, she reaches for the door handle and yanks it open.

"I don't care if nobody ever loves me," she says, raspy and low. "*I* love me. You two were *lucky* I ever even acknowledged your existence."

She slams the door shut on their raucous laughter and breaks into a run.

CHAPTER SIXTY-SEVEN
VERONICA

THE HALLS move around her.

Veronica's trying to find her way to the basement, and it should be easy, she should know where she's going, but every time she turns a corner the way before her is not the way she wanted, not the place she thought she would be. And no matter how hard she tries to focus, the house seems to slip from place to place, stripes sliding down the walls and carpet crawling up onto the ceiling.

It's just the strigoi, she tells herself. *They're just playing tricks on me.*

But it doesn't matter how many times she reminds herself of the truth. The house still shifts beyond her control, and she can still feel the spider's sticky web on her skin, and she can still hear her father and Archie calling her a pathetic, stupid little brat.

"I don't have time for this," Veronica says, unsure whether she's speaking to the strigoi or to herself. "I have to finish this, for my friends—I have to put an end to this."

She's sweating as she runs through the never-ending halls, but then she turns a corner and *look*—her bedroom door. There, with the ornate *V.L.* stenciled in gold on the doorknob.

She's never been so relieved to see her bedroom in her life.

Veronica heads straight for it, keeping her eyes locked on her destination, determined not to let it slip out of her grasp. She reaches the door and sighs in relief, twisting the knob and opening it.

But when she steps inside, everything has shifted again.

Inside is not her bedroom. It's an entirely foreign room, although beautiful: wide windows looking out onto treetops, a four-poster canopy bed, and a gorgeous gilded mirror stretching from floor to ceiling, showing the reflection of a white woman in an ivory gown, her blond hair falling in delicate curls to her shoulder blades.

"Oh," Veronica says, a small noise of surprise. "I'm sorry, I— *Betty?*"

The woman in the gown turns and clasps her hands to her chest. "V! There you are," she says. "Oh my goodness, you're still not dressed? Listen, I know you're just being a good maid of honor and handling whatever crises are happening so that I don't have to deal with them, but come on, we *have* to get you ready. You can't walk down the aisle in that!"

It *is* Betty standing before Veronica. She looks older, maybe, but it's definitely Betty there in a wedding dress, veil hanging off the end of the bed; she looks breathtaking, but Veronica shakes her head. "Maid of honor?"

"I know," Betty says, smoothing her hands down the silk skirt of her wedding gown. "Doesn't it seem like just yesterday that we were fighting over Archie? And now I'm marrying him. Isn't it *wild*? I'm so glad you finally admitted that you weren't good enough for him and let him be with the girl he really wanted all along."

"You're—" Veronica glances around the room, trying to get her bearings, but of course she can't, because of course this room doesn't belong here. She doesn't belong here, Betty doesn't belong here. "You're marrying Archie?"

Betty smiles at her, her signature bright, sincere, glowing Betty Cooper smile. "Of course I am, V. What? Did you think I would have second thoughts?" Her smile turns sharper. "Is that what you wanted? Is that why you're not dressed? You thought I wasn't going to go through with it, or you thought he was going to change his mind and choose *you* instead?"

"No, Betty! I—"

"I should have known you were lying," Betty says, and she bares her teeth and begins to run at Veronica, her eyes wild. "He loves me! He loves *me*, and he'll never love you! You're a lying piece of—"

Veronica slams the door shut and holds it closed tight as the Betty behind the door hammers on it, the force of her hits vibrating through the wood and into Veronica's spine.

Then they stop, a sudden absence of sound and sensation.

Of course they stopped. It was never really happening.

Veronica sags against the door and lets out a wild yell, a noise that holds all her anger and deep-down self-loathing and fear. "Is that all you have?" she calls out into the silent dark. "You think that's enough to scare me off? You think I'm so afraid of *you*? You can't even come out here and face me. You're hiding away trying to trick me out of finding you, but I don't go down so easily. So fine, keep it coming! I can do this all night!"

The echo of her voice replays down the hallway for longer than is possible, the cracked yell coming back to her over and over.

It's not true, is it? She can't do this all night. She has limited time to find the strigoi before her friends won't be able to hold off all the newly turned Riverdale vampires any longer.

I shouldn't have left them there, she thinks. *Why did I leave them? Betty, and Cheryl, and Archie and Dilton—if they die, it's all on me. Their blood, their deaths, it'll all be on me.*

A laugh carries down the stairs.

Veronica's head snaps to the sound, and she peels herself off the door. Follow it? It could be the strigoi.

Or it could be another trick, another illusion.

Only one way to find out.

Veronica climbs the stairs, stairs she finds suddenly right in front of her, as if they've been there all along, and she climbs and she climbs and she comes to a door. She puts her hand on the door and feels the warmth from behind it. Not the basement, but maybe she was wrong. Maybe this is where the strigoi has chosen to hide.

She turns the handle slowly and opens the door.

CHAPTER SIXTY-EIGHT
CHERYL

CHERYL'S BEEN TREADING water for what feels like hours, and she's beginning to tire.

"How much longer?" Betty says, her voice shaking with the effort of staying afloat.

Cheryl looks up at the vampires gathered, watching them. Waiting. "We'll be okay," she says, although she can barely feel her legs anymore, and she's beginning to struggle to stay above the surface. "Veronica's going to do it, you'll see. And then we can get out of here."

"Uh . . ." Dilton sounds alarmed. "Not to put a hole in that plan, Cheryl, but—does it seem like the water's getting lower to anyone else?"

"What?" Cheryl's teeth click together as she scans the edge of the water. No. Dilton's wrong. He's just seeing things, he's just panicking—

Her toe scrapes the bottom of the pool.

Oh.

She couldn't do that before. She couldn't reach the bottom of the

271

pool before, and Cheryl's torn between relief and a new fear.

Relief: She can put her feet down now, and give herself a break.

Fear: *Oh god oh god—*

Cheryl looks at the others. "The water's going down," she says. "Someone's draining the pool."

Archie looks so pale he could be dead, and maybe he will be soon. Cheryl can't stop herself from thinking it. They'll all be dead if the pool completely empties. This holy water dip is the only barrier between them and the hungry moroi, who are no longer staring blankly. No: They're beginning to smile now, some of them, others reaching out toward their trapped prey, as if to say, *It won't be long now.*

"What do we do when it's empty?" Archie says.

"Veronica will kill the strigoi before that happens," Betty says. "Right, Cheryl?"

Cheryl feels her feet find the floor of the pool once more, and she swallows the wave of water that laps over her mouth. "Yes," she says, unable to keep the tremble out of her words. "She's going to do it."

We're running out of time, V. I need you to do this.

CHAPTER SIXTY-NINE
VERONICA

"DARLING." A DARK-HAIRED white man in a black suit takes Veronica by the elbow and kisses her on the cheek. "There you are. Carolyn's been waiting to meet you."

Veronica blinks at the scene before her. Some kind of cocktail party, guests milling in a low-lit room while servers pass out tiny canapés and shiny drinks in delicate glasses. "Carolyn?"

The man leans close again, as if kissing her other cheek, but what he actually does is speak directly into her ear, a cold harsh whisper that's a thousand miles away from the warm tone he was just using. "Yes, Carolyn Heatherton, Michael Heatherton's wife. Don't tell me you're drunk already. Go over there and talk to her and, for the love of god, don't embarrass me."

He pushes Veronica in the direction of a tall dark-skinned woman in a yellow silk dress that seems to move with the light. *Talk to her?* Veronica thinks. About what? What is this party for, and who is that man?

Her questions are answered a second later, when she sees the picture blown up to almost comical proportions and propped up near the entrance of the room. It's a picture of her, and that man, and a small dark-haired child, and a matching black poodle. *Mr. and Mrs. Porter welcome you to tonight's fundraiser*, it reads beneath the image, and below that, in large red and blue letters, *Jasper Porter for Congress*.

Veronica scans the room and a sick feeling rises in her.

This is it, isn't it? Her future.

Her society-wife future, where she's no more than a prop for a husband who doesn't love her at all—just an actor costarring in the play of a political campaign.

She closes her eyes, squeezing them so tight the light through her eyelids splinters and blurs, like one of those kaleidoscope toys she had as a kid, the ones that you put your eye to and watch the psychedelic patterns spin at the end of the cylinder. *Okay, this is too real. This is too much.*

She can feel her breath coming faster and shallower, that panicked sound. *It's all an illusion*, she reminds herself, and this time she does know it, but it makes it worse, somehow. Because even as an illusion, this is all far too close to the truth.

This is the life Veronica sees herself having. Unhappy, trapped with a man just like her father, a man who belittles her and berates her and wants nothing more than for her to smile and look pretty. Who believes deep down that she is capable of nothing more than smiling and looking pretty.

She backs into a corner, grasping for something real to hold on to. Something to anchor her in reality, but this husband of hers suddenly appears at her side and slides his arm around her waist, the gesture outwardly sweet but with his hand behind her back he pinches at her skin, hard enough to bruise. A warning, Veronica knows: *Get it together and act like the sweet, demure little wifey you're supposed to be.*

"Honey," he says, and his voice oozes with it, a thick coating over the razor venom beneath. "What are you doing hiding over here?"

"I'm not hiding." Her voice shakes when she speaks, but Veronica feels emboldened by the anger that strobes over his face. "I'm leaving."

Veronica shakes him off and breaks for the door. *This is not my life and this is never going to be my life,* she thinks. *You don't own my future, and I am not afraid of it. This is not me.*

She feels hands ripping at her as she tries to escape, claws of strength that seek to keep her there, in her place. That try to hold her down and pin her to this empty-shell version of herself. But Veronica is strong now, is determined, and she lets them bruise and scrape her as she pushes through, fights her way free.

And then she is on the other side of the door and she slams it shut and it's over.

She's free.

She bends at the waist, catching her breath, and when she straightens, the walls around her are solid again. Stairs straight ahead leading down, down, and if she takes them she'll find her way to the basement, she knows.

"Not free," Veronica says, dragging a hand through her hair, adjusting her gem-studded hoop earrings. "Not yet."

She makes her way over to the stairs and looks down into the darkness ahead. Whatever nightmare awaits her below, she's ready for it. Time to put an end to all of this.

Time to put an end to the sire.

She descends.

CHAPTER SEVENTY
CHERYL

THE WATER'S AT waist level now. Cheryl has her crossbow up and ready to fly, not that she'll be able to hold off any more than a handful of vamps with it. It feels better than just sitting here, waiting to die, though.

"Hey," Betty calls. "Is it just me, or does it look like there are less of them now?"

Cheryl scans the watching moroi. Actually—yeah, the crowd does look thinned out. "Where are the others?"

"Look." Archie sloshes through the water and points to the ballroom behind them. Inside, at least half the vampires are working as one, taking the chairs and tables that are scattered across the room and piling them up in the center. "What are they doing?"

"Building something," Dilton says, and a shadow passes over his face.

Cheryl looks up and flinches. Veronica's father is standing directly in front of her, his cold red eyes focused on her. "Not *something*," he says. "A gift. For you, Cheryl."

Her blood runs cold, if it's possible for her to even get any colder than she already is. "What?"

"You'll see." He crouches, looking down at the sinking water level. "Shouldn't be too long now." He stands and flicks a hand in Cheryl's direction. "Then we'll get you nice and warmed up."

What the hell is that supposed to mean? Cheryl cocks her crossbow, aiming right at Mr. Lodge's heart. One move from her and he'll be dead.

She shuts one eye, narrowing her aim. *Bam*, she thinks.

And then Betty's on her. "Don't!" She pushes the crossbow right as Cheryl lets fly, the bolt careening wild, high in the air, and Mr. Lodge barely reacts, only laughing as he walks away, the vampires parting to let him through and then swallowing him up.

Cheryl glares at Betty. "What did you do that for?"

"You can't *kill* Veronica's dad!" Betty looks aghast. "What would Veronica do? God, Cheryl."

"You're talking about the same girl who killed two of her own friends," Cheryl says. "She knows what might happen. She knows that there's only one way to stop them when they start coming." Then she ducks beneath the water to retrieve her weapon, where it fell after Betty's shove. "What do you want me to do, Betty, just sit here? I'm supposed to let him threaten me?"

"We're supposed to wait for Veronica to—"

"I know," Cheryl snaps. "But what if she doesn't do it, Betty? What if the strigoi kills *her* first?"

It makes her feel sick to even say it, but look at them. Look at the situation they're in—they'd be stupid not to consider it. If Veronica doesn't pull it off, then there's no magic solution coming to rescue them. They're in this by themselves, and at the rate the water's disappearing, they don't have long to come up with a plan. "Betty," Cheryl says, and her voice has lost its edge. She's scared. That's the honest truth of it. "I don't want to die tonight."

Betty puts a hand on Cheryl's shoulder and shakes her. "You're not going to die tonight," she says, and she turns to the boys, raising her voice. "None of us are dying tonight. Do you hear me?"

I hear you, Cheryl thinks. But she raises her crossbow again anyway.

CHAPTER SEVENTY-ONE
VERONICA

VERONICA SLIPS THROUGH the darkened basement. She's turned on the light, but the bulb flickers and the glow it gives off is weak at best.

In the back corner was where she saw it last time: the coffin.

And Veronica sees it there again, as if it's waiting for her. She's so close she can taste victory, sweeter than the thick chocolate shake she always gets at Pop's.

When she reaches the coffin, Veronica runs her hands over the top, just like she did that first time. The etched symbol is still as unfamiliar as before, but Veronica ignores it, hooking her fingertips under the lip of the lid instead. Inside here lies the other strigoi, the real sire; she's sure of it. Open it up, stab a stake through the heart, and everything's over.

She stops, a breath away from cracking the lid.

That's true, isn't it? It'll all be over the minute she puts her stake into this creature's chest. Riverdale will return to the way it was before all this mess: Her parents will become human again; her friends will be saved. And Veronica will no longer be a vampire.

It's *that* which makes her hesitate. She knew this before, of course she knew this before, but in the rush and heat of the attack at the hotel there had been no time for her to truly consider the ramifications of what she was doing. She had to kill Theodore so fast she didn't have the luxury of considering the impact his death would have on her.

Veronica stares down at the closed coffin. It's just her and this strigoi, in this dark lonely basement. Now she has time (*You don't, you don't have time, think of Betty and Cheryl waiting at the hotel, surrounded*) and now she can think about how soon, so soon, she'll no longer be this new vampire version of herself. She'll go back to being Human Veronica, and with her comes all the trappings of her former self: the perfect, role-playing daughter-friend-cheerleader she's always been.

The teenage version of the girl who goes on to be the wife she briefly was upstairs, the woman with the husband she hates and the empty sad heart.

Veronica swallows. That's the problem, isn't it? Vampires are monsters. Look at her parents, look at Theodore. If she's truly good, the light-side vamp she and her friends have cast her as during this whole ordeal, then surely she wants to go back to being human. It's what a good girl would want.

But I like being a vampire.

That's the deep-down truth.

There's no feeling like it, none that Veronica has ever experienced. In her human life she was Veronica Lodge, always trying so hard to be all things at once: hot and funny and kind and smart. Ambitious but not too much, flirty but not too needy. Determined but not greedy. And it was exhausting, draining, to always be trying to do all those things and somehow pulling them off—but at what cost? Trying to convince her father she's worthy of taking over the company one day when he'll never believe in her. Spending all that time calculating what will make Archie like her more than Betty; but really, does she even like Archie like that anymore? Or has it always been that she's stuck in this love triangle because that's what people expect?

Veronica begins to ease the coffin open, more out of curiosity than anything now. The strigoi inside is powerful enough to play with her perception of reality while being knocked out in this box. Powerful enough to control the minds of all these newly made moroi.

That's the other part of this that Veronica has grown to love: the sheer power, most of which she hasn't even gotten to explore yet. Not just the strength, or the speed, but the shape-shifting, the mind trickery that has been used against her so much. She'd be lying if she said she wasn't curious, if she pretended she didn't want to explore those parts of herself, too. But in the space of just a week she's gotten into more physical fights than she had in the rest of her life. Actually—she'd *never* gotten in a physical fight before she turned. And now she can more than handle herself. She casts fear with just a look; she sees it in people's eyes.

Being a vampire has blown up her existing world, and Veronica—

She's not sure if she wants to set it back.

The lid slips off the coffin and lands on the basement's cement floor with a harsh crack. Veronica looks at what's within and inhales sharply.

"No," she says quietly. "No no no."

Inside the coffin the strigoi lies perfectly still, waxy. Hands together at heart height, clasping a single white hydrangea between its palms. And its face—

Veronica holds the confused keening inside.

The strigoi is wearing her face.

It is her, and she is it.

"Not real not real not real," Veronica finds herself whispering again, but this time she's not so sure. Maybe it is her. Maybe this is another vision of her future, the life she could have if she remains a vampire forevermore.

A cold blade runs up the length of her spine, and there's a voice in her head—her own—telling her to do it. To remember her friends, her family, the rest of this town she calls her home, and save them all.

Veronica reaches into the coffin. She just wants to see. She just wants to feel.

Her fingers slip around a cold, waxy wrist, and—

The strigoi snaps her eyes open, grabs Veronica's wrist, and holds tight, her fingers so cold they sear like a burn. "Hello," she says. "I've been waiting."

CHAPTER SEVENTY-TWO
VERONICA

THE STRIGOI RELEASES Veronica and climbs out of the coffin. No; *climb* is not the right word, Veronica thinks. She doesn't move like a lowly human so much as slink and shift and creep like a rolling ocean wave slip-sliding onto the shore. She is liquid, melted ice.

"Who are you?" Veronica swallows and licks her dry lips. Her voice is ragged, not strong at all, and she tries again. "I'm going to kill you."

The strigoi—the mirror version of Veronica—laughs, her head thrown back. "No, you're not," she says, and then her face seems to change. *Does* change: features morphing and rearranging themselves until Veronica's face has entirely faded and the one that replaces it is different but familiar; Veronica doesn't know why until the strigoi smiles again, her own smile this time, and the memory snaps into place.

Veronica has seen this girl before. Because she is still a girl, a little taller than Veronica but with a young face, an innocent sheen to her, and it's the same version of her that lives inside the photograph they saw in that old book. The Finch family portrait.

"Odette," Veronica breathes. "You're Odette Finch."

Odette's smile widens. "Yes," she says. "I am."

Veronica blinks. "You're supposed to be dead."

"But I am," Odette says. "Don't you see?"

CHAPTER SEVENTY-THREE
VERONICA

"YOU'RE THE STRIGOI. You're the sire."

Veronica says it, and Odette makes a pained face. "God, it sounds so boring when you say it that way," she says. "But you are right. *And* you're smart." Odette gives her a nod. "I didn't expect you to make it through all those nightmares I conjured up for you. I'm impressed, little girl Lodge."

Odette Finch died in the fire that wiped out her family, Veronica knows. Except Theodore was supposed to have died in that fire, too, and yet Veronica just put a stake through his heart.

He escaped, she thinks. *And so did Odette.* "You were trying to stop me," Veronica says. "But you couldn't."

"Stop you?" Odette turns and runs a pale finger along the edge of the coffin's velvet lining. "No. I was trying to challenge you. See if you would rise to the occasion or fail me. But you're made of sturdy stuff, I see now. And it pleases me, Veronica. Look at how far you've come! If I'm honest, it's not that I didn't expect you to make it through all of that up there." She waves a hand toward the ceiling. "I hoped you would. But I couldn't make it too easy for you. I had to see that you truly were the girl I thought you might be."

Veronica shifts her weight, watching Odette warily. "I *am* going to kill you," she says. "For what you've done to this town, my friends, to me—"

"To you?" Odette rushes to her and has her hand around Veronica's neck before she can so much as think of moving. "Look at you. Before, you were so weak, and now you can do whatever you want. You can live the kind of life you've only dreamed about!"

"What, like you are?" Veronica says, her words choked. "Trapped in a tragic coffin in the basement of somebody else's house? Yeah, no thank you."

Odette releases her, pushes her away hard. "You don't know the half of it," Odette says.

"I know you're supposed to be dead." Veronica rubs at her neck. Odette's grip is stronger than her father's, her mother's, stronger even than Theodore's. "I know you were supposed to have burned in that fire that killed the rest of your family. Or that everybody *believed* killed the rest of your family. But here you are."

"Here I am," Odette agrees. "A survivor."

"You *and* your brother," Veronica says. "Except—bad news." She smiles darkly, because she's almost excited to tell Odette what she did. It's not like the pain she felt when she killed Reggie and Moose. This time, she's proud. "I killed him."

Odette's eyes flutter closed, and she sighs. "I know," she says, only slightly mournful. "And I suppose I should thank you, really. Because you did what I couldn't do."

"What?" Veronica shakes her head.

No. This isn't how Odette is supposed to react. She's supposed to be hurt, in pain, or at the very least *act* like she is. Veronica destroyed her brother, like Odette is trying to destroy her parents. She should be *sickened*. "Do you even care? Do you have any feelings at all, or is this what happens when you live for far longer than you ever should have? You become an empty monster, is that it?"

Odette opens her eyes. "You think I don't have any feelings?"

Odette circles Veronica, brushing at her hair, her dress, the exposed skin on her back. "Would you like to hear a story?" she says, in a singsong voice. "It's really rather good. Here, sit—"

She shoves on Veronica's shoulders and Veronica finds herself sinking to the ground, and try as she might, she can't fight it. "You and I, we're alike," Odette says, and her words snake into Veronica's ears. "Let me tell you about the night I died."

CHAPTER SEVENTY-FOUR
ODETTE

IT'S PITCH-BLACK when Odette wakes.

She smells it first: smoke. It takes her a minute to understand what's happening, why the air around her smells like burning, and then the sleep falls from her and she sees the glow beneath her bedroom door.

"Fire," she breathes, soft and awestruck. "Fire. Mother!" She almost falls out of bed and runs to her door, the lace edging of her nightgown twisting around her knees. "Father! Theo!"

She touches the door handle and snatches her hand back. "Ah!" It's monstrously hot, the skin on her fingers and palm instantly swelling where she touched the metal.

Odette coughs. The smoke is thicker than it was only a moment ago, and it's getting harder to breathe. If she can't escape through the door—

She turns to her bedroom window. There's a trellis below her window; she had used it in the past to welcome romantic partners to her bedroom without her parents knowing. Griselda Thomas lost a shoe climbing back down once, and Odette had to get up early and pick through the rosebushes at the side of the house to find it before any of the house staff could.

I can break the window and climb out, *she thinks, searching*

frantically for something to use to smash the glass. Her eyes alight on the chair that accompanies her dressing table.

She can hear the flames now, and it's a wonder that she slept for so long through the noise of the crackling and burning, through the smoke that's seeped in and polluted the air surrounding her. Odette picks up the chair and braces herself before ramming it at the glass. The window shatters, the wooden frame groaning as it splinters and then falls apart. It leaves a jagged rim of wood and glass spikes around the hole Odette needs to climb through, and she pulls the heirloom quilt from her bed, uses it to pad the frame. It'll have to be enough; she doesn't have anything else on hand to help, nor the time to think too much about it.

Odette leans out, gulping a lungful of air. She looks down: The trellis is lower than she thought, a gap between her window and where the trellis begins that means she'll have to jump, and hope she can catch on.

What other choice do I have?

Odette places her hands on the covered window frame and feels the glass beneath begin to pierce the quilt, the soft flesh of her hands. Without giving herself the chance to fear it, she launches forward and begins to fall.

CHAPTER SEVENTY-FIVE
BETTY

THEY MOVE WHEN the water's at Betty's ankles.

The vampires begin to drop down into the near-empty pool, hissing as what little is left of the laced water touches them. But it's not enough to stop them, not even enough to slow them.

Betty backs into the others, frantic. "Now would be a good time for—"

Cheryl fires before Betty can finish, and the nearest vampire drops in a heap.

But there's way too many for them to defeat. Betty knows it, she can feel the cold grip of their fate around her heart, but she draws her knife anyway and looks to Archie, then to Dilton. "Ready?"

She raises her knife in front of her, her only protection, and braces herself for the fight.

But then the vampires stop. As before, as one, they just cease moving, and it sends a shiver through Betty.

"What are they doing?" Archie asks.

"I think—" Dilton sounds afraid, as afraid as Betty is. "I think the strigoi is doing this."

And then the moroi move as one again, the slightest but creepiest shift. Just their eyes, all turning to focus on one person.

On Cheryl.

Cheryl reloads her crossbow and fires again, cracking one through the shoulder, the spray of blood warm on Betty's shocked face. "Come on," Cheryl says, teeth gritted. "Is that all you got?"

She's about to fire again when the vampires converge on her, a rush so fast that Betty can't even try to stop them. "Cheryl!"

Archie's arms circle Betty's waist, pulling her back. "Stop! You're gonna get yourself killed!"

The vampires part, revealing two of them holding Cheryl in an iron grip.

"What—" Betty yanks herself free of Archie's grip. "What are they doing? Where are they taking her?"

Betty watches as the vampires pull Cheryl up and out of the pool, Cheryl fighting them the whole way, and begin carrying her back toward the ballroom.

CHAPTER SEVENTY-SIX
ODETTE

ODETTE FALLS FOR *what seems like forever, until her hands find the trellis and she grabs on, bringing her body slamming into the side of the house so hard it knocks what little breath she has left out of her.*

· *No time to cling on; she begins her climb down, wooden splinters digging themselves into her fingertips. When she reaches the bottom she stares up, amazed.* I made it. I'm alive, *she thinks.*

Odette runs to the front of the house and what she sees, she knows, will remain scarred in her brain and her heart for as long as she lives.

Their home is ablaze. It's not just the wing where her bedroom is; it's the entire structure, their entire house; it's burning bright and wild, and the heat of it is unbearable even at this distance.

"Mother!" Odette calls into the blaze even as she knows nobody could survive the intensity of that burn. "Theo!" The only way any of them will still be alive is if they did as she has done, found some way out.

But if they did, then they would have come for me, *she thinks.* Theo, at least, would have found a way to me, and I wouldn't have woken up to the flames licking at my door.

"Theo!" She screams his name now, her burned and bloodied palms

292

throbbing. *Why is nobody here? Why is she all alone as her world burns down around her?*

Odette stumbles forward, bare feet stinging on the scorched grass, but she has to hold a hand up as there's a loud boom and a cloud of fire explodes from what used to be the drawing room, rippling up and into the night air.

And then, a movement behind her.

Odette whips around, long black hair trailing with the motion. "Hello?" she calls, her throat gritty and painful. "Is somebody there? Theo? Anyone, please, help!"

She scans the trees in front of her, the woods their estate is nestled within. She could have sworn there was somebody there, but now the night is still again, only the fire behind her—

There. It's just a flash, something lit up under the cover of the trees for a second, but Odette is certain this time. Somebody's out there.

She's about to call again when she sees the figure side-on. Slipping away from her, running under the cover of dark along the road that leads up to the Finch estate.

It's a silhouette she knows too well, and it comes crashing at her then, the truth of it all.

This fire is no accident; somebody set it on purpose. Somebody wanted them all to die.

Odette falls to her knees and works to stand again, takes another few steps forward as if chasing after the culprit, but her legs and lungs give out before she can even really try. "Jeremiah" is all she can say, a strangled call after the figure leaving her there.

Jeremiah Blossom.

I thought we had a deal, *she thinks, even as she lies there with the heat*

singeing the back of her. I thought we were on the same side. And yet you tried to kill me.

She calls for her brother, her parents, one more time, but it's too late, she knows. They are gone, and maybe it would be better if she were gone, too. She should have stayed in that room and let herself be swallowed up by the flames, because what does she have now? Her family gone, her home and all possessions lost. Betrayed by her supposed business partner. Leave me here to die, *she thinks, and closes her eyes to the orange heat.*

And then she feels it, or is she dreaming, or is she already dead? A hallucination, it must be, the feeling of somebody's cool hands on her hot ones.

The sensation of being dragged, the heat slowly diminishing.

Odette opens her eyes and the sky above is starry.

She closes them and opens, and now she is under the canopy of the woods and she wants to see her savior.

She wants to know who finally came for her, but then she feels burning again, except it's inside her this time, and it radiates through every part of her—

She screams into the night, a broken pained cry, and then the blackness comes and the burn tears her to pieces.

CHAPTER SEVENTY-SEVEN
VERONICA

"*I WOKE UP* in the woods," Odette says, walking dizzying circles around Veronica. "I woke up all alone, and I was changed. I imagine you can understand how that feels."

"Blossom?" Veronica repeats the name Odette uttered only moments ago. "Jeremiah Blossom torched your house? Why would he do that?"

"Why do the Blossoms do anything they do?" Odette says. "Why does your family? Why did mine?" She bends, bringing her face close to Veronica's. "Money, power, greed, you name it." She straightens. "See, I had made a deal with the Blossoms. I worked with my father, and I always hoped that he would choose me to be his successor. I knew it would be unusual, but there were other women in positions of power; it was a possibility. And I worked hard for him—I was a good second-in-command, not that he would ever admit to me fulfilling that position. No, that always went to my dear sweet brother, who cared more about drinking and women than the business. Which was fine with me—Theo wasn't a bad person, just not cut out for the world my father and I inhabited. Again—" Odette glances at Veronica. "You understand what I mean."

Of course she does; of course Veronica knows what it is to be the dutiful daughter clawing her way up the ladder. She had wondered before, looking at that smiling photo of the Finch family, what Odette was like. Had she known that all she really had to do was look at herself for the answer . . . ?

What? What would that have changed about anything?

"So you made a deal with Jeremiah Blossom," Veronica says. "For what?"

"There was a piece of land just outside town," Odette says, and she drags a chair over to sit in front of Veronica, her legs crossed in her deep blue dress. "A very plain, very boring piece of land. On the surface, at least. But if you were curious enough to actually consider what was beneath there, and pay attention to the geological surveys like I did, and keep watch on the price of oil like I did, then you would know that the land was actually *extremely* valuable. So I took it to my father, with the idea being that we could purchase the land at dirt cheap prices and then collect the spoils; and once the land was tapped, we could develop it into housing or commerce, whatever. We would have the profit from the oil and it would, at the very least, double our net worth."

Odette leans in, her red eyes gleaming. "Of course, I predicted that for my diligence and hard work, I would be justly rewarded. I would head up the project and officially become a leading associate in my father's company. But can you guess what happened?"

Veronica gives her a small smile. "Daddies don't like it when their little girls get too bold," she says.

"Exactly," Odette says. "You're exactly right, Veronica. And *my* daddy didn't like it at all. Oh, he liked the land and he liked the oil and he liked the money he knew he would make, but he didn't want *me* to be in charge. He gave it to Theo. Theo! Who spent most of his time in the casino or traveling or spending time with the women he met while traveling. Theo who could tell an excellent joke, always had his friends' backs in a bar fight, but couldn't command a business to save his damn life."

Veronica's putting the pieces together. Odette is a girl after her own heart, it seems. "So you took the proposition elsewhere," she says.

Odette nods. "Our families—yours and mine and the Blossoms— we existed in a delicate balance. The town thrived as long as we each played our part, and if any one of us got too far into the others' realm, things quickly started to go sideways. So we stuck to our own, mostly. But I was sick of being dismissed by my father and the way he chose my brother over me, time and time again, even though he had not even a *fraction* of my skill and work ethic." She stands again. "I took it to the Blossoms so they could undercut my father. Buy the land first, and of course, as a thank-you for alerting them to the deal in the first place, they'd place me in charge of running it. But—"

"The Blossoms are the Blossoms," Veronica says, cutting Odette off. "That was your biggest mistake. Trusting them."

"Well now, who's the girl who's been running around with Cheryl Blossom lately?" Odette bares her teeth at Veronica. "Not exactly one to lecture me on trust, are you?"

"That's different—"

"Is it?" Odette flies in front of her again, so close Veronica can see her reflection in Odette's black pupils. "She's a Blossom, through and through, just like you're a Lodge. We all run with the traits of our families, for better and worse. Jeremiah Blossom was only a few years older than me. We had known each other almost all our lives, and there wasn't a time I could remember without him in it. So I went to him as an ally, as a friend. And what did he do? *He stabbed me in the back.* Cut me out of the deal, and then—because that just wasn't enough—he came to destroy my entire family." Odette's breathing heavily, the sweet-sour scent of blood on her breath. "I saw him that night. I saw him running from the fire he set. My family was dead, and I was nearly dead, but I was alive, still. Until . . ."

"Until somebody found you, and turned you," Veronica says, and then, almost to herself, "Yeah. I've been there."

Then Veronica looks up at her. There's a big part Odette has left out of her little tale. "But your family wasn't dead," she says. "Not all of them."

"My dear brother." Odette smiles grimly. "You're quite right. He wasn't dead, was he?"

She circles Veronica again, her voice taking on a distant quality, as if she's right back there in the wreckage of the fire. "Of course I thought he was dead, because if he were alive, he would have come for me when the fire started. He was my big brother, and we had a bond, you know? He understood how our father hurt me; I understood that he didn't want the responsibility Daddy gave him."

"But he didn't come for you."

"No," Odette says, and flicks her dark hair over her shoulder. "When I woke up changed, I didn't know what to do. The house was still on fire. I walked back to it. I had nowhere else to go, and I didn't really want to leave it. I just wanted to stay until the end, or something. But—" She laughs now. "There he was! In front of the fountain, lying there. There was my brother! And at first I thought he was dead, that perhaps he'd crawled out this far before the fire completely took him, so I ran to him. To what I thought was my brother's body. But when I got there, and I knelt by his side, and I called his name—well, he *woke up*."

Veronica swallows, remembering the moment when she'd seen her parents' bodies on the study floor. Imagining what it would have been like if they had opened their eyes as she knelt over them.

"He wasn't dead," Odette continues. "All these thoughts rushed through my head. How stupid I was to have believed he cared enough about me, his *sister*, to rescue me; how angry I was that he was there, seemingly fine, while I was changed; how hurt I was that he would be known as the only remaining member of the Finch family. All of that, over and over, but it was all eclipsed by the biggest, most urgent feeling of all."

Odette pauses, the moment crackling with tension, and Veronica knows exactly what she means. "The hunger," she breathes.

"I didn't mean to kill him," Odette says, and she sounds more like she's trying to convince herself than Veronica. "It just took over, and I had to feed. I didn't *mean* to drink until he was dead, except— when I saw he was dead, I felt *good*. It felt like he got everything he deserved, after the way he'd left me for dead." She rolls her eyes. "Of course, I didn't really know what I was doing, and I tried to feed again, after he was gone. How was I supposed to know that the second bite would bring him back?"

"You could have killed him again," Veronica says. "For real."

Odette nods. "I could have," she agrees. "But once I understood what he was, I didn't need to. For the first time in my life, our positions were reversed: *I* had all the power. To the outside, I was still just a girl, and he was still the all-powerful man; but they didn't know the truth. They didn't know that I could make Theo do whatever I wanted, whenever I wanted."

She comes close to Veronica now, her red eyes gleaming with excitement. "There's nothing like it, is there?" she says. "The power it brings you. How alive it makes you feel—and it's funny, because you're undead! But it was a different time, and there was this kind of freedom for girls like the one I remade myself into. I traveled all over, ruled every place I deigned to land with my brother at my side, and I banished Riverdale from my mind. What did it have that Paris couldn't give me, or Hollywood, or Berlin? Nothing at all."

"But you're here now," Veronica says. "You came back."

"I came back."

"And you hid." Veronica looks up at her, curious. "Why? You could do whatever you wanted now. Why put Theodore out there like he was in control?"

Odette sits again, her legs wide this time. "Because I could," she says simply. "Because I wanted to. I know you want me to tell you I had some big, complicated plan, but really—" She grins. "Why do the dirty work when I can pin it all on somebody else? Why risk my own life when I could risk Theodore's? See, I didn't count on you getting in my way *quite* so much, but I knew there was a risk of things going wrong. There's always a risk, and I always make sure I'm the last person it might hit."

She shakes her head. "But I'm getting off topic. What were we talking about? Oh, yes, why I came back. I mean, for the town, sure. I have everybody here that I could need to run this place, and I will. But why stop there? There's always Pembrooke and Midvale and wherever else I choose." She holds her hands out wide. "The Blossoms stole my future from me. I should have had this town in the palm of my hand a century ago, so here I am now, to take it back."

Revenge, Veronica thinks. *A simple motive, but so pure.*

"And now that I have all the forces I need, I can get on with the very sweetest part of my plan," Odette says, and she smiles, her fangs gleaming. "Burning those Blossoms to the ground, just like they did to me."

CHAPTER SEVENTY-EIGHT
CHERYL

CHERYL STRUGGLES ALL the way back toward the hotel, but she truly begins to lose it when she sees exactly where the vampires are taking her.

When she sees what it is they've been building within the wreckage of the ballroom.

"No!" She thrashes, ineffective against the strength of the moroi. The structure in the middle of the room is unmistakable now. Cheryl saw them on their ninth-grade field trip to nearby Harperville, studying the local witch trials. The pyres where the accused were burned.

This is where I die.

Cheryl kicks out and is rewarded with a crack to her skull, hard enough to dizzy her. Her eyes roll as she feels herself hoisted high and rope is wound around her.

She is tied tight to the post, her feet resting on the remains of the chairs she'd spent so long picking out with her mother and the head designer. Now they will be the kindling for the fire that ends her.

Cheryl fights to remain conscious, and when she can focus again, it's the pattern on the painted ceiling that catches her eye. Paint swirled like soft clouds, and she begins to cry.

This might be the last thing she ever sees.

CHAPTER SEVENTY-NINE
VERONICA

"YOU'RE GOING *to burn her?"*

Veronica turns her head and retches, bringing up nothing but sour blood-tinged spit, and then she flinches when she feels Odette smoothing a hand across her forehead.

"Sweet Veronica," Odette says, a rueful smile on her beautiful face. "I thought you'd understand."

"She's my *friend!*" Veronica stares up at her. "You thought I'd be okay with you killing my friend?"

Odette sits back on her heels. "She's your 'friend,' huh? And how long have you two been friends? Would you say she's loyal? Would you say she'd do anything for you? Do you think she'd lay down her life for you? Do you think she'd care *at all* if your roles were reversed right now?" Odette's eyes narrow. "Don't act so holier than thou, Veronica. You're just like me."

I'm nothing like you, Veronica wants to say, but it would be a lie. Hasn't she just listened to Odette's story thinking the entire time how oddly similar their lives are? Daughters of founding families. Ambitious and driven but held back by dismissive fathers.

Drawn to the darkness of being a mythic creature turned real.

And besides, she knows none of that is even what Odette means right now.

"I had to do what I did." Veronica shuts her eyes against the image of the ragged grave that floods her mind, the dead bodies of Moose and Reggie piled in there together, limbs tangled and blood still slicked across their skin. "I had to kill them. Or they would have killed Cheryl and probably half the town."

"Of course," Odette says smoothly. "Of course you *had* to. And you didn't like it at all, did you? I'm sure you didn't. I'm sure you didn't take any pleasure in the way you defeated those boys, in the way it felt to take a life. Two lives. Veronica? Tell me. You didn't like it, did you?"

Veronica squeezes her eyes tighter shut.

They're underwater and she aims her stake right for Moose's heart, and it sinks into him, and she watches the un-life drain out of his eyes.

She rises out of the water, dragging their corpses like prizes, like they're her reward for being such a good vampire girl.

She digs the grave and pretends to feel sad and sickened, but there is a small, powerful part of her hidden somewhere deep inside that is awed by what she's done. No one will mess with her anymore. No one will tell her what she can and can't do—not now.

She feels a tear snake its way under her eyelid and down her cheek. "I killed them," she says quietly.

Odette makes a sad sound. "Because they deserved it," she says. "And because that's what you're made to do. Veronica—"

Odette's hands tug at hers and Veronica opens her eyes, finds now that she can move again. She rises when Odette pulls her up and lets herself be guided to the back wall of the basement.

Odette's hands are soft and delicate, cold as they are, and there's a kind of relief in letting her take charge, Veronica finds. Odette leans forward and whips a cloth from a frame, unveiling the mirror behind it, and then she takes her place at Veronica's shoulder.

"Look," she says, and Veronica does as she says. The two of them reflected there together, Odette's dress pristine where Veronica's is battle-worn, Odette's skin pale white where Veronica's is warm honey, but outside of that they are so similar. Dark hair and intense red eyes, a wildness to the shape of their mouths, the flash of their fangs inside. "People see small, insignificant girls when they look at us. Not because that's what we are, but because it's what they want us to be. They can't stand the idea that we could ever be more than that—can't stand the idea that we could force our way out of the places they've put us in. But look at us. You know what power feels like now, don't you?"

Veronica nods, her eyes fixed on Odette's mirror ones.

"You know what happens if you kill me?" Odette speaks into her ear. "You lose all of that. You have to go back to the girl you were before, and no one will ever respect you the way you deserve to be respected. But—" She draws a hand down the side of Veronica's face. "You could join me. Take your rightful place in control of this town, like I'm going to. A Lodge and a Finch daughter, ruling like we always should have. Don't you want that?"

Veronica can see it clearly, the life Odette is offering her. No one ever telling her she's not smart enough. Not having to answer to her father, to smile and curtsy like the princess he likes to call her. And best of all: No more pretending that she is palatable and perfect. She will be the New and Improved Veronica Lodge, the one with the razor-wire teeth and loud heart, and she'll rule with Odette, the daughters of Riverdale taking this town for all it has. There'll be no Stepford wife future for her, and no more fighting over stupid boys that mean nothing to her, really, and most thrilling of all, no need to act like she's disturbed by what she's capable of.

Don't you want that? Veronica hears Odette's voice slip-sliding its way around her brain and down deep into her heart, and she thinks, *Yes, I want that, I want to be this me for the rest of time, and I want to show everybody what a mistake they've made underestimating Veronica Lodge for so freakin' long, and I want to tell Betty—*

Her heart thuds to a crashing stop. Betty.

Betty's waiting for you, remember? That voice is not Odette's; it's her own, a thin and desperate part of herself calling up through the rapture Veronica's twisted up in as she watches Odette smile in the mirror. *Betty's waiting for you, and if you don't do what you came here to do, she's going to die. And Dilton—he helped you survive; he found you scared and did everything you asked of him. And then Archie, you saved him from death once, are you just going to leave him to it this time?*

And Cheryl.

Cheryl.

"You're going to burn the Blossoms," Veronica says, careful to keep her voice neutral.

"*We're* going the burn the Blossoms." Odette smiles, wide and proud. "Well, we're going to burn Cheryl. Poetic, don't you think? The lone surviving Finch daughter taking the lone Blossom daughter from Penelope and Clifford. And now that they've been turned, they can have the rest of their existences to feel that loss. It's what they deserve. I wanted to put an end to them years ago, but I realized just killing them would be so *boring*. This is so much sweeter. I think it's all worked out perfectly. Now I can have everything I want *and* I have you."

Veronica stills. Odette *has* her.

That's what everyone always thinks, that they /have Veronica. Archie, when he deigns to choose her, and Reggie, when she'd let him kiss her, and even sometimes Betty, when she expects her picture-perfect best friend, even if she doesn't realize that's what she's doing. Every other person in her pre-vamp life always thinks she's something to have.

You're just like them, she realizes as she stares at Odette, almost her twin in the mirror. *You don't see me for me. I'm just another trinket for you to own, another prize on your path to being the richest, bestest vampire ruler in Riverdale and beyond.*

"Okay." Veronica nods, her reflection's head bobbing, and for a moment Odette looks so pleased with her that Veronica's heart swells and she won't, she can't—

No. I will.

"We're going to have such *fun*," Odette says. "You won't—"

Veronica moves.

She pushes Odette back so suddenly that Odette flies clear across the room and Veronica twists as she crouches to snatch her last remaining stake from its place at her ankle. She covers the distance between her and Odette, on the floor, in half a second.

Odette opens her mouth to let loose a piercing, grinding cry, and it rips at Veronica's ears; the walls begin to move as they had upstairs earlier, but Veronica is singularly focused.

"I might be a bitch," she says, "but I'm not going to be *your* bitch."

She drives the stake deep into Odette's heart.

CHAPTER EIGHTY

CHERYL

THE HEAT IS creeping up her legs.

Cheryl cries out, desperate, for someone—anyone—to help her. It's pointless, she knows: Betty and Dilton and Archie are outnumbered so thoroughly that any attempt to save her would only lead to their own deaths. And even then it might be too late.

If she looks down, she will see the flames taking hold. The vampire who lit the pyre stands back, the torchlight illuminating her face. "Mom." Cheryl sobs the words, watching the light dance over her mother's blank face. It's not her, it's not really her, she knows, but what does that matter now.

Except then, a change comes over her mother's face. One moment she's blank, and the next . . .

It's like the life has slipped back into her, as if she's suddenly herself again, and as her eyes focus on her daughter a scream rips from her mouth. "Cheryl!"

"Mom!"

For a moment Cheryl sees the horrified realization play out on her mom's face, the realization that she's about to watch her daughter burn to death.

Mom, Cheryl wants to call out again, but the smoke from the pyre chokes the word from her.

This is it, she thinks. *I'm going to die.*

She locks eyes with her mom, trying to say all the most important things with just a look.

And then—

Her mother's eyes roll back and she drops to the ground.

The wood crackles, loud snaps and rips. Cheryl struggles against the rope binding her to the pyre, holding her close to the fire creeping closer and closer to her flesh, and at the same time she watches in wonder as the vampires surrounding the pyre drop, just as her mother did.

Veronica, she thinks.

The army falls, and Cheryl calls out with renewed ferocity. *"Betty!"*

The flames lick her feet.

CHAPTER EIGHTY-ONE
VERONICA

THE NOISE ODETTE makes is unholy.

Veronica twists the stake as deep as she can go and throws her head back, letting out her own wild wail.

Beneath her Odette's body begins to collapse in on itself: her pretty face goes first, those red eyes rolling as her eye sockets cave in, and the flush on her cheeks becomes blood vessels bursting, a rush of dark, sticky blood oozing through the cracks in her skin.

Veronica pants as she watches Odette die. It's not like when she killed Theodore, or Reggie and Moose: It's as if Odette's soul is fighting with every remaining piece of herself to cling on to life, even as her body decays, acid and blood and shredded flesh ripping and separating from bone.

I did it, Veronica thinks, and she allows herself a triumphant smile, a loud laugh. *I did it! I killed her!*

She swings her legs over the remains of Odette, her dying cry stuttering and fading out. "Sorry," she says. "I don't think the dry cleaner's going to be able to get the blood out."

Odette's voice finally falls silent; Veronica turns away from her, but stops.

Take no chances, she thinks, and spins back.

There's a toolbox in one corner, and Veronica throws it open, draws out a large saw with a gleaming silver blade. How do you kill a vampire?

A stake through the heart, or decapitation.

"Both feels good," she says to herself, and goes back to the body that used to house Odette, a sunken mess there on the floor.

Veronica straddles the remains and presses the blade to its throat, takes a deep breath. "This is for Cheryl," she says, and begins to saw.

CHAPTER EIGHTY-TWO
CHERYL

THE FLAMES HISS as they're extinguished, and Cheryl mimics the sound as Dilton unties her. "My feet," she says thickly. "I don't think I can walk."

Archie takes her in his arms, and Cheryl winces when she catches sight of her feet and ankles. The skin is red and blistered, throbbing so intensely it's all she can do not to pass out.

But she's alive.

And so is everyone around them. The former mob is shifting, waking, and Cheryl can see the mayor rubbing at her eyes, their high school principal sitting up, her own mother coming to with a shocked expression on her face.

The destroyed ballroom is filled with the hum of confused voices. Cheryl catches pieces of them: *What happened— Why are we— Smells like— Some kind of attack— What's that noise?—*

She snaps out of her haze. "Veronica!"

She points and the others follow her finger. Yes, *that noise* is Veronica, roaring back up to the hotel on a motorcycle, her dress and hair streaming behind her.

"She's alive!" Betty says. "V! Veronica!"

And then, knowing that it's all over, that they're all alive, that Veronica is *okay*, thank god, Cheryl lets the sweet blackness take her.

CHAPTER EIGHTY-THREE
VERONICA

VERONICA SPRINTS THROUGH the waking crowd to reach her friends. Are they all—yes, they're all there: Dilton and Archie and Betty and Cheryl—and she exhales, panic seeping out with it. All she's thought about as she raced from her house back to the hotel was whether she had acted in time, or if she had let Odette seduce her for too long and now her friends would be dead; Cheryl would be on fire.

But Veronica careens into Betty, throwing her arms around her. "You're okay!"

"Because of you." Betty squeezes Veronica tight. "You did it, V."

Behind Betty, Veronica can see her father. He's sitting up against the wall, raking a hand through his always artfully disheveled hair, and when he looks up his eyes meet Veronica's.

His face fills with surprise.

"Veronica?"

"Daddy." She disentangles herself from Betty and passes through her friends, pausing briefly to look at Cheryl in Archie's arms. She looks a little hurt, but she's alive, and Veronica almost can't believe it. That Cheryl came so close to death, that Veronica came so close to losing her new friend.

Then she continues over to her father. When she gets there, she stares down at him, and it's all she can do not to walk back the way she came. Instead, she puts her hands on her waist. "Guess your plan didn't exactly work out, did it?"

He frowns up at her. "Plan?"

"Oh, don't try to play that confused little innocent act," Veronica says. "You know what you did, Daddy. And guess what? I finished it. *Me*."

Her father slumps, but his face stays confused. "I really don't know what you're talking about, Veronica," he says. "I don't even—I mean, what the hell happened here? Was there some kind of accident?"

Veronica takes a deep breath and exhales shakily. She hasn't been sure this whole time—ever since her mother said that they had agreed to Theodore's plan before he turned them—whether they were really involved or not. But her father's confusion seems to tell her exactly what she wanted to know.

They weren't a part of this. It was all Theodore's—no, *Odette's*— lies. And that means her parents are *hers* again.

She drops to her knees and throws her arms around her father. "Yes," she says. "Yes, an accident. That's exactly what happened." She pulls back, scanning the rest of the residents coming back to their human selves. Everybody looks lost, bewildered. Like they have no memory at all of the havoc they were part of.

Then she spots the face she was looking for and jumps to her feet. "Mom!"

She leaves her father there and rushes to her mother, who is gently probing a small cut on her forehead. "Veronica," her mom says, sounding as lost as she looks. "What happened to me? Are you okay?"

"I'm fine," Veronica says. "And you're going to be fine, too. Come on—" She helps her mom to her feet and leads her over to join her father. "There was . . . a gas leak," she says to both of them, the only explanation that comes to mind. Will it explain the damage, or the drained pool, or the general sense of chaos pervading the night? Maybe not, but gas leaks make people do weird things. A gas leak could, like, *totally* make a group of people build a pyre in the middle of a hotel ballroom.

"You should go home," Veronica says, and then remembers the havoc *she* wreaked at their home. "Or . . . maybe get a room for tonight. I mean, not here. Another hotel that *isn't* leaking gas. Sound good?"

Her father shakes his head, brow furrowed in confusion still. "A gas leak—"

"Yes," Veronica says, cutting him off. "So you should probably get out of here, in case it gets bad again. Or, like, goes *boom* or something. Maybe spread the word to everyone else, too—okay? Perfect."

She leaves her parents staring at each other and makes her way through the ballroom back to her friends. "They don't remember," she says when she reaches them. "Look around—it looks like *nobody* remembers anything."

Dilton adjusts his glasses and screws his face up as he thinks. "It makes sense, sort of," he says. "If you consider the mind-control aspect—if they weren't in control of their nervous system at all, then it follows they might—"

Veronica tunes him out and looks back toward her father. He's plucking at his clothes, the spot of blood on his shirt collar. And suddenly Veronica is not intimidated in the slightest by this heap of a man, this arrogant man who never seems to see what Veronica truly has to offer.

He didn't save the town; *she* did. He didn't kill Odette. He has no clue who Odette even is, can't remember being manipulated by Theodore. So really, who has the power now?

You were never in control, Daddy, she thinks, but she's not angry so much as satisfied. *And you will never be in control of me, ever again.*

Veronica turns back to her friends. Archie looks tired, Cheryl still half passed out in his arms. Dilton's shivering, and Betty looks like she needs a *really* good shower, but overall they seem to be okay. It could have been so much worse.

For a moment, I was willing to let it be worse.

"We should get out of here," Betty says. "Cheryl could probably use some bandages."

Veronica nods and smiles as Cheryl opens her eyes and focuses on her. "Wakey wakey, princess."

"Veronica." Cheryl frowns, her head rolling against Archie's chest. "Like, could you have taken any longer to kill the freakin' strigoi? I don't think I'll be able to wear heels *ever* again."

Veronica makes a face. "Still a pain in the ass," she says.

And Cheryl smiles. "Oh, you wouldn't have it any other way."

"Come on," Betty says. "Let's get the hell out of here before people start asking more questions we can't really answer."

The five of them carve a path through the mess, leaving the smoke-filled ballroom and carcass of a pool and the confused once-vampires in their wake. The hotel is still lit brightly against the dark night, and Veronica takes a moment to look at the stars hovering above the trees.

This is what Odette saw on that night, lying with the fire eating her home, half-alive under the night sky. Veronica watches the pin-prick lights blink in and out on the velvet night, and for a second, she is filled with sorrow. For the girl that Odette could have been if she hadn't so thoroughly corrupted herself, and for the wreckage of her body that Veronica left behind.

But then she looks at her friends ahead of her, walking out of a night she wasn't sure they'd all make it through, and the sorrow evaporates.

I did what I had to do.

Betty turns. "V! Come on!"

So she goes.

CHAPTER EIGHTY-FOUR
VERONICA

WHEN THEY PUSH open the door to Pop's, the bell jingles and the waitress at the counter gives them a cursory glance, not the slightest reaction to this gang of kids in bedraggled ball gowns and suits.

"Be with you in a sec," she says in a flat, bored voice, and Veronica scans the diner as they walk in. It's completely normal. Like nothing's been going on in town at all, and oh, it's such a relief to realize that while she and her friends have been battling a demon-vampire takeover, Pop's has just been ticking along in its own little world.

Veronica laughs behind her hand. "Thank god for Pop's Chock'Lit Shoppe," she says.

They crowd into a large booth at the back—Betty and Archie and Dilton on one side, Cheryl and Veronica on the other—and Betty picks up a menu, like they haven't had every item in this place memorized for years. "So Theodore Finch was just another zombie vamp?" she says. "And his sister *was* alive?"

"Not quite alive," Dilton corrects.

Betty waves him off. "You know what I mean," she says, but looks at Veronica. "So this was all about her, really?"

Veronica nods. On the way over, Betty driving, she'd told them how she'd discovered the strigoi in the basement and who she had turned out to be.

She hadn't told them about the hallucinations-slash-illusions-slash-visions, though. And she wasn't really sure why, except that they had been targeted as her biggest fears, hadn't they? So telling everyone what she'd had to fight her way through would mean they all knew exactly what she was afraid of.

Veronica wasn't ready for that.

"The weird thing is, I understood where she was coming from," Veronica says. "In a way. You know, she wanted to be treated a certain way and she was never able to get that. She made a deal with someone she thought was a friend and he betrayed her. And when she thought she was dying, somebody—some*thing*—turned her into a vampire and she had nobody to guide her through that. So I get why she was angry, but—" She shakes her head. "I couldn't let her get the revenge she wanted. She was killing innocent people because of what happened to her a century ago and that's not justice, is it? That's just a fantasy."

The waitress comes over and Betty orders almost every single item on the menu, and when they all turn to her, she widens her eyes. "What? We had a big night! Don't worry, I'll pay for it."

Dilton leans his elbows on the table and behind his glasses, he's making his thinking face that Veronica's come to know so well, inside the chem lab and now out of it. "So Odette was a strigoi," he says. "Interesting. I wonder who it was that turned her, then, if she never knew, even afterward. I mean, you'd think if Riverdale had a rogue vampire running around a hundred years ago, there'd be some kind of story about it, but I've never heard anything."

"Well, we'll never know," Archie says, and he sounds relieved. "Odette's dead, and it's over; everybody's human again. I can't wait till Jug gets back from his trip. He won't *believe* he missed all of this."

Veronica plays with a straw, twisting it between her fingers. *Everybody's human again* . . .

"And nobody seems to remember anything that happened," Cheryl says. "Does that mean—we're the only ones? Only we'll ever know what happened?"

"Seems like it," Betty says. "But maybe it's better this way."

Cheryl looks at Veronica, and Veronica knows exactly what she's thinking.

Reggie and Moose are dead—not vampire dead, not *undead* dead, but for real, buried-in-an-amateur-grave-decaying dead.

When they were vampires, it was explainable. But now? If the town's memory is completely absent of all of this?

How do we explain what happened to them?

"Here you go, kids." The waitress arrives with a groaning tray of food and drinks, and the others busy themselves passing burgers around and stealing fries from one another.

Veronica doesn't move. For them, she knows, they can be normal again. They'll remember what happened, but none of them were changed. And now that Veronica has destroyed Odette, she's lifted the dark cloud that fell over Riverdale. On Monday they'll go back to school and no one will be any the wiser. Return to the way things were.

Except I can't, Veronica thinks, and she digs her nails into the red vinyl of the booth. *I can't go back.*

Betty nods at the food in front of Veronica and speaks with her mouth full of burger. "Eat, V! You just battled a vampire queen and came out the victor. You can chill now."

Veronica looks at the plate before her. Usually she loves Pop's cheeseburgers, and this one is doctored exactly the way she likes it—no lettuce, extra pickles, bacon grilled crispy.

But she pushes it away. There's only one thing that can quell her hunger, and it's not on the diner menu. "There's something I have to tell you," she says, and she fights the urge to close her eyes so she won't have to see her friends' faces when she says it.

"What?" Cheryl drops the fry she was about to put in her mouth. "V, what is it?"

Archie leans across the table. "Ronnie," he says. "You're kind of freaking me out."

Veronica exhales. It should have worked, it worked for everybody else, but—

Not for her.

"That whole reverting-to-human thing?" Veronica shrugs, and then she bares her teeth, wide and almost feral, and Betty gasps.

"Oh my god," Betty says. "Oh my *god. What?*"

"Yeah." Veronica runs her tongue along her teeth, feeling at the sharp points of the fangs she has let out, the fangs that should have disappeared when she killed Odette and regained her human self—except that didn't happen. It didn't happen at all. "I'm still a vampire. Surprise!"

CHAPTER EIGHTY-FIVE
VERONICA

ODETTE'S SEVERED HEAD hits the floor with a sticky thump, and Veronica sits back, breathing heavily, still straddling Odette's remains. It's over, *she thinks*. It's all over.

How will it come? The humanity, flooding back into her. How does it happen?

Veronica lifts her hands and watches them, waiting. For what, exactly?

She's still panting, and her hands are covered in Odette's almost-black blood, and there's a severed head in front of her, but Veronica—

She feels no different.

She scrambles off Odette and rushes back to the mirror. Eyes still tinged red, and when she tries to flick out her fangs, they come easily. Sharp and ready to feed on the blood her body is singing for.

I'm not human.

It didn't work, *she thinks*, and then she knows she has to leave.

She abandons the gruesome remains and sprints through the house, back to the stolen bike. Speeds her way back to the hotel, wondering what further carnage she's going to find.

But when she gets there, all she sees is people slowly coming back to life.

And then she knows: It did work.

Just not for her.

CHAPTER EIGHTY-SIX
VERONICA

BETTY PRESSES HERSELF back against the booth. "What the *hell*?"

Veronica retracts her fangs and gives Betty a soft, sad smile. "Exactly what I thought."

"So—if you didn't change back, but Odette's dead, and everybody else reverted—" Cheryl's brown eyes widen even further. "I don't understand."

All that fighting and all that Veronica did to save the town, and she's still not back to what they all thought she would be.

And here, of course, is the strange thing:

Veronica isn't so sure she minds.

"God, I'm sorry, V," Betty says. "Do you think—I mean, Dilton, is it possible there's yet *another* strigoi still out there?"

Dilton steeples his fingers. "I suppose it's not beyond the realm of possibility. As far as we know, it's all about the bloodline. Kill the strigoi sire, and everyone they've turned reverts. But if you're not part of the bloodline—" His eyes light up. "Think about it—somebody had to turn Odette herself. What if that vampire also turned *you*, Veronica?"

Betty nods. "Didn't you say she was turned in the woods outside their estate? So—outside where the hotel is now?"

"Right," Veronica says, twisting a hand through her dark hair. "The night their house burned."

"Those woods," Betty says. "They run all the way along the edge of town. Up to your house and the road in. And isn't that where you were turned?"

Veronica nods slowly. "But it doesn't matter," she says. "It's like you said earlier, Dilton. Who even knows if the vampire who turned Odette—and maybe, probably, turned me—is around here still? Wouldn't we have heard scary stories? Wouldn't it be a legend?"

"They *have* to be here," Archie says. "It can't be a coincidence that you were both turned in the same woods. Unless there's just, like, a hundred different vamps running around out there, undetected. In which case—Dilton, we should get to work on a new water gun prototype."

"Archie!"

He's only joking, Veronica knows, but Betty looks outraged anyway. As if they can't joke about killing vampires, not when V still is one, and not when there's no immediately obvious solution for that—even though Veronica's killed her fair share of vampires this week.

Betty reaches across the table and grabs Veronica's hands, looking into her best friend's eyes. "It's gonna be okay, V," she says, and Veronica can feel how much she means it. How much she *wants* it. "We're going to figure out what's going on and we're going to do every single thing we can to get you out of this mess.

We'll have you back to human before you even know it. I promise. We all do, right?"

The others nod and murmur their agreement, and Veronica nods. "Okay," she says. "Whatever you say."

Betty squeezes her hands. "So we have to wait a little longer to get our old V back. The important thing is that we will—we'll figure out this new mystery, and then old Veronica will be back in our lives for good."

Veronica swallows hard and pinches her thigh under the table. It's that or scream.

Because she knows this is what Betty wants, and Archie, and everybody. For her to go back to who she used to be. That's how this story is supposed to end, isn't it? Veronica reverts back to not just her human self, but the old perfect girl they all adore.

But she can't.

And more important—she won't.

Even if we do figure this out, Veronica thinks, *even if I do go back to being human eventually, I'll never be that girl again.* Not now that she knows how it feels to shatter the grip her old life had her in. She is New Veronica now: fishnets and fighting and dreams beyond this place, and none of that can be undone.

She looks at Betty. She won't understand. None of them will. "Yeah," she says, the lie easy. "It'll all be like it was before."

CHAPTER EIGHTY-SEVEN
VERONICA

VERONICA WAITS UNTIL Archie and Dilton are at the old jukebox and Cheryl and Betty have gone to the bathroom before slipping outside.

She's not running away. Not leaving.

She just—needs air.

The stars are bright, even with the neon lights of the diner behind her, and Veronica hops on the hood of Betty's car. *It's just me and me now, kid*, she thinks, and blows a breathy sigh into the night. They're gonna have a hell of a cleanup job on their hands—gotta take care of that body in the basement, and come up with a plausible story for the destruction and bloodshed at the Blossoms' hotel. And what about—

"Hey."

Veronica jumps, hand to her heart. "Cheryl, you scared me."

"Me?" Cheryl tries to jump up next to her but winces from the pain in her feet, and Veronica helps her up. When she's settled on the hood she starts again. "Me? Scared you, the big bad vampire?"

Veronica tries to laugh but nothing comes out. "I know," she says. "Not what anyone wanted."

"Isn't it?"

"What?"

Cheryl smiles at her. "We're friends now, right? So don't worry. I won't tell anyone how you feel about this whole vampire thing. But just so you know—if it's what you want, to stay this way forever—then it's cool with me."

Veronica doesn't quite know what to say, and so she just stares at Cheryl for a long time, longer than should be comfortable. But she supposes Cheryl's right, now, and they are friends. *The kind of friends who can sit in silence*, Veronica thinks. "Forever is a long time," she says eventually, and then, quickly, so she can't chicken out, "You don't think I'm a monster, then?"

"Hello," Cheryl says. "I just found out that really, it was *my* ancestor who was responsible for this whole thing. He *burned* their *house* down. I'm descended from a murderer, V. If you're a monster, then I'm a monster, too."

Now Veronica does smile. "You did help me bury a couple bodies," she says.

"Yeah." Cheryl sighs. "What the hell are we going to do about that?"

"I don't know." Veronica turns her face up to the inky sky. "If nobody in town remembers what happened, then no one will ever understand why I did what I did."

"Why *we* did it."

"You didn't kill them."

"No," Cheryl says. "But you were saving me. And I buried them. I filled that grave in, V. It's not just you, okay? I mean it." And then she sounds unsure. "I mean, we *are* friends now. Aren't we?"

Veronica laughs, but it's not the way she used to laugh at Cheryl, defensive or bitchy. "Yeah," she says. "We're friends."

"Right," Cheryl says, and she sounds relieved. "So we make a pact. That's what friends do, right? If you go down, then I go down. But we won't. Because we're going to stick together on this. You have nothing to feel guilty about."

Tell that to Reggie's parents, Veronica thinks. *Tell that to Moose's little sister.*

"Promise me." Cheryl elbows her and then holds up her hand, pinky finger out. "You won't torture yourself thinking about what happened. We're moving on. Promise?"

Veronica hesitates for a second. "Okay," she says, and she knows what she's about to say is only half-true, but she's tired and ready to give in. And Cheryl's looking at her so hopeful that Veronica doesn't want to disappoint her. The only one of her friends who's willing to accept her not as she used to be, or not as she might be in the future, but as the messy, monster girl she is right in this moment.

So Veronica holds her hand up, too, and links her finger with Cheryl's. "I promise."

ABOUT THE AUTHOR

Rebecca Barrow writes stories about girls and all the wonders they can be. A lipstick obsessive with the ability to quote the entirety of *Mean Girls*, she lives in England, where it rains a considerable amount more than in the fictional worlds of her characters. She collects tattoos, cats, and more books than she could ever possibly read.